Forever Kind of Love

by

Susan Elizabeth Bagby

Cedar Hill Series

Forever Kind of Love

Cover Art by *Teddi Black*

The Wild Rose Press, Inc.
PO Box 708
Adams Basin, NY 14410-0708
Visit us at www.thewildrosepress.com

Publishing History
First Edition, 2026
Trade Paperback Print ISBN 978-1-5092-6430-8
Digital ISBN 978-1-5092-6431-5

Cedar Hill Series
Published in the United States of America

Dedication

To my bestie from grade school, Cathy Kunkel, who welcomed me back to my hometown in Ohio with unconditional love and caring. I will forever be grateful to you. xo

Acknowledgments

Thank you to The Wild Rose Press for welcoming me into your writing community. I'm excited to embark upon this journey with such a wonderful group of supportive authors and editors. I look forward to sharing and celebrating my stories alongside all of you.

To Leanne Morgena, my editor extraordinaire—thank you for your patience, clarity, expertise, and hard work in bringing *Forever Kind of Love* to its final form. I have learned so much from you—from dangling modifiers and the correct placement of commas to techniques for enriching a story and making it stronger. You're amazing.

To my "chicks with sticks" group—Cathy, Jan, Nikki, Marian, Pam, and Georgia. Thank you for buying my books, leaving me reviews, and listening to me as I discuss my hopes and fears about the publishing world while we're out on the golf course. Your friendship is priceless.

And to all my friends and readers who support me by buying books and following me on social media—an author can't make it in this world without you. Thank you.

Chapter One

Caught unaware by her husband's financial crimes, Willow Barton lost everything. Money, home, hopes and dreams were gone…down the toilet…kaput. *How did I miss the signs?* Or did she ignore them?

Didn't matter now. Willow fled New York City and landed back home in Ohio, living with her mother. She was determined to make ends meet and needed a job. She leaned her shoulder against the front door of the crowded coffee shop, pushing her way inside, and slid up to the counter. *I can do this. But first, caffeine.*

When she opened her purse, hunting cash for the barista, she couldn't stop a credit card from falling out. *Damn, forgot to cut it up.* She stuffed it back inside her wallet and slapped a five-dollar bill onto the counter while standing in line. Willow tapped her foot, her shoe flapping in rapid rhythm, and waited for her cappuccino.

She scrolled on her phone, checking out local events, and shook her head. Not even a decent fine arts gallery in the small town of Cedar Hill with its ten thousand inhabitants to incite her talents. *Guess I'm starting over again.* She tilted her head, breathing deep into the intense aroma of coffee beans grinding and brewing, already giving her a heady buzz. *How much longer?* Stretching her neck, she sought the location of her order and grinned.

The server called her name, setting the cup on the counter.

Willow grabbed her coffee and sat at a nearby table with the local newspaper and her tablet, scouring the want ads for work. With furrowed brow, she twisted her hair around a finger. *I can't work at a coffee shop or restaurant. I'd make a terrible barista and an even worse server.*

"Willow Barton! Is that you?"

Willow glanced up. "Marcy Brewster! Haven't seen you since high school."

A woman, towing a young boy in one hand and juggling her coffee in the other, approached. "Did you move back to Cedar Hill?"

"Yep." Willow eyed the little boy. "He's adorable. How many do you have?"

"One. He's in preschool half a day and can run me ragged." Marcy peeked over Willow's shoulder at the circled want ads. "Are you looking for a job?"

"Yes." Willow lowered her head, fiddling with her collar. Heat radiated around her neck and cheeks. "I might be getting a divorce."

"Oh, sorry to hear that." She paused, taking a sip of her coffee. "How would you feel about overseeing a bookstore on Main Street? My manager quit yesterday. My husband and I started this business without a clue of what we were doing." Marcy shook her head, readjusting her grip on her child. "Being a single mom, I'm way too busy to handle it now."

The young boy tugged harder.

She struggled to keep her coffee from spilling all over the floor.

Willow tapped her fingers on the table. "Are you

divorced, too?"

Marcy glanced at the laminate floor and exhaled a breath through pursed lips. "A widow. I lost Chet a year ago to cancer."

"I'm so sorry, Marcy." She touched her friend's arm. "Losing a loved one is tough."

"Thanks." She readjusted her faltering hold on her squirming toddler son. "This bookstore was an extra investment. I might not pay you as much as what you made working in New York, but I'd love to have someone I trust in the position. What do you say?"

Willow's pulse quickened. "Yes! Of course. I love reading books." At least reading and writing were creative endeavors. Living in New York, she immersed herself in the art world—even if her job was only as a gallery assistant. But hopes of finishing a portfolio and making a career in fine arts photography were squashed after her husband's arrest. Launching a career took extra money. *Not happening now.*

Marcy shrugged. "Do you want to see it? The shop is up the street, about three blocks." She pointed at the window in the store's direction.

"Lead the way. And I'm changing my name back to Mason."

"I'm glad you came back to your hometown, Willow. You still have friends here."

"Thanks. Lord knows, I could use another friend." Willow stuffed everything in her backpack, practically skipping after Marcy as they headed down the street. She had just accepted a job she had no clue of how to do. *God help me.*

****

The following week, Willow squinted, peering out

the bookstore window at two burly men with surveying equipment. *What are they doing?* She noticed them the day before but didn't bother investigating them further. *Hmm.* She scratched her head, then straightened several books on a shelf. Her phone buzzed.

Willow slid it out of her back pocket. *Leah.* "Hey, what's up?"

Leah Hayes, her best friend since kindergarten, was thrilled when Willow decided to move back to Cedar Hill after her breakup in New York. "Sorry to bother you at the store. Are you still able to check on my dad today?"

"Yep. I'll arrive at four and can stay until seven or later, if he needs anything. Don't worry. I've got you covered. Besides, I can use the extra cash, although I hate you're paying me."

"Oh, stop, Willow. We'd be paying somebody else if he'd let them in the house. He still thinks you're trying out recipes for a cookbook you're writing." Leah chuckled.

Willow shuffled her stance. "I guess the one good thing about memory loss is he forgets if I made the same lasagna a couple of days ago. Every meal is new, sadly to say." She found cooking for Mr. Hayes to be a meditative exercise and needed calm in her life after the fiasco in New York.

"Yeah, this dementia thing isn't easy. At least, he still knows us. Liam's working long hours at our hardware store, and I need to take care of Rosie in the evenings."

"You're a great mom, Leah, and Liam's a lucky guy to have you as his wife. Your mother would have been proud."

"Yeah, I wish she was still with us."

"Me, too." Willow fiddled with her watch on her wrist. "I need to open the store in ten minutes. I'll text you later."

"What would I do without you? Thanks, Willow." She ended the call.

Willow peered around The Readers Bookshop, stopping to focus on her black-and-white photographs for sale on the wall. She drew nearer, adjusting the frames and straightening the edges. Smiling, she folded her fingers together, hoping for a sale soon.

When her phone rang, she grasped it from her back pocket as her attorney's name flashed on the front. "Hi, Tim." Timothy Louden was handling both the pending divorce and the aftermath of issues stemming from Charles's crimes. She would never forget the horrible day—federal agents hauling out filing cabinets, Charles's computer, artwork, and all their valuable items. She cried, screamed, and even threw some of Charles's belongings in the trash to make herself feel better—but nothing did. Marriage or not, she wasn't sticking around for a man she no longer trusted.

"I'm mailing you some papers to sign, and I'll keep you informed about Charles's pending court date. Any questions?"

"No." She quivered on the intake of air. "I don't have to come to the trial, do I?" Willow twiddled her pen back and forth, her nerves firing in rapid, relentless pulses.

"Not if you don't want to. I can readily deal with everything here."

"Great. Thanks, Tim." Willow tapped the End button and took another deep breath. Somehow, she would get through all of this. Who would have imagined the handsome, charismatic Charles Barton was capable of fraud? Certainly not her. Charles swept her off her feet during her college years, and she wholeheartedly trusted him—until she didn't.

As she finished unpacking a new shipment and set up the cash register, Willow wiped the sweat from her forehead. Main Street was one block from the walkway along the Crestview River, and people loved to shop at the charming boutique stores and stroll along the Riverwalk on the weekends. Expanding maple trees, their leaves transforming to gold, stood tall, still shading pedestrians meandering the streets.

When a tune blared from her phone by Zachary Hayes—famous country music star, a local boy, and Leah's brother—Willow turned up the volume on her playlist. She bobbed her head up and down, her hips swaying to the beat. *My childhood crush.*

Years ago, he settled in Nashville, and she hadn't seen him much since. He and his father had a falling-out after Zach refused to take over the family hardware business, and the rift never healed, according to Leah.

Around noon, Willow bent over boxes in the back, checking inventory.

"Auntie Wiwow, where are you?" A child's voice bellowed from the front of the store.

Willow put down the books. "Back here, honey."

Rosie burst through the storeroom, running as fast as her little legs could carry her, and jumped into Willow's arms. "Mommy and I are getting ice kweam. Can you come?"

Willow peered up at Leah as she neared her daughter's side, out of breath. "I believe I could." She winked at Leah.

"Sorry to bother you during work, but she wouldn't stop bugging me until we convinced you to join us too."

Willow palmed a hand on Rosie's face, studying the mischievous spark in her eyes. "Let me grab my purse and see if Deedee, our new part-time hire, can handle the store by herself. She should be ready." Willow grabbed Rosie's hand. "Let's go."

Rosie was six years old, almost seven, and small for her age. She had been diagnosed with Down's syndrome at birth but never let anything stop her from doing what she wanted. Leah fought hard for inclusion in a regular classroom where her daughter now thrived and received tutoring when she needed extra help. Rosie's loving personality always lifted Willow's spirits.

The three of them grabbed their favorite flavor on cones and strolled to the benches overlooking the river, its steady current mesmerizing them. Fall was on the horizon, but the day was warm, and a few trees, lush with greenery, swayed in the gentle wind. Ohio's winters could be brutal, but the rest of the seasons in Cedar Hill were spectacular.

Willow closed her eyes, soaking in the rushing sound of the water. The current's *swishing* over the rocks lulled her to rest. "I could sit here all day."

"Reminds me to slow down." Leah paused. "If possible."

Rosie hummed, licking the sides of the cone. Not one drip of double-chocolate chip escaped her lips.

Willow opened her eyes and offered Rosie a napkin. "Someone is enjoying herself."

Leah rescued a stray hair about to land in the

melting mess of ice cream on her daughter's face.

"How was your dad this morning?" Willow popped the last of her cone into her mouth and wiped her sticky lips.

"Irritable." Leah sucked in a breath, then forced it out. "He wants to go to the hardware store, but Liam doesn't want him there. He doesn't have time to keep his eye on him, and after several screwups with customers, he's unsure of what else to do. I've got Dad interested in a project in the garage, so once he's engaged in work, he seems okay. He's making birdhouses for me now. Tell me if you want one. I'm keeping this project going for as long as possible." Leah chuckled as she handed Rosie another napkin.

"I'll have him show me after dinner and put in an order. Mom would love a couple of new birdhouses hanging in her backyard. Seems bird-watching is becoming one of her favorite pastimes on bad days." Her mother, a retired schoolteacher, had been diagnosed with lupus right before Willow returned to Cedar Hill. Some days were more challenging than others with the autoimmune disorder, but Willow helped whenever she could. Fatigue was the worst symptom.

Leah squeezed Willow's right shoulder. "We'll get through this. At least, we have each other."

Willow patted Leah's leg next to hers. "Yep. For sure."

"I'm done." Rosie stuffed the last bit of sugar cone straight into her mouth. "Let's go see the ribber."

Leah leaned over, her raspy voice in a whisper. "Rosie started speech therapy, and she loves it."

"Awesome." Willow stretched both legs out in

front. "You two go. I trust Deedee, but if a ton of people show up today, she might be in over her head."

"Okay." Rosie threw both arms around Willow, sticky fingers smearing chocolate across Willow's shirt in the back.

Seeing the dark-brown goo spread across Willow's shirt, Leah grimaced. "Your shirt is a mess. Sorry."

Willow shrugged. "No problem. We've got a washing machine." She kissed Rosie's cheek, then stood. "See you guys later."

Leah took her daughter's hands, cleaned them first with a damp wipe from her purse, then trotted off toward the Riverwalk with Rosie skipping beside her.

Willow headed back to the store to finish the nitty-gritty tasks at her mundane job. She sighed, kicked a stone on the pavement, and shuffled back to Readers Bookshop. Would she ever find the time to pursue her artistic dreams again?

****

When she arrived at the Hayes's house after work, Willow jumped off her bicycle. Her mom's house and Leah's childhood home were close enough to the bookstore so she could bike around on sunny days, which saved her gas. *Gotta save every penny I can.* She shook her head, still in shock at how her world had been rocked in the worst way during the aftermath of Charles's escapades in New York. Every penny was gone, wiped out of their savings account, and she would never get it back. Weeks passed before she fathomed what happened. She couldn't believe she had been so clueless not to notice or realize what her husband was doing all those late nights and weekends he told her he traveled for conference trips. *Did I have an inkling something wasn't right?* The finance and venture capital world sounded so exotic and exciting—until it wasn't.

She rapped on the front door. No answer. She knocked louder. Still no answer. Remembering Mr. Hayes had projects in the garage, she scurried around back. The side door was open to the garage. "George! Are you in here?"

Nothing. He'd left his tools scattered on the workbench, abandoned in the middle of a task. The smell of sawed wood and fresh paint filled her nostrils, but a sickened feeling clenched her gut. She ran to the back door and grabbed the extra key from the ledge above. Opening the door, she yelled his name, frantically searching each room downstairs and upstairs, including the basement. Mr. Hayes was nowhere to be found. Hands shaking, she yanked out her phone. "Leah, your dad's not here. Where could he have gone?"

"Oh, my God. I knew this would happen. Since I relocated his car to my house, he can't drive, so he must be on foot. He might head toward the hardware store. Why don't you ride in the direction of the shop? I'll call Liam. Rosie and I will start roaming the surrounding streets as well."

"Don't worry, Leah. We'll find him." Willow shut the door behind her and climbed on her bike, scoping out the best route to the store in town. As she pedaled faster, she scanned every street she passed, hoping to see Mr. Hayes strolling along, safe and sound. She made it all the way to Hayes Hardware without a single sighting.

Liam stood outside.

Leah skidded into the parking lot, dust flying up from the wheels.

Liam, a tall, broad-chested man with wavy brown hair, stepped closer. "Let's divide up the neighborhoods before we call the police. I'm sure he was headed here, took a wrong turn, and got lost."

"I hope you're right." Leah wrung both hands together, rocking side to side.

Willow winced, seeing the fear on Leah's face, and leaped on her bike, maneuvering up and down streets between the store and the Hayes's residence. She glanced down a familiar street.

George hung his head, strolling in the opposite direction of the store and his home.

After she sent a text to Leah, she snuck up behind him and cleared her throat. "Hello, Mr. Hayes."

He spun in a half-circle. "Oh. Hi, Willow. What are you doing here?"

"I wondered if you wanted to go back to the house and try one of my new recipes for dinner."

"Sounds good. I need to get some more paint for my building project. I was headed to the store but must have taken a wrong turn." George shook his head. "Seems I've been making a lot of mistakes lately."

Willow could see he was mustering up a smile but wasn't happy with himself. "We all forget stuff, George. Let's make dinner, and then you can show me your new project. I might have a couple of orders for you."

His eyes widened. "You don't say. All right, you lead the way."

Willow hopped off her bike and swiveled, pointing in the opposite direction. "We're going this way."

George nodded and stepped beside her as they headed toward his home. He rambled on about the inner workings of making birdhouses, his animated voice resonating.

After they arrived back the house, she started dinner.

He retired to his recliner chair in the den to watch a favorite television program.

Willow stirred the marinara sauce, then pulled out her phone, tapping Leah's number. "Don't worry. He's settled in the den and dinner's cooking. You were right. He was headed to the store for more paint for his birdhouses. You might want to take him after dinner, or I could go home, get my car, and do it. I've got nothing else going on."

"Do you mind? I'm kind of busy with Rosie. I'll make sure Liam meets you. Text me. Willow, I can't thank you enough for today."

"No problem. But Leah…" She stopped.

"Before you say it, I want to hire someone during the day. Liam is furious we haven't done so already. I'm calling my brother—Zach needs to step in and help. I wish he'd come home and see for himself."

"Good luck with convincing him." Zachary Hayes loved his life in Nashville or, at least, it appeared so in all the tabloid magazines she read. But Leah needed help. She hoped he could be useful but had her doubts.

"I'll keep you posted."

"All right. Talk to you later." Willow ended the call and returned to kitchen duties. As she peeled a potato, she daydreamed about Zach. Would she still have a crush on him? But she feared her heart had slammed shut after Charles, never to open again—at least, for a very long time. And Zachary Hayes was one of those men who couldn't be trusted—the kind of man she would never, ever date again.

Chapter Two

As Zach opened his eyes and glanced toward the window, he moaned. Sunlight seeped into the hotel room, its rays dancing on his bedspread. He sighed, picturing the blonde-haired woman he danced and cavorted with at their after-party. *What was her name? Emma? Erica?* He scratched the stubble on his jaw and grinned. *One wild night.* With the end of his tour complete, he would fly back to Nashville in the afternoon.

He picked up his phone. Three more texts from his sister—she wanted to *talk.* If her incessant efforts had been an emergency, she would have contacted his manager. Reveling in the last show, partying got way out of hand after the concert. His head throbbed, so he climbed out of bed in search of ibuprofen. He strode to the hotel phone, placed a large breakfast order with room service, including plenty of coffee, and jumped into the shower.

By the time he was done in the bathroom, he had a short wait before the room service arrived. Lifting the dome cover, he breathed in the tantalizing aroma of crisp bacon and scrambled eggs alongside a fresh pot of coffee. He popped a strip of the greasy pork in his mouth, then glanced at his cellphone when an incoming text appeared from last night's woman.

—*Last night was off the charts! We should do it*

again sometime—
    —Yeah—
    His nonchalant response was brief. Then he caught a glimpse of her heart emoji and dropped his phone on the table without texting back. He grabbed a coffee, poured plenty of cream and sugar in it, then called his sister.

    "Geez, Zach. How many times do I have to text you before you respond?"

    "Don't be mad, Leah. If you had an emergency, you'd have said so or called my manager. A *talk* can wait until I'm not busy. But now, you have my full, undivided attention." He leaned back in the chair and sipped his coffee.

    "All right, I'll take it. We need to talk about Dad. He wandered off yesterday afternoon and roamed down a side street, searching for the hardware store. Zach, you need to come home. I can't do this alone. We need to figure something out for him. I check in on him after I drop Rosie at school, and Willow stops by in the afternoon after her shift at the bookstore. He needs more care, I'm afraid."

    "Freckle-faced Willow? Doesn't she live in New York?"

    "She did. I told you she moved back here after a tough break-up. You never listen."

    Zach threw up a hand. "Okay, okay. I got it. Listen, my tour ended, and I'm headed home this afternoon. Let me talk to Mike and see what I can arrange. Could be perfect timing. Are you sure Dad's going to want me around? Our bickering matches annoyed him last visit."

    "It might be different this time, Zach. Since Liam took over the store, he's feeling better since the business is staying in the family—just not with you."

Zac puckered his lips sideways, contemplating his challenging relationship with his father over the last ten years. Since he picked up and left for Nashville, he'd suffered his dad's fury. The old man insisted he was crazy for giving up such a lucrative business opportunity as Hayes Hardware in Cedar Hill to pursue a rock star dream. Zach loved his dad, but the riff had gotten way too intense. Shoved away in some obscure place in his mind, he pretended it didn't exist. "Glad to hear it. Let's hope so."

"So, you'll come?"

She's softening. "Yes, I will come. I'll call you tomorrow with more details."

"Thanks, Zach. You'll be glad you did. How long he will remember us as he does today is unclear with dementia hovering over him. He can still function day-to-day, but the forgetfulness and wandering are getting dangerous. And you'll have to help convince him to accept help. Willow is the only one he lets inside the house besides us."

Zach chuckled at the image of goofy, skinny Willow, his sister's best friend, helping his dad. "Talk to you soon. Don't worry. We'll figure this out."

Leah sighed. "I hope so."

Zach shoveled the last bite of his eggs into his mouth, then grabbed his wallet. He removed a worn photo of his dad and him before he left for Nashville. His dad's arm circled him, and they had just finished working on some house project. Could he ever get close to him again? In this visit, he was determined to put in the effort and hoped for the best.

****

As Zach strode along a popular street in Nashville to meet Mike Kincaid, his longtime manager, he tapped his digital watch, reading a text. They needed to discuss what was next in his career and his trip to Ohio. Arriving, Zach waved at him, sitting at an outdoor table on the back patio of Demarco's, one of his favorite Italian restaurants. Cooked garlic in bubbling tomato sauce poured over pasta from a neighboring patron permeated his olfactory glands, stimulating the growling in his stomach. The secluded seating gave Zach more privacy, away from the crowd of tourists roaming around the area.

He greeted him with a brief hug, and Zach dropped onto his seat. "Thanks, man, for meeting me in person."

"Anything for my most lucrative client. Your tour was a huge success, by the way, even without a new album or hit song." Mike adjusted his glasses and ran his fingers through his curly hair.

Ouch. Mike could be direct—straight to the problem with Zach's career. No new album and no new hit song. "See. I still got it anyway." He shifted his body. "Listen, I want to discuss some personal things."

"Sure." Mike smiled at the server placing glasses of water on the table.

Zach told Mike about his father and his trip back home. "I'm not sure how long I'll be gone, but I'll get back in the studio soon. I've been working on some new stuff." *Liar.* He scratched his head, pretending to peruse the menu.

"Good, because the label is breathing down my neck. Write some songs while you're away since you're returning to your hometown. They might like the sound of you getting back to your roots and all."

Zach nodded, toying with his silverware. His roots were thin, almost non-existent at this time. *Can I find them again?* But he would put up a solid front—he always did. He was a master at hiding feelings and problems. "Yeah. I'll keep you posted. Now, let's focus on food, and you can tell me what I've missed here since I've been on the road."

Mike picked up the menu. "I've got a few crazy stories."

"I bet you do." Zach grinned as he steered the conversation in a whole new direction but wondered if he would he ever find his roots again. A gnawing knot in his gut warned him he needed to find his muse—and soon.

****

The sun beat down on Willow's back as she climbed the rickety steps to the back-garage apartment, keys in hand. When her family was planning to house her grandmother years ago, her dad built it, but Grandma and Dad both died before the unit was finished. She stopped to breathe in the sweet and woodsy air of lingering warm weather. She stepped, the wood creaking as her shoe caught in a split section of wood on the steps. *Oops. Gotta fix this.*

As she unlocked the door and rotated the knob to enter, she held her breath. She scanned the room, taking in the cobwebs, dust, and musty smell permeating the area. One vast, open space with a small kitchen expanded into what could be a living room. A small kitchen table for two fit into the corner, and a tiny bathroom and bedroom were off to the side. Not much, but it could do. At least, she'd have her own space, away from her mom yet close enough if she needed help. Not the fancy loft she lived in for five years in New York with Charles, but the home was hers, and no one could take it away.

She offered to pay rent for staying in the house, but her mom wouldn't hear of it.

She wanted Willow to get back on her feet, save money, and create a new life.

Willow wandered around the rooms, inspecting windows, floorboards, lighting, and the few pieces of furniture remaining. Cleaning was the first step, so she opened the windows to air out the lingering, stale odor. Glass cracked in one of them as she cranked it open. "Damn! One more thing." *Can't get a break.* She returned to the house for supplies, opening cupboards, and checking out what was available.

Mom sat at the kitchen table, reading the morning newspaper, and drinking coffee.

"Hi, Mom."

Evelyn, a middle-aged woman with short, curly brown hair, set her cup on a coaster. "Good morning, dear. What are you up to today?" She folded her newspaper in half and placed it to the side.

"I'm working on the apartment. Cleaning is first on the agenda. Mind if I use your stuff until I have a chance to go to the store?"

"Of course not. Anything here is yours." Mom wrapped her fingers around her mug. "How bad is it?"

"The structure is okay, but it needs new plumbing, which will be the biggest expense. I should have enough saved by the end of the month. Meanwhile, I can clean and paint the walls a new color. Should be perfect."

"And your darkroom?"

"Same as I left it ten years ago. Should be easier to get up and running." Willow felt a tingle race up her spine. A new darkroom meant her dreams were still alive.

Mom tilted her face. "Sit and eat breakfast before you go all crazy with your projects."

"Okay." Willow smiled, grabbed a mug, and tossed a slice of bread into the toaster. She was anxious to start, but finding quiet moments to sit and chat with her mother were too rare these days. She was always in work mode. *I guess with two jobs, I am.*

"How's Mr. Hayes?"

She told her about the previous episode of wandering and being found.

Mom shook her head. "What is Leah going to do? The inevitable is on the horizon. I feel for her."

"She told me yesterday Zach is coming to town to see the situation for himself and agreed to help her make decisions. When the time comes, they'll have the money to pay for more care."

"Good. I'm sure he has plenty of resources and should be here helping Leah. She has enough on her plate. I'm glad you're able to help her out." Evelyn stood, grabbed her mug, and strode to the counter for a refill.

"Yeah, me, too." Willow stared into her coffee cup. Mr. Hayes's condition was a big unknown for the future, and her heart hurt for her best friend.

****

As dusk settled in, Willow sat on the apartment wood floor, drinking an iced tea and inspecting her work. She brushed the sweat on her forehead with her sleeve. She had scrubbed and disinfected every corner, nook, and cupboard. Willow wiped her runny nose affected by the antiseptic smell of cleaning liquids still hanging in the air. Fresh paint would brighten up the place, and the bed and dresser appeared in good condition beneath all the dust.

Willow picked at her dirty nails. If she was honest, her heart still ached. She loved Charles and had consumed herself in his way of living and social lifestyle. His friends became her friends, who no longer wanted anything to do with her. She didn't blame them. Some were financially burned by him as well. She couldn't believe she had been so naïve not to see what he was doing or so stupid she lost herself in the fantasy of being Mrs. Charles Barton, an up-and-coming socialite in the big city.

Back in Ohio, could she find herself again? Or at least discover a new Willow, wiser and better equipped to stand on her own two feet and see a train wreck coming. She stood and grabbed some of the supplies. *Can't think about this anymore. Time to tackle the darkroom.*

Chapter Three

Zach bounced his head up and down as a Nashville buddy's song blasted through the truck's radio speakers. He made plenty of friends over the last ten years, and some grew into fame with him. As they got older, though, most married and settled on the outskirts of town, raising kids and a swarm of animals. He did want kids someday but didn't want to give up the free lifestyle of touring and the road yet—too exhilarating. And the women—too tempting. For now, he needed to focus on his dad and his music.

Nearing Cedar Hill, he called Leah. "Hey, I'm about an hour away. Want to give Dad a heads-up I'll be home soon? You did tell him, didn't you?"

"Don't patronize me, big brother. Of course, I did. Willow is with him, and I told her to make enough dinner for you, too, so don't stop for anything."

"Willow?"

"Yes, I told you. Willow has been helping in the evenings."

"Right, right." Zach hadn't seen her in years. *What does she look like now?* She was kind of nerdy in high school—her head always in a book. *Thump, thump.* As Zach hit a pothole, he tightened his grip on the steering wheel.

"I'll be over in the morning after I drop Rosie off to school. I put clean sheets on your bed."

"Thanks, sis. We'll figure this out. Don't worry."

"I hope so. Thanks for coming home."

"I was long overdue, Leah. See you tomorrow." He tapped his phone and ended the call. Zach scanned the stretch of rolling green hills and forest landscape unfolding along the road. The air was fragrant with a crisp, woodsy smell of early autumn, and Zach immersed himself in memories as he exited the highway, taking side streets the rest of the way. But as he curved the familiar road to his childhood home, he inhaled, tightness seizing his chest. A tightening filled with fear and apprehension. He had waited too long to confront his father, and now he was sick. Not physically yet, but mentally losing his grasp on the world—which scared him more. What was coming gripped his heart like a vise, and he couldn't shake it loose.

The tires crunched along the graveled stones in the driveway—home sweet home. Zach sat for a moment before getting out, taking it all in. His heart pounded, and a gnawing fear settled in the pit of his gut, taunting the unknown future surrounding his dad.

****

From her stance by the kitchen window, Willow saw Zach's arrival. A wave of excitement washed over her body like a tsunami, a rapid tingling from head to toe. Was she anxious about seeing Zach again? *No, couldn't be.* In grade school, she ran into him occasionally at Leah's house and observed him from the sidelines all through junior high and high school, although they never hung out. She was too shy, and, if she admitted it, too nerdy to be social with Leah's older brother and his friends—who were way out of her league. But now, she was a grown woman. Scorned and broken, yes, but still a single woman. She was curious, like an experiment, to see if he still made her heart pitter-patter. No other interest. *None whatsoever.* "Hey, Mr. Hayes. Zach's here."

"Oh, yeah?" George lifted from the chair, pivoting to greet his son.

Zach strolled up to the porch, carrying a suitcase and a duffle bag slung over his shoulder.

George opened the screen door. "Well, I don't believe it. You're here."

Zach stopped in his tracks, his eyelids pooling with tears. Blinking them away, he put down his bags. "Hi, Dad." He hugged the old man. "Time for a visit, huh?"

His dad released the grasp of his son's arms and patted him on the shoulder. "You got that right, son. Come on in."

Zach retrieved his bags and followed his dad into the living room. When his view landed on the kitchen doorway, he dropped his jaw.

Willow stood facing him and brushed a hair dangling in her face. "Welcome home, Zachary Hayes." *He's more attractive than in the magazine photos.* His well-defined arms and muscles filling out his tight T-shirt made her heart spring forward, spinning in a frenzy. But she halted it, controlling her feelings with every ounce of energy she had. *Uh-oh, I might be in trouble.*

Zach's eyes widened, his eyebrows shooting into his forehead. "Willow Mason? Damn, you grew up."

A surprising heat spread across Willow's face. "Yes, I did. Dinner's almost ready. I'll call you guys." She bolted back to the kitchen to finish the food prep but kept glancing into the living room as she worked.

"She's quite the gal. Been making me dinner every night, trying out new recipes. I'm happy to help her any way I can." George patted Zach's shoulder. "Let's get you settled. I heard you might be staying a bit."

"Yeah, Pops, we'll see. Let me unload the truck, and we'll talk more at dinner." Zach washed up and joined his dad at the dinner table.

Willow served a roasted chicken, baked potatoes, a vegetable side dish, and a salad.

Zach inhaled and exhaled with a muffled sigh. "These last six months I've been on the road full-time, and I haven't had a home-cooked meal like this in ages. Looks and smells amazing."

Willow poured him a drink of lemonade.

"Hope you didn't go through all of this trouble on my account."

Their gazes collided, and a ripple of nerves fluttered across her belly, making breathing difficult. The chemistry she encountered as a freckle-faced kid still existed, but now the attraction was infused with an itching in her adult body, stirring up desire on a whole different level. "Well, I couldn't serve hot dogs, could I, on your first day back home? Leah and your dad made a special request, and I was happy to oblige." She glimpsed him again for an instant but averted her gaze afterward. No way was she engaging in any fantasies or flirting with this man. *No way.*

"Are you joining us?"

"No, no. I'll let you two catch up."

"And miss this great meal?" George pointed toward the empty chair. "You sit, young lady. I insist."

Willow took a deep breath. *Guess I'm not getting*

out of this one.

"Yes, I insist as well." Zach's steadfast gaze didn't move.

"All right. Let me get a plate. You two start before it gets cold." She whisked around to retrieve a dish.

"Smells delicious, Willow." Zach's voice boomed toward the kitchen.

Willow entered the dining room again. "Thanks."

George motioned to his son with his fork. "How long are you staying?"

"I'm not sure. If you need anything done, I could help you out around here. I've got some writing to do too." Zach picked up a knife.

"Great. Maybe you can go into the store with me tomorrow. I can show you the upgrades, and you can work awhile." George scooped mashed potatoes on his fork with a piece of chicken.

Zach's gaze darted to Willow.

She caught his glance and nodded. *He's getting it.*

"Yeah. Leah told me you've also got some projects going on in the garage. I'd like to see those." He gripped his fork tighter.

"Sure. I can show you after dinner." He returned to eating, and silence fell upon the table.

"So, Willow, Leah tells me you recently moved back here from New York City. Small-town living is a big transition."

"Yes." *In more ways than I'm telling you about.*

"Has Cedar Hill changed much since you last lived here?"

"A little." *Don't be rude.* "You should wander around Main Street. More boutique stores have opened, a charming riverwalk wanders through the city park, and a couple of new upscale restaurants have taken up residence. Cedar Hill's not the big city, but I like it."

"How about giving me a tour, if you're not too busy one day?"

Willow caught a playful glint sparkling in his eyes. "I work a lot of hours. Not sure if I'll have time." *Don't be a snob.* She wrapped an unruly hair around her ear and rose. "Maybe next week. I'm starting on these dishes. Do either of you want coffee?"

"I'll have a cup, dear. Any pie tonight?"

"Of course. Peach, your favorite."

"She's my girl. See, what did I tell you? She takes terrific care of me at dinner."

She smiled, then turned, scurrying into the kitchen.

"You're a terrific cook, Mason." Zach yelled out to Willow working at the counter. "I'll take a cup, too, if you don't mind." He stood. "Let me help you clear the table." He slipped past with a chicken platter and vegetable dish, grazing her arm.

A shiver rushed up her spine as the arm brushed hers. *Too close.* "Thanks." She created some distance and prepared the after-dinner desserts.

"I can help, if you like." Zach's drawl lingered in the air.

"No, thank you. Spend time with your dad while you can. Coffee and pie will be ready in a minute." She was doing everything she could to clear the kitchen of this sexy man. The fact she fantasized about him tightened every muscle in her body. She served the men their pie and coffee and hurried back to the kitchen to clean the mess, eager to go. She stretched, putting the last clean dish in the cupboard.

Zach slid two more dirty plates in the sink. "I'll get

these last two. No need for you to do everything."

She glanced into his eyes and held eye contact for a fleeting second or two. Willow's guard was up, locked and secure, and her emotions hidden. She bent at the waist, tying the overflowing garbage bag. "Okay, I've got something I have to do at home." She struggled to lift the bag.

But Zach grabbed it, brushing a hand over hers.

Innocent, yes, but a prickling sensation crawled up her spinal column. Sweat formed on the back of her neck—not a good sign.

"I've got this." He swung it over his shoulder and flew out the kitchen door.

She couldn't say anything. Willow peeked out the window, watching Zach toss the bag into the can. He stood tall, about six feet, with broad shoulders and wavy brown hair brushing his collar. An image of a sculpted, toned body underneath his clothes flashed through her mind. She shook her head. *Squash that idea. This is Leah's big brother.* The one who never gave her the time of day and never bothered to talk to her much, if ever. As the screen door opened, she twisted around to face him. "Thank you."

"I appreciate you've been coming over here to help, Willow. Don't worry. Leah and I will figure this out." He kept his voice low.

"No problem. But you are paying me, and I'm serious about my work. I'll say goodbye to your dad and leave now. Glad you made it here." Willow eyed him briefly, then headed toward the living room.

George retired in his favorite easy chair with a remote, searching the channels. "Willow, would you be a dear and find my show? I can't seem to find it."

He was becoming more confused using the TV remote this past week, and Willow made a mental note to tell Leah. "Sure, Mr. Hayes." She fixed it and headed for the front door.

Zach stepped into the foyer. "Thanks for dinner again. Are you coming tomorrow?" He cocked his head. "I'm not a very good cook."

His flirtatious, crooked grin did not go unnoticed. "Whatever you guys need, I'm here. Have Leah call me after you've made some decisions."

"Will do."

She darted out of the house. Zach's seductive eyes and overpowering presence were too much.

****

Willow's beauty, even in jeans and an apron, intrigued Zach. Her curly, brown hair, olive skin, and dark eyes were still the same, but she was nothing like the kid he remembered. A sadness set in her eyes, like a dimmed light, once solid and bright, but was no longer. What happened in her last relationship? Leah told him the whole breakup was devastating on more levels than the heart—whatever that meant. He'd have to get more details from Leah and was more than curious now. This little writing retreat might not be so bad. Willow Mason was tempting him, and he was up for the challenge, wherever it led.

When Zach entered the living room, he noticed his dad was engaged in some game show. "Hey, Pops. I'm taking a shower and then unpacking. Need anything?"

"No. How long are you staying?"

"I'm not sure yet. At least a week. Is it okay with you?" Zach searched his dad's demeanor for any resistance. The usual edge had magically softened. Did he forget how angry he had been at Zach all these years for not taking over the hardware business and following in his footsteps? *Is it possible?*

"Sure." And he returned to his show.

Zach rubbed the stubble on his chin. *What's with this new attitude?* Dad's anger from a year ago had dissipated. *Is it his condition?*

After showering, he toweled his wet hair, catching a glimpse of himself in the mirror. In his early thirties, he still portrayed a youthful appearance. Yes, he achieved great success and amassed wealth, but did the shallowness of his lifestyle affect his writing? Nothing new or deep emerged in quite a while.

He sat on his childhood bed and picked up his phone, scrolling through messages and social media. At this point in his career, he paid a professional in Nashville to handle his social media accounts for the most part, but occasionally, he posted. He leaned back against the pillows and scanned the room. His dad had never thrown anything away since he left. The wall was adorned with dated country music posters of singers and album covers. Old baseball trophies from junior high school lined the top of the dresser, along with one for football in high school. An athletic youngster, Zach made every sports team he tried out for in school.

Zach's focus rested on his dad's old guitar leaning against the wall in the corner, and his heart leapt. Zach learned how to play on it as a kid. His dad had been his first teacher, and when Zach committed to practicing music, he'd been gifted an expensive brand he still owned and played. The same one he'd brought home with him.

He climbed off the bed and picked up the

instrument by its neck. Sitting on the edge of a nearby chair, he ran his fingers across the wood, basking in the memories of himself as a kid with his dad—the first chords, the first songs, and the exhilaration of playing something sounding halfway decent. After his parents bought him the new guitar, he used to play folk songs and simple country tunes with his dad, strumming and singing along at the top of their lungs. *Can Dad still play?* Residual anger might harbor inside of his dad but playing together might ease a bit of the remaining angst. He wasn't sure what his relationship was with his father anymore and guessed he would find out soon enough.

****

The screen door slammed behind her, and Willow tossed her purse on the kitchen counter at home. She rubbed her neck as every muscle in her body was tense from spending so much time with Zachary Hayes. *Why am I so nervous around him?* Now she understood why all his groupies lapsed into mush, blubbering, and giggling around him. His charm was magnetic, and you'd have to be an idiot not to feel it. *A normal reaction to a star. Nothing to worry about.* Satisfied, she ventured into the living room to see if her mom needed anything. "Hey, are you hungry? I have leftovers from the Hayes's house."

"No, thanks. I already ate. Put them in the fridge, and I'll heat them up tomorrow. How was your day? Come sit and tell me everything." She patted the couch. "Did Zach make it home?"

"Yeah. In time for dinner. They insisted I eat with them, or I would have been home sooner."

"And?"

31

She wants more details about Zachary Hayes. Who wouldn't? She plopped onto the sofa. "He was kind and gracious and as handsome as all the tabloid pictures make him out to be. Seeing his dad so quiet and mildly confused at this stage surprised him, I think. I'm not sure, though. We didn't talk much."

"I hope he and Leah figure things out. George Hayes is a good man, and this diagnosis has been hard for the whole family."

Willow tugged at her hair scrunchy. "I need a shower and want to read my book. I'm beat." She stood and kissed her mom on the cheek.

"Goodnight, dear. Get some rest."

After showering, Willow sprawled out on her bed, holding a paperback. Before opening it, she lay still, staring at the ceiling. Her brain was full of Zachary Hayes. Oh, dear God, she didn't need this kind of distraction now or ever. She would not allow another charismatic man to suck her into his life and knock her off course—even if the thoughts were one-sided. Erasing them should be easier, since they were all in her head at this point. *Yes, I delete the thoughts as they come in.* She chuckled at the analogy of deleting him from her brain's inbox each time, but it could work. But if it didn't, she'd have a problem—and a big one.

Chapter Four

The next morning, Zach poured himself a cup of coffee and retrieved a slice of toast from the toaster. The ancient toaster was the same one he had growing up. *Need some upgrades around here.* He mixed eggs and was about to scramble them in a pan. Breakfast, he could do.

Dad appeared from around the corner wearing a clean but wrinkled shirt, half tucked in his baggy pants.

"Coffee? I'm scrambling some eggs too."

"Sure. Then we can head over to the store."

"Leah is stopping by first, okay?" He would try and stall the store visit for as long as possible. That much he could do.

George shook his head and sat at the kitchen table, fixing his coffee. "How long are you staying?"

"At least a week. I've got to write some new songs for my next album. I finished my tour and don't have to play anywhere for a few weeks." He searched his father's eyes for a response.

"Hmm." Dad drank his coffee, staring straight ahead.

Zach had no clue what was going through his father's mind, which was strange and unlike him. Usually, he would say things like, *'When are you moving back?'* or *'When can you start working at the store?'* Zach side-puckered his lips, his gut uneasy.

Where's the fight? Where's the argument? He shrugged, then peeked out the window. Tires screeched, skidding into the driveway—his sister, hell on wheels. "Leah's here, Dad."

Leah bounded into the house, out of breath. "Hey, everybody!" She kissed her dad and then grabbed her brother, hugging him with a firm embrace. When she released him, she kept her sight locked in with his. "About time you came home."

"Not holding back, huh?" No pussyfooting around the topic of his longtime absences. A straight shooter, Leah dealt with any nonsense with a firm resolve and was one of the most dedicated and loyal people on the planet. Standing in the kitchen, Zach felt devoured by a wave of guilt for not coming home to support her earlier. "Yeah, you're right." He lowered his head, face flushed. "And I'm sorry."

Leah eyed him with both hands on her hips. "I guess you're forgiven." She tossed her curly blonde hair back and chuckled. "Breakfast?"

"Coming right up." Zach turned, hurrying back to the kitchen.

After the three were seated, Leah related stories about Rosie and her first days in school with an animated voice.

Zach told a few about his recent tour, minus the escapades with the women he'd met along the way.

George listened but didn't ask questions. When they were cleaning up, he stood. "Time to get to the store, son."

Leah eyed Zach with a raised brow. "Let us clean up, Dad, and then I need to talk to Zach for a minute about something. We'll come get you."

"I don't want to be late, so don't take too long." He turned to leave.

"We won't." Leah kissed him on the cheek. After her dad settled in the living room, she confronted Zach. "Let's go outside."

Zach followed her.

"How's he been since you've been home?"

"Weird. He hasn't argued with me once. He's quieter and subdued but doesn't seem sad or unhappy. He does keep talking about the store. Would it be okay if I took him later? He needs to get used to becoming a customer rather than the boss."

"As long as you're with him. You're right. Let him take on his new role gradually and with your support—if you're up to it."

"I'm here to help, sis. I'll be staying for at least a week, or it could be more. Let's assess the situation later. But I would like Willow to stay on for dinner prep, if possible. Cooking isn't my forte beyond scrambled eggs." His intentions for the attractive woman were more than getting meals served. *She's hot.* And he loved a challenge.

"She needs the money, so I'm sure she'll continue. No problem." She swept a dangling hair strand away from her face.

"Not to be nosey or anything, but what happened in New York?"

"Messy divorce in the works and devastating on many levels. Really did a number on her."

"Like how?" He shifted his stance, kicking at the patio cement beneath his boot.

"You'll have to ask her yourself—not my story to tell, Zach. She is my best friend and feels ashamed about the whole ordeal. She blames herself for the mess she's in, but I trust Willow. She'll bounce back."

His curiosity was more than piqued, but he could see he wasn't getting any information out of his sister. He'd have to try another route. "Tell Liam we'll stop by later."

Leah touched him. "Thanks. I'm glad you're here."

He wrapped her in a solid embrace. "Me too."

Inside, Zach found his father sitting in the easy chair, staring into space.

Dad craned his neck, peering around. "I can't find the remote. Do you see it anywhere?"

Zach searched until he found it on the floor behind his chair. "Here you go, Pops."

"Is my game show on now?"

Leah stepped forward. "No, Dad. It comes on tonight. Why don't you show Zach your projects out in the garage? He might want to order one too." She winked at Zach.

"Oh. All right." He stood. "I've got to get to the store."

Zach touched his shoulder. "We'll go, Dad. A little later. Do we need more things for your projects? Let's make a list."

"Good idea. How long are you staying?" He tilted his head upward and shoved his hands into his back jean pockets.

Zach told him and realized the question would be repeated frequently. Inside, his heart sagged, its aching wrapped around his chest. His father was not the same man he had been a year ago. Gone was the feisty, argumentative person who challenged Zach's every act and decision. In his place was a more complacent man.

He was still kind but lacked the driving spirit Zach found familiar or inspiring. After he moved to Nashville, Zach struggled to be around him, but now, he missed the gutsy, outspoken man. "Probably a week or longer. Show me what you're working on."

Dad turned and headed toward the garage.

Zach followed and waved goodbye to his sister as she left. He wrestled with his emotions, but he found he could only put one foot in front of the other as he followed the crooked path to the garage.

****

When a truck screeched into a parking space across the street, Willow lifted her head from working on the front window display of the bookstore. The same guys again. *What are they doing?* Curious, she observed as they carried some surveying equipment and set it up close to the store.

A shiny black luxury car parked behind them, and an attractive man dressed in a navy suit climbed out and approached the men. They greeted each other and pointed to Readers Bookshop, discussing something, and gesturing with hand movements.

I should find out what's going on. Willow stood, tucked her shirt into her jeans, and opened the front door. The store didn't open for another fifteen minutes, so she could leave. She waited until the man with the fancy suit was headed back to his car and intercepted him. "Excuse me, sir. Can I talk to you a second?"

The man lowered his phone. "What can I do for you, miss?"

Willow approached. "I work at the store across the street. Are you doing renovations or something?"

"I'm putting in a bid to buy this portion of the

block—building condos. The market's on fire."

Willow glided a hand over the gut punch slammed to her stomach. *Condos? Here?* "Condos?" She couldn't get another word out.

"Yep. Perfect place. Still in the beginning phase. The surveyors are for my presentation to the town council since the building is next to a historical landmark site. Just protocol. I do this all the time." He stared.

Is he checking me out? Willow cringed. "Oh."

"Do you own the bookstore?"

"No. I'm the manager." Willow shifted her weight, brushing a hair from her eye.

"I'm sure the owner will be willing to relocate somewhere else. I'll be offering a tempting price." He dug inside of his jacket. "Here's my card, if you have more questions."

He sure is full of himself. "Thanks." Willow left and headed straight to the store, getting away from the man as fast as possible. Was this true? Did Marcy have a clue? She had a sinking feeling her livelihood was in danger again, and she could do nothing about it. She dropped her forehead onto her palm, shaking it side to side.

Willow plucked her phone out of her jeans pocket and called Marcy. "I've got something to tell you." She informed her about the surveying and the man in the suit.

"I'll stop by and pick up the card around lunch time. I might as well get ahead of this before any big surprises. Thanks, Willow."

After the phone call, Willow sat at the register and gaped at the books lining the shelves and displays.

Nausea rippled inside, its movement tormenting her. She didn't want to find another job. This one suited her fine for now, and she doubted Marcy would want to relocate the store. As she shuffled some papers on the counter, she slumped. Her future was becoming murkier. The stability she worked hard at establishing since leaving New York was unraveling. Searching for a new job was not part of her plan—not in the least.

****

Zach and his dad spent the morning in the garage, cutting mini-size boards, gluing them together, and making sturdy birdhouses. Dad had built a complete workshop in half of the garage years ago and was skillful at making almost anything. Owning a hardware store, he understood a thing or two about construction, electricity, plumbing, or anything else related to tools or equipment supplies.

Zach reminisced about fond memories as a teenager. He spent hours in the same spot, learning to use a block plane and table saw. "Hey, Pops. How's this one?" Zach turned, holding up his almost-finished base structure.

"Not bad. Give it here." George grasped the wood frame, inspecting it from every angle. "See this nail?"

"Yeah."

"It would be better placed down here for strength but overall, pretty good, son." He handed the wood back to Zach and paused. "We need to go the store now. They're waiting for me."

Zach wasn't quite sure who *they* were. Old employees? But he agreed to take him for a buying expedition. "We could use some more paint in different colors. Let's go after I finish nailing the roof together."

"All right." George immersed himself in fitting pieces together.

"How about I make us a couple of sandwiches after this before we head to the store? I'm starving."

George nodded and kept working.

Zach also needed to return a few calls. His manager had left two messages, and a couple of his buddies were also weighing in on his visit. Manager first.

"How's it going? Any creativity flowing yet?"

Mike was pushing hard, and less than a day had passed. "No, but I'm settling into being with my dad. He's changed, and I'm wrapping my head around that first. I did find my guitar he taught me my first chords on last night—sparked some fond memories."

"If I didn't bug you, I wouldn't be doing my job, right?"

"Yeah. Give me the week. I need this time." No matter what, Zach was the boss in this situation. He lived his life the way he wanted, and no one could tell him otherwise. He always believed in himself, and the belief never failed him.

"I hear ya. Enjoy Ohio." Mike ended the call.

Zach shuffled back to the house, determined to make a connection with his dad, be it bologna sandwiches or birdhouses. He curled his lips upward as he gathered the meat, cheese, bread, and whatever else he could find. *Who does the grocery shopping? Leah? Or Willow?* Willow. *What a stunner.* He was still shocked at her beauty—and very attracted to those melancholy brown eyes, hinting at a trace of mysterious secrets. He'd research her later to read her New York story. At least, he secured a daily encounter by hiring her as their dinner chef. He was happy to keep her cooking for as long as possible.

****

Marcy worked most of the morning with Willow, reviewing and balancing the thick accounting ledgers for Readers Bookshop. She insisted on staying over lunch, so Willow could run an errand.

Willow wanted to buy paint for her bedroom and hoped to get a first coat on at least one wall after making dinner for the Hayes men. Her heart did a little flip, as she daydreamed about Zachary, but she was determined to secure the wall between them. Her female hormones had jumped to attention seeing him, but no matter how challenging ignoring him might be, she could do it. The thought of Charles alone was enough to reinforce the wall, as anger and hurt from his betrayal surged through her. She steered into the Hayes Hardware parking lot and rushed inside to select her paint.

She perused the color charts on the wall until she found a pale-peach hue she liked. After giving her order to the guy behind the counter, she turned and jumped, startled to find herself inches from Zach's chest, standing right behind her. "Oh, hi." *What are you doing here?*

"I guess great minds think alike. Got a painting project?" He grinned and swiped at a fallen strand across his eye.

She peeked over at George, who was talking to an employee with Liam by his side. "Uh, yes." She didn't plan on this encounter today.

"What is it?"

His intent stare prevented her from slipping away.

"My bedroom. Or rather future bedroom in my new apartment." Did she mention her *bedroom* to this man? *Yikes, I'm in trouble.*

"Are you getting a new apartment? Leah told me you were living in your old house with your mom." He shifted his stance, hooking a thumb on the belt loop of his jeans.

"I'm fixing up the old mother-in-law's apartment above the garage my dad built when my grandma was alive. The unit was supposed to be for her, but she died. Then he died, and it never got finished."

"Very impressive. You're a woman of many talents, I see." He bent his head sideways, and the edges of his mouth pulled upward.

She tapped a foot, shifting her weight back and forth. *When will the paint be ready?* "I'm giving it my best shot." She retrieved her cans from the employee and exhaled over pursed lips. "I've got to get back to the store. See you later." Willow waved to George and Liam, paid at the front counter, and exited as fast as she could, dumping the paint cans into her trunk and hopping into the front seat. She gripped the steering wheel and focused on her breathing. *Whoosh, in and out. Easy does it.* Zachary Hayes was throwing a wrench into her plans of recovery. Did she have the strength to endure his daily presence? At least, he lived in Nashville and would have to leave at some point. Sooner than later would be better.

****

Mesmerized by the endless whirling of the mixing machine, Zach stood and waited for the paint. When finished, he attended to his dad, who was still talking to his brother-in-law. Zach caught a look from Liam and

42

angled his head—time to redirect George. He listened to the conversation and couldn't help but reflect on Willow. She quickened to escape their every encounter. *What's up with her?* He was used to women flaunting themselves, desperate to get his attention. This deflection made his pulse accelerate in anticipation of winning her over, and the floral scent of hers drove him crazy. But she was his sister's best friend, not a typical woman. A casual hookup wouldn't work. He shook his head. *Best not to get involved with anyone right now.* "Hey, Dad. Let's check out the paints."

"Okay, I'm coming." George turned and walked with him.

Zach noticed the relief on Liam's face.

He followed his dad to the color charts and purchased five bright colors, a cheery assortment to use on the birdhouses. Leah was building a customer base, so if Dad was content filling those orders, his days would be active and productive. Keeping busy was important, but another conversation about the store would be forthcoming. *Not looking forward to that.*

After loading the cans and a few other supplies into the truck, Zach glanced at his dad and noticed a blank expression in his eyes, which were fixed straight ahead. "Everything all right, Pops?"

George took a breath in and let it out through puckered lips. "You guys don't think I understand what's happening, but I do. When I got the diagnosis in the doctor's office, I read up on the disease before my mind started playing tricks on me. I can't run this business anymore. When I tried, I made mistakes, but, son, if you've poured all your heart and sweat into something, you can't walk away easily."

Silence stilled the air. Zach arched his forehead upward, stunned his father shared his feelings and was so clear in his communication. This dementia thing had not completely taken him. He was dealing with it in his own way, and Zach wanted to support him. "Yeah, I can only imagine." He patted his dad's shoulder. "We'll get through it."

George lifted the corners of his mouth. "Let's go home."

New feelings of compassion, shaded by sorrow, erupted in his gut, and Zach bit his lip. His father's courage was inspiring, and his unusual silence had been his mechanism for dealing with all the changes in his life. Given his father's tendency to avoid emotional discussions, Zach was caught off guard with his dad's introspection. He yearned to hurry home, pick up a pen and paper with his guitar, and write. *Is Dad becoming my muse?*

Chapter Five

Willow locked the front door of Readers Bookshop and flipped the *Closed* sign on the entry window. The afternoon had been busy, so notions of Zach took a back seat. *Thank God.*

Marcy spoke to Robert Matthews, the big-shot investor from earlier, and her fears were confirmed. He told Marcy the same thing and would await the town's council approval before taking the next steps. The meeting was scheduled for next week.

Great. Just what I need. Willow scrolled her phone, then thumbed through a magazine while waiting in line at the local grocery. Something simple tonight, like pasta and salad. *Can't wait to go home and start painting.*

Willow parked her car at George's house and lifted the grocery bags out of the trunk, both arms balancing them with precise skill.

Zach rushed out the kitchen door and plucked one of the bags. "Here, let me help."

She glanced at his bulging biceps and the tousled hair hanging above his brow, making her butterflies flip into cartwheels. *Here we go.* "Thanks." *No avoiding this man—might as well surrender.*

"What's for dinner tonight?"

"Pasta and salad. Okay?" *I need to find out what he likes to eat.* George was easy, but Zach might have different tastes. She wanted to maintain a professional relationship with him while cooking in their kitchen.

"Sounds great. I'm starved." He tucked his right hand into his jeans pocket and tilted his head. "I can help."

She peeked in his direction, and a tremor surged across her belly. "No, I've got it but thank you. Could you write down some of your favorite meals? Your dad eats anything, but what do you like?"

"I pretty much eat anything, too." He grabbed a bottle of water from the refrigerator. "If you don't need help, then I want to check on Pops. When I left him an hour ago, he was deep into birdhouse mode. Leah was right. He needs to stay active and productive."

She lowered her gaze, busying herself with prepping vegetables for the salad.

"I'll be back in a minute." He tugged the screen door open and strode to the garage.

Willow lowered her cutting knife and peered out the window. Zach's hips swayed, strutting across the lawn, his long arms hung to his side. *Cocky kind of guy, eh?* His sturdy build, accentuated by faded jeans and a tight T-shirt, highlighted his broad chest and slim waistline. *Too distracting.* But today, he seemed more like a regular guy and not the famous country music star clamoring for attention.

After dinner was served, she returned to the kitchen. She wanted to go home and start painting. She lied and told Zach and his dad she was eating with her mom. She finished cleaning up the pots and pans, then wiped the counter and stove with a sponge.

Zach appeared with the dirty dishes. "Delicious, Willow. You're quite the cook." He placed them on the counter.

She didn't lift her gaze but could hear his soft breathing, teasing her senses and sending goose bumps up her spinal column. Faint hints of a woodsy cologne enticed her nostrils, weakening her knees. "Thanks."

"When are you starting your painting project?"

She didn't want to be curt. *A little conversation couldn't hurt, could it?* "Tonight, I hope. I'm excited to see if the color I picked out looks just as good on the wall as it does on the color chart."

"Yeah, one of our blues is brighter than on the sample at the store. But I guess brighter is better for a birdhouse, so it attracts the birds." He shifted his body weight back and forth, not moving from the kitchen. "If you like, I could help you tonight. Dad enjoys his evening television shows, and I'm sure he won't leave. During the day is when he gets restless."

"I agree, and you don't have to help me. I can do it myself." *Can't trust myself alone with you.*

"I insist. Besides, I'm a little restless at night. I'm used to working evenings, remember?"

What should she do? Be rude? He was Leah's big brother and would be gone soon. He was more like family—the skinny kid from grade school who rode his bike around the neighborhood, terrorizing the girls, including herself. "Well, if you insist. Two hands are better than one."

"Great. I'll be over right after you leave. I need to check some emails and answer a phone call."

"Okay." Ready or not, she had just invited this gorgeous hunk of an irresistible man to help paint her new bedroom—a risky move on her part. And possibly a dumb one.

****

Thirty minutes later, Willow bent over, spreading out a plastic sheet across the floor. She covered the bed frame but slumped to her knees while attempting to move it. She couldn't do it by herself—she *did* need help. A creaking noise echoed from the back stairs, and she shot up her head.

Zach filled the doorway, shoulders almost touching the sides. "Your steps could need a coat, too, and they need to be repaired in a few places."

As she blocked the bedroom with the bed, she lifted her gaze. "Yeah, I noticed." Knees wobbling, she motioned him into the room. *Friend, friend, friend. Keep the mantra going.*

"Let's try and get this frame into the living room." He reached for the metal structure.

"Yeah, I needed another pair of hands." Willow rubbed her sweaty palms against her jeans.

He reversed it on its side. "Grab it like this."

After a few moments, she stood in the living room and broke into a smile.

"Much better." Zach swatted at a fallen strand over his eyelid.

"You're right. Thank you." She pivoted, pressing a hand to her rollercoaster stomach. "I've got brushes and supplies in here. Let me show you."

He saluted. "At your service, Miss Mason."

She bit her bottom lip, holding back a chuckle. "Better watch what you say, Hayes. A lot of work needs to be done here."

"Hard work never scared me." He bent over with a screwdriver in hand to open a can. "Let's see what we've got."

Picking up a brush from the tray she held, Willow ignored the potent odor of paint chemicals and focused on the rhythm of smooth straight lines. She moved to another wall and checked out Zach—to make sure he was getting the corners. *Can't keep my eyes off him.* "A little different than making a record in Nashville, eh?"

He hummed something, shrugged, and dabbed his brush against the surface.

Willow shook her head and angled back to the wall. "Long straight lines." She instructed him in firm voice. *Is he messing with me?* She stepped back to check her own progress, and newspaper crunched, then slipped. A foot shot upward, and paint and brush flew high. Willow squealed and landed on the hardwood floor, butt first. Face hot, she peered up at Zach and pointed a finger. "Don't you dare laugh!"

Zach threw up both hands. "Never." He lowered his brush onto the plastic tray.

The intense smell of paint was stronger now, and Willow's backside throbbed.

"Let me help you." Zach extended a hand.

She took it, slowly standing, and then remained still, aware of his strong grip. He smelled more like a musky spice than paint and was staring with such intensity her heart jumped. "Thanks."

"No problem."

His smirk toyed with her. *He's enjoying this a little too much.* Willow shifted away, anxious to forget the warmth of his hand squeezing hers. Grabbing a clean rag, she wiped the excess paint off her bum, ignoring the warmth settled in her cheeks. After an hour, she stood and admired the work. "I love it."

"Fantastic, I must say. We're a good team, Mason.

What's next?"

"Bathroom and living room?"

He peeked into the bathroom. "Easy. Let's do this tomorrow." He stepped to the sink to wash his dirty hands. Nothing poured out of the faucet. "This could be a problem."

"Yeah, plumbing is on my list. All of it needs to be redone. I could afford the painting first, but I'll have enough saved next month to hire a plumber." She just exposed her dire financial situation. *Pathetic. Should have kept my mouth shut.*

"My dad did teach me a simple thing or two about plumbing. I could at least look at it."

"You've done enough. I'll figure it out."

"Whatever you say." He returned to the living room, picked up the lids, and secured them on the paint cans.

She grabbed some clean rags. "We can wash up outside at the spigot by Mom's house."

He followed her, carrying the brushes and rollers.

Willow shivered while descending the stairs. Dusk settled in around her, draping her surroundings in a soft, fading glow and bringing cooler temperatures. She switched on the water and rushed in at the same time as Zach. She bumped his hands, splashing water across her face. As she wiped away the wetness, Willow laughed. "You go first."

"Ladies, first. I insist."

She scrubbed the dirty brushes, wiping them with vigorous strokes, and stepped away when finished.

Zach did the same and stood.

She handed him a dry towel. "Thanks."

"No problem. How about I grill some hamburgers

tomorrow? Pops loves them, and you'd only have to do the sides."

"Sounds easy." She curled a loose hair behind her ear.

He handed her back the towel. "We'll tackle the bathroom tomorrow." He smiled his self-assured grin and headed for his truck.

Seeing Zach's truck disappear, Willow headed toward the garage. *What am I doing?* She accepted help from Zachary Hayes, the famous country music star, to fix her apartment—more time together and more angst. *I need a therapy session with Leah.* Her sister would give her the feedback she needed to keep her head straight. But what about her heart? Could she protect it? Maybe. Maybe not.

Chapter Six

The next day, Willow dropped her butt on the park
bench overlooking a wide Crestview River. The rushing
current swirled by, enticing her to let go of any worries
harbored within. Holding sandwiches in a bag, she
scooted over to make room for Leah.

"This never gets old." Leah passed her an iced tea.
"Love the warm weather in early September." She tilted
her head toward the sun for a moment and closed her
eyes.

"Thanks for taking your lunch break with me."
Willow grinned, admiring the massive oak and hickory
trees still clinging to their lavish leaves, and handed her
a sandwich and a bag of chips.

Leah shared a small therapy practice with two
other professionals at the edge of town. She worked
part-time to be available for Rosie before and after
school. "What's up?"

Willow told her of the events which transpired over
the last two days and about her interactions with Zach.
"I'm ashamed to say, I still have a crush on your
brother. Different from when I was fifteen, but I'm an
adult now, with unwanted baggage. I can't get involved
with anyone. I'm not even divorced yet." She slumped
back against the bench. "I feel like I'm damaged goods,
Leah. I'm ashamed I didn't see what was right in front
of me with Charles. I feel foolish. How do I get over it?

And I'm mad at myself for crushing on your brother. He's your dashing, famous brother, and I can't help noticing his charm and charisma—all-star quality." She blew air out through pursed lips.

"He's quite the magnet for women. Don't beat yourself up, Willow. Your feelings are normal, and I'm glad you have them for another man. Gives me hope you'll one day get over that sneaky liar, Charles." Leah bit into her turkey sandwich, and a huge glob of mayonnaise dribbled down her chin. She wiped it with a napkin.

"And another thing. I accepted his offer to help me paint my new apartment. Was it a mistake?" She set down her drink, a crease forming between her brows.

"Oh, Willow. You've got to rewire your brain, girl. First, Zach is my brother, so he's also your friend. Friends help friends—very simple. You're overthinking this."

Willow sat silent for a moment, staring at the water hastening downstream in front of her. "You're right." She crunched on a potato chip, contemplating her emotions.

"I am."

"I…I'm feeling attracted to him and don't want to be. I can't. A long time will pass before I'm ready to open to another man again."

"So, be friends. Concentrate on friendship, not courtship." Leah paused and tilted her head. "You need to forgive yourself, Willow. If you were my client, I would tell you to focus on forgiving first, so a deeper healing can happen for you and your precious heart." She patted an arm. "I'm always here if you need me."

Willow grabbed Leah's hand. "You're the best.

Thank you."

"And about your apartment. He'll be here for a week. I'd be surprised if he stays longer. Take all the help you can get. As his friend, you allow him to leave the house when Dad is safe and occupied. And besides, he can be a little selfish and self-centered, so giving to others does him good. He could use some mental readjusting, too." Leah flipped her hair back and laughed. "I can say such a thing because I'm his sister—and a therapist."

Willow straightened her posture. "Friends it will be then. I can do friends."

"Yes, you can." Leah stood and tossed her garbage in a nearby trash can. "Sorry, I've got to head back. I have a client at one. Thanks for lunch."

Willow hugged Leah and walked with her toward Main Street.

"Don't forget about Rosie's birthday party on Saturday. You'll have another day off dinner duty. I'll make sure they have plenty of leftovers for later if they get hungry. Zach can handle the microwave."

"I hope so. I found the perfect present." Willow discovered a pink ballet skirt covered in silver sequins in the window of *Dreamy Treasures*, a children's boutique store on Main Street. Rosie adored pink and loved to dance. *Should be a hit.*

Leah waved goodbye.

As Willow strolled back to the store, she reflected on their conversation. Could she see Zach as her new buddy? She had her doubts but hoped so.

****

Willow arrived at the Hayes's house and stared at Zach hunched over the grill. Ash dusted both hands, the air smelled of lighter fluid, and an empty charcoal bag lay crumpled on the back porch.

He bent over to do some magic with the coals, stretching his jeans even tighter.

Oh, no. She wiped the sweat dripping on her brow.

Turning, he nudged the lush, wavy hair out of his eyes, exchanging looks.

Focus, girl. On the groceries…he's just a friend. Bags in arms and gaze cast down, she darted for the door.

And Zach grabbed the bags out of her hands.

"Thanks. How's your dad?" *Just my friend. But those tight-fitting jeans—way too hot. And that smile—too sexy.*

He put the bags on the counter. "Okay. We've been busy together in the garage, checked out the river, and I even messed around on my guitar."

"Leah said you were working on a new album. How's it going?" She reached for her apron hanging on a hook by the stove.

"I'm feeling pressure from my record label to write, but nothing's coming. Emotions and melodies are stirring, but if I'm honest, I'm a little stuck. But I'm giving myself time to let the inspiration come. Can't hurry the muse." He squeezed his dimples into his cheeks.

"I'm sure you'll figure it out." She took out the ingredients for the sides and placed them on the counter. "You can light the coals now. This won't take long."

"Okay." He plucked a spatula out of the drawer. "I like your company, Mason."

Willow shifted her stance, a prickling rising in her

spine. "Thanks. I like cooking for you guys."

He left to build a fire and wipe down a few patio chairs.

Did he compliment me? Willow shook her head, then prepped a green salad, and placed the store-bought potato salad into a bowl. *Keep busy. Ignore him.* She wanted his help and liked hanging out. If she focused on just the easy *friend* relationship, would the attraction dissipate?

Zach marched inside. "Charcoal's almost ready, and I cleaned off the table on the porch. We can eat outside." Sidling nearer, he peeked over her shoulder. "*Mmm.* Nice salad."

His breath tickled her neck, triggering a shiver. "Want to grab the condiments in the refrigerator and buns on the counter?"

"Sure. I'll tell Dad dinner's almost ready, too."

"Thanks."

Before sitting at the table, Zach served the hamburgers on a platter, grilled to perfection.

Willow lowered onto a chair, breathing deep into the smoky, slightly charred aroma of the burgers. Her stomach growled.

George reached for a bun. "Is there ketchup?"

Willow gave him the plastic bottle and caught Zach smiling. *Is he grateful I'm sharing this journey?* Suddenly, he became her friend, her neighbor, and her best friend's brother—not the celebrity. She exhaled, then bit into the juicy, fatty goodness of the meat. She quickly dabbed her mouth's edge as the excess trickled along her jaw. When dinner was finished, Willow held out a platter of freshly baked cookies from a local bakery under their noses, enticing them with a whiff of chocolate and sugary dough oozing out into the air. "Anyone for dessert?"

George grabbed one. "Thanks, dear."

Zach snatched a cookie. "Thanks." He locked in a stare with Willow.

She didn't avoid him. "You're welcome."

"Ready to tackle the bathroom tonight?"

"Yes, if you're still okay with it." The tingling in her body was nonstop.

"No problem. We can start on the living room, as well. Do you have the color?"

"I have one can. We'll need more, but I can get it if I like this shade."

George shoved his chair away from the table, his attention shifting toward Willow. "Can you help me find my show?"

"Of course. It comes on in about ten minutes." Keeping busy would dull the escalating frenzy in her body being near Zach.

"I'll help you clean up in the garage, Pops." Zach hovered over his dad.

"Not much to do. I finished before dinner, but let's go check. With my brain, I seem to forget much more these days." Without another word, he stood.

Willow felt a wave of compassion bubbling up inside for Zach. *This must be hard.* All the money and fame can't shield a person from the pain of watching a loved one's illness or disease progress. "I'll clean up in the kitchen and find your show's channel for you. Then I'll head home, Mr. Hayes."

"Please. Call me George. You're part of the family, Willow."

Family. Did he include her in the Hayes family? As

she took in his words, she felt a calming sensation envelope her heart. Yes, she had her mom, but having more support was welcomed as she stumbled toward finding herself again. "Okay, George. I enjoy making you dinner, and my mom loves the leftovers I save for her." She peered across the patio.

Zach wiped his hands on a napkin and studied her expression.

"Glad to hear it." George stood, then headed for his workshop.

Zach faced her before following him to the garage. "See you in a bit."

"Thanks for helping. I really appreciate it." Willow caught a glint in his eye.

"What are friends for?" He shrugged, then joined his dad.

Yes. Friend, friend, friend.

****

A half hour later, Willow spread the drop cloths over the floor and sink in the bathroom. She heard Zach's footsteps pound on the steps, and her neck muscles seized into a knot.

"Hello! Anybody home?"

"In here!" She lifted her chin and gazed toward the doorway.

Zach saluted her, then tossed his hat onto the table. "Reporting for duty. Which wall do you want me to work on first?"

"It worked out best when you did the higher spots, and I took the lower ones. Let's keep the same pattern going."

"Will do." He bent over, poured a warm, golden-peach paint with soft, honey undertones into a plastic tray, and grabbed a brush.

The night before, she kept her physical distance intact because of the size of the room. But the bathroom was tiny, and now, she grazed an arm or leg passing underneath him. The nearness of his body was closing in, making breathing difficult. The muskiness of his cologne mixed with paint chemicals fogged her brain. *Didn't plan on this.* She sat back on her heels, inspecting her work, and brushed a hair out of her face.

Zach leaned in to wipe smeared paint from her cheek. "You have a glob there."

His fingers touched her skin, and heat sizzled, sending shock waves throughout her body. The simple, innocent touch was too much. She grabbed his hand. "No need. I'll get it. Let me find a rag." She fled the room before he could argue. After getting some fresh air, she returned a few minutes later. "How about I start in the living room? We're almost finished in here. Can you handle it?"

"Of course. I'll step out when I'm ready for your inspection."

She returned to the living room, happy for the respite from Zach's alluring charm. An innocent touch, but she liked it and wanted more. She wanted Zach Hayes to touch her, and she mustered every ounce of her strength to stop him. *Not now. Not ever.*

When finished for the evening, Zach grabbed his hat, carried supplies out the door, and waited.

After locking up, she squatted by the door and put the key underneath a terra-cotta flowerpot.

"Are you sure you want to put your key in the most obvious place? Aren't you worried about burglars?" Zach's eyebrows lifted.

"No. Who would be interested in old furniture and empty paint cans?" She grinned, then descended the steps.

"Yeah. You're right." Zach joined her in washing out paintbrushes under the spigot, then stood. "Guess I'll see you tomorrow. Have a good night, Willow." He rubbed his jaw, then retreated abruptly, and climbed into the truck.

"Thanks again." She called out to him. "And don't feel like you have to help me every night." She wanted to let him off the hook of his verbal commitment.

"No problem. I'm kind of enjoying it." He tipped his black, worn cowboy hat toward her and drove away.

She fixated on the back of his truck cruising down the street. *Unfortunately, so am I.*

****

Willow put the clean brushes and rollers away in the garage but couldn't stop the pondering in her head. The touch of Zach's fingers on her face was imprinted on her skin. *What would his fingers feel like on the rest of my body?* She unleashed a muffled groan, then distracted herself by inspecting the darkroom once more. She gripped the door handle, stepped inside, and flipped the light switch.

She managed to clean most of the cobwebs out, but the working space still needed attention. The wood on the table had splinters, requiring sanding and repainting. And she needed more shelves built. She didn't have time to develop any film, nor had she shot anything in recent months. She missed her muse visiting and understood Zach's internal affliction for new songwriting ideas. He shared something personal, and his vulnerability surprised her. When he was around his dad, the same uneasiness for the future was evident. He struggled to comprehend what was unfolding right in front of him. Willow was glad he came home, even if his presence was causing significant torment.

****

After showering, Willow slipped on her soft silk nightgown—one of the many gifts Charles had brought her from his business trips or wherever he had been. Crawling into bed with her journal, she contemplated what she and Leah discussed earlier about forgiving herself. She spent months blaming herself for not realizing the truth about Charles. *How did I miss the signs?*

So here she was, not quite thirty, and with no photography career. She sighed, grabbed a pen, and opened her journal. *Forgiveness.* She began writing all the things she needed to forgive herself for in this past year, or ten years, including her failure as a fine arts photographer. She read her list, her mind spinning on the truth. *These failures make me question every step I take forward.* Time to believe in herself and change the trajectory of her life. Tomorrow, she would start forgiving herself, one item at a time, and take as long as she needed to heal her heart and pride—both wounded by unforeseen circumstances.

Before turning the light out, Willow scrolled through her phone, stopping on an online video of Zach's. Unable to control herself, she glued her gaze to the screen as he sang, strummed his guitar, and swung his hips on the stage. The charismatic star firmly held an audience captive. Hundreds of women surrounded him, singing, waving their hands, and hoping for a touch or some attention. She shook her head. Women would always swarm Zach, and he would love it. *Who wouldn't? Just look at that contagious smile, that ripped body, and his sexy dance moves.* He was a player and nothing else.

Chapter Seven

The next morning, after breakfast, Zach cleaned the kitchen, then picked up his notebook and pen, eager to write. "Hey, Pops. I've got some work to do. Mind if I don't join you in the workshop?"

"No. How long are you staying?"

"A week or two." Zach was used to the repetition of questions. "I need some new songs for my next album and want to spend more time getting new lyrics written on paper."

"Okay. I'll be in my workshop if you need me." George stood, put his dishes in the sink, and headed outside.

Zach trailed his father's steps to the garage, still baffled by his father's lack of argumentative outbreaks. He felt consumed by guilt for leaving Cedar Hill and the family business, but he never regretted his decision. He came home on multiple occasions, only to get into shouting matches with his dad and storm back to Nashville without a word. *Time to heal the rifts between us—before I lose him completely.*

He grabbed his guitar, an extra cup of coffee, and plopped onto a back-patio chair, surveying the expansive backyard with its two large oak trees shading the lawn. He picked around at chords and daydreamed about Willow. He wasn't sorry he touched her yesterday. He couldn't put the brakes on his flirting, but he imagined, when it came to men and relationships, she was still fragile. He adored the way her laughter brought a rare glimpse of unfiltered, carefree joy, which didn't happen often. Perfect songwriting material, especially the line, *She was lit like an angel.* Zach hummed a melody, wrote some chord progressions, and got lost in the new song. At the point he spotted his dad, he still needed another verse.

George strode over, grabbed another chair, and sat. "Show me what you got."

Zach hadn't played a song for him in years. "I've got the hook, but I'm stuck on the verses." He plucked the strings, bellowing out the chorus. When finished, he rested both hands on the base of the guitar. "Well?"

"Sounds like a winner. Play me one of your songs I hear on the radio."

Zach peered at his dad for a fleeting moment, eyes widening. "You listen to my songs?"

"Of course, I do. You're my son."

Images of being sixteen again and playing music for his dad drifted through his mind, and Zach fought back the wetness behind his eyes.

Dad leaned forward. "Do the one about love tangled up in blue."

"Okay." A tingle of surprise flickered in Zach's gut, shocked by his dad's interest, but the feeling vanished as his rich, melodic voice echoed out toward the lawn. As the song ended, he hung his hands over the instrument, motionless in the quiet.

"I always liked that one."

Zach expanded his chest, his lungs taking in a deep breath and letting it out with a forced sigh. "Dad, I'm sorry."

"Sorry about what?"

"Sorry I didn't come to work at the store. But I couldn't. I had to give country music a try." He tapped his fingers against the fretboard.

"I know, son." He rubbed his hands back and forth on his thighs, brushing against the fabric of his jeans. "And I'm sorry I let it get out of hand. Too many years were lost between us, and I'm sorry."

Zach put down his guitar. "I'm sorry I always blew out of here before we could even talk about our differences. What else was I supposed to do? Those arguments made me so mad all the time."

"Yep, it made me mad, too. What do you say we call it water under the bridge and enjoy as much time as we can together?" George stood and patted him on the back.

Zach rose to his feet. "I'd like that." Then he grabbed his father and wrapped both arms around his frail frame in a voracious hug. He felt all the tension and anger slip away into liberated memories of the past. As he released him, Zach's eyes pooled with tears. "I love you, Pops."

"I love you, too, son. Keep writing. You've got talent. I always knew it."

"Thanks." He wiped the residual wetness with his sleeve. "I'm tired of bologna sandwiches. How about going into town for lunch today?"

"Sounds good. How about Chuck's Diner? They've got a tasty pulled pork sandwich."

"I'm in. Let me put this stuff away and clean up."

"Tell me when you're ready." As George entered the house, he let the screen door slam.

Zach gathered his notebook and guitar and

followed him inside. As he put on a clean shirt, he felt his phone ping with a text from Mike.

—*Check your email*—

—*Taking Dad to lunch*—

—Thumbs-up emoji—

Whatever Mike sent, it could wait. He didn't want to dwell on anything but his dad right now. Forgiving each other for years of unnecessary conflict was a welcomed miracle and a blessing. For as long as possible, he wanted to hold onto this feeling.

****

After Willow rang up the last customer before her lunch break, she grasped the manila envelope from a shelf under the counter. It arrived yesterday, but she hadn't opened it yet. Her lawyer mailed it from New York and, most likely, the envelope contained the final divorce papers. She couldn't sign them soon enough. He texted earlier, asking her to call him after she read the contents. As she took a deep breath, she brushed her fingers across the front, the smooth touch of the paper calming her. *I look forward to the day when nothing reminds me of the past.*

She lifted the sealed flap and removed the cover letter. As she read, she pressed a hand against her stomach coiling into a knot, nausea overtaking her. Yes, the rest of the papers were about her divorce, but her lawyer recommended she come to New York for the trial date involving Charles's wrongdoings. He had enclosed an official letter from the prosecutor requesting her voluntary appearance as a witness, even though she had already given a statement to federal agents confirming her lack of involvement. In court, they would probe her for details she might have forgotten. If she didn't come, they would subpoena her. As Willow picked up the phone to contact Timothy, she couldn't keep her hands from shaking, but the bells on the front door jingled before she could make the call.

Zach strutted into the store and threw both hands in the air. "Surprise!"

Willow's breath caught in her throat, and her heart pounded against her ribcage. "What are you doing here?"

"Dad and I had lunch at the diner, and a couple of his buddies arrived while we ate. They wanted to hang out for a bit, so I wandered over here. I remembered you worked at a bookstore, and this is the only one on Main Street." He hesitated, staring at the envelope she held. "You're kind of pale, Mason. Something else going on?"

"Yes. No. I got some disturbing news." She squeezed her fists, stopping the tremors. "I'll deal with it later. Don't need to talk about it." She shoved the letter back into the envelope and jammed it into her purse. Zachary Hayes would not hear about her dirty laundry today.

"If you ever need someone to talk to, consider me. I can be a good listener. Or at least I would try to be one for you."

She looked away from his compassionate gaze, shuffling some papers on the counter. "Thanks."

"Mind if I take a look around?"

"Be my guest. Holler if you need help, but the sections are well marked." She wasn't ready to deal with him yet. The letter was enough stress for one day.

He browsed the shelves, stopping in front of a framed photograph on the wall of a close-up picture of a couple, sitting in a park somewhere in New York City. The woman was laughing, and the man held her outstretched hand. "The carefree expressions on their faces strike me with a feeling of wistfulness. Not an easy emotion to capture in an image. Who did this?" Zach pointed to the picture.

"I did." Willow felt warmth spreading across her cheeks. *Oh, God. I'm blushing.*

"You've got talent—another surprising quality you possess. And this one?" He indicated another photo on the opposite wall.

"Yes." She chewed on the end of her pen, watching him.

"Why aren't you pursuing this as a career?"

She lowered her pen. "I've always wanted to, but life got in the way." She was determined to stay tight-lipped about her endeavors in New York and failed career as a fine arts photographer.

"Don't let adverse circumstances prevent you from following your dreams, Willow. No matter what happens externally, don't lose touch with your inner calling." He lifted the photo and placed it by the cash register. "I want to buy this, please."

Willow observed his facial expression, which bordered on flirtatious. "You don't have to. Please don't feel you need to buy one because we know each other. I won't be offended."

"You see, your problem is you don't believe in yourself. I want this because the photo is an exquisite piece of art. I have a perfect place for it in my house. Don't argue." He grinned and eyed her with both hands on his hips, then slapped his credit card onto the counter.

She dropped her shoulders. Zach was right. She didn't believe in herself. And this sale could buy more paint. "Okay. And thank you." She wrapped the frame in paper, then wrote a receipt. She was grateful Marcy insisted that Willow receive a one-hundred-percent commission for any photographs sold in the store.

"See. Making a sale wasn't so hard, was it? You do have talent, Mason." He trailed his fingers along the package. "See you tonight?"

"Yes, for dinner, and then if you're up for painting again. But no pressure." Willow busied herself with the receipt pad, flipping a sheet.

"Can't wait." He grabbed his package and left the store.

Willow peered out the window, tracking the broad-chested man in cowboy boots, flaunting a seductive swagger, crossing the street and being every bit as dashing in his jeans and T-shirt. Yes, he made her head spin with a desire beyond a friendship, but underneath he was a decent guy—no denying it.

She stood over the counter, dug out her purse, and grasped the letter again. *Deep breath.* She tapped Tim's number. *I need to deal with this, no matter how difficult.*

"Willow. Thanks for getting back. Did you get the package?"

"Yes, and I'm not happy. I wasn't supposed to testify in court. Wasn't my statement enough?"

"I'm sorry. As they prepared the case, some new evidence surfaced, and the prosecutors wanted the judge and jury to hear your side personally. You're on the witness list now for the trial."

She felt the muscles in her neck tighten into a knot

as she lifted her shoulder blades higher. Seeing Charles again and facing what he had done to their marriage and finances was too much to bear. "Can I get out of it? Do I *have* to come to New York?"

"Yes, to both of your questions. If you don't come voluntarily, you'll be subpoenaed."

As a sour taste crept up her throat, she touched her belly, shoving down an urge to throw up. This legal entanglement was not on her radar. "When?"

"In a week or two. Yes, the request is last minute, but they just informed me. I have a meeting with them tomorrow and will call you with more details. I'm sorry, Willow, but I can't get you out of this. When I speak to the prosecutors, I'll try one more time."

"You could mention the duress it would cause me because it will."

"Hang in there, Willow. I'll be in touch."

She had nothing left to say and felt a moistness forming behind her eyelids, threatening to spill if she didn't stop it. She dabbed the edges of her eyes with a tissue and stared into space until the bells on the door jingled. She jerked back to the present moment to help a customer and cast away her feelings to be dealt with later.

****

Zach adjusted his sunglasses to avoid the glare from the sunlight piercing through the front windshield of his truck. He headed into the driveway and glanced at his dad, who was staring out the window with slumped shoulders and a distant gaze. Did hanging with his buddies exhaust him too much? Tracking conversations appeared to be getting harder.

As Dad traipsed into the house, he turned to Zach.

"I'm taking a nap. Wake me if I'm not up in an hour."

"Sure thing, Pops." Zach needed to check his email and call Mike back. He walked to the patio with his computer and planted himself at the table. Scanning his inbox, he found the email with an attached contract. He narrowed his eyebrows. *What's this about?*

As he read through it, he curled his lips upward. Trent Adler, a major star and friend, requested he record a song with him for his next album. Trent had been on a roll of producing hit after hit in the last two years. Singing with him would almost guarantee a spot on the country charts' top-selling songs for its release. And give Zach some breathing room to get his next album finished—at least, he hoped. He grabbed his phone and called Mike.

"Took you long enough." Mike picked up right away.

"Sorry. We just got home. Wow, this is an incredible offer. Yes, I'll record with Trent. Should be a blast. When is the recording session scheduled?"

"Next week. Will you be home by then?"

Zach pressed a hand against his stomach as it lurched unexpectedly. *I'm not ready to leave Cedar Hill.* Silence hung in the air.

"Wasn't the original plan for this to be a week-long trip?" Mike's voice elevated.

Zach took a deep breath. "Yeah. But I was hoping to spend more time with Dad. *And* I started a new song. The muse is here for my next album, Mike, but I don't want to give up this chance."

"Yes, you can't pass this up."

"I can fly down for a couple days, leave my truck here, and return when the session is done."

"Sounds like a doable plan."

"Okay, I'm in. I'll sign the contract and send it back. Email me the details and the tracks. I'll give Trent a call later to thank him."

"You've got it."

Zach pressed the *End* button and glanced out at the backyard, scanning the treetops as they swept across an endless blue sky above. He smiled—his hometown never felt so sweet. He breathed deep into his chest and was grateful for the time spent with his dad. With the thought of leaving Willow, he felt stirred emotions—he wanted more of her. Sexual tension he could handle, but he had no clue how to manage this other blocked emotion. Would she ever trust him enough to talk about what happened in New York? He never researched her, so he opened his computer again.

The signature on his photograph read, *Willow Barton*, which was probably her married name. He searched and found an article about Charles Barton with a wife named Willow. *Must be her.* As he read, imagining what she faced, he groaned and shook his head. *This is why she is so tight-lipped about discussing her personal affairs and feels ashamed.*

His heart ached for her. It's one thing to get a divorce. It's another thing when your husband's arrest for fraud was printed in the newspapers and spread throughout the Internet—a devastating humiliation haunting her at every turn. He was determined to do whatever he could to help her get back on her feet. Even if she held him at arm's length, he would find a way to get in.

****

Later in the evening, Willow returned home after

making dinner and tried hard not to stew about the trial—too upsetting. Zach had been in an upbeat mood and respected her space, not asking questions or talking too much. Painting was a helpful outlet for her emotions, and she welcomed Zach's presence, even if she wasn't good company herself. As a friend, she wasn't letting him in. *Does he sense my wall?* But she appreciated that he stopped his constant flirting, allowing time to develop a relationship as friends. But she couldn't deny she missed the womanly attention.

Willow changed her clothes and headed toward the apartment. She spread the plastic sheets, shoved furniture to the center of the room but struggled with a table.

Zach stomped up the stairs and appeared in the doorway. "Let me help you." He grabbed the other end, and it landed with a *thud*. He glanced in her direction. "Perfect."

"Thanks. I opened the paints." She handed him a brush. "You can start on the side wall, and I'll take this one."

"Whatever you say, Mason." He tossed his hat on a chair and bent toward the floor, grasping a tray.

Willow suppressed her amusement at his witty banter, but she needed his friendship now. She decided to ask him some questions, before he could inquire about her life which was messy and getting messier. "What do you love most about being a country music star?"

"Playing with my band and touring. Nothing excites me more than performing in front of a large crowd—singing my songs and experiencing the energy from my fans as they sing along or dance to my tunes.

And recording. When something I've written comes together in the studio, and I hear it for the first time on the radio—pure magic."

"Sounds amazing. Do you ever miss Ohio?" Willow kept her focus on painting as she talked.

"When I first left, Nashville was so exciting I didn't miss Cedar Hill. I was happy to get away from this small town. I got caught up in the fame and thrill of it all and forgot about it. When I wasn't getting along with my dad, I stayed away. Coming home feels like a respite from all the hype and pressure I've been feeling about the job lately. And with Pops and me talking again, I needed this trip to re-energize and re-prioritize my direction in life."

"And have you figured it out yet? I mean, your direction in life. How would it be different?"

He lowered his paintbrush. "Are you digging into my soul, Mason?" He cocked his head. "Believe it or not, I've been wondering what it would be like to have a family of my own, scary as it sounds. Most of the guys who are at my level in the business are getting married and having babies. I guess I've enjoyed the party life a little too much." He looked her way.

His twinkling gaze pinned her. "Yes, I've seen the trashy tabloids." She grinned.

"Oh, yeah? You've been following me?"

"Well, you are my best friend's brother. We talk about you from time to time, but don't get too full of yourself. I've never been a groupie." *Until now.*

"Good to know." He resumed spreading the color on the wall.

Willow stilled her paintbrush for a minute to inspect her work. "You never had a girlfriend you wanted to settle down with in Nashville?" *What am I doing?* If she asked personal questions, she risked discussing her own miserable life, but she couldn't help herself.

"I dated someone a couple of years ago, but she didn't like when I toured. She became jealous, and the jealousy tainted the relationship. I wasn't ready to commit, and she knew it." He grabbed a rag and wiped a paint smear off Willow's face.

She didn't deflect and touched the place where he wiped it. "Is it gone?"

"Yep."

"Thanks." She inspected the paint cans. "We have enough for the kitchen. Should we start tonight or tomorrow? If you're free. No pressure."

"I say tomorrow."

"All right. Let's clean up." Willow closed the paint cans and trotted down the wooden steps toward the outdoor spigot.

Zach grabbed the dirty brushes and his hat, then followed close behind, his whistling ringing in the air. "I'll take measurements of these boards. You need to replace a few. I can get some for free at Dad's store—scraps in the back lumberyard. What do you say?"

As she lowered a brush, she locked her sight with his. "Getting free wood would be awesome. Are you sure?"

"Yes. The task will give me something to do with Dad."

"Sounds good." She picked up the scattered wet paintbrushes. "See you tomorrow."

"Yep. Tomorrow." He brushed his hair back, putting on his hat before heading back toward his truck.

Willow leaned against the house, scratched her jeans spotted with paint speckles, and sighed. She watched him take off, swatted a loose hair falling from her ponytail, and waved, grateful for his help but undeniably crushing on him—big time.

Chapter Eight

The next afternoon, Willow completed the last transaction for the day and checked her phone. A text from Zach.

—Dad wants pizza. And salad? Easy night for you—

—Thumbs-up emoji *Thank you—*

—You work too hard. Laugh emoji—

—Maybe. Silly-face emoji—

—See you soon—

This past week was nothing like she ever imagined, even with the devastating news from the lawyer and her job threats. As she heard a Zachary Hayes song blasting through the speakers on the radio, she increased the volume and swung her hips side to side. The sound of his voice squeezed her heart—no stopping it.

Willow dropped off a prescription for her mom, then headed home. Pulling into the driveway, she noticed an assortment of wooden boards in a pile by the apartment stairs. She smiled—Zach remembered. She burst into the living room, greeting her mom. "Was Zach here today?"

"Yes, dear. He and his dad stopped by with those boards for you. I invited them in for tea and some fresh-baked brownies. Zach's quite the storyteller. I enjoyed our little chat."

Zach was here, socializing with Mom? "About

what?"

"Oh, your apartment, George's birdhouses, Zach's life in Nashville. Don't worry, I didn't reveal any of your private affairs, but I did order two birdhouses." She thumbed through a magazine and chuckled.

Willow wasn't sure what she was feeling at this moment. "I put your pills on the counter in the kitchen, then I'm heading over to make them dinner. Zach is helping me again tonight to finish the painting."

"I peeked inside today. Your dad would have been proud, dear."

Willow walked closer to her mom, but her attention drifted to a photo displayed on the mantel from her parents' wedding day. "Yeah, I hope so. When I'm working in the apartment, I feel his spirit around me—like I'm in the right place at the right time, finally, after all the turmoil in New York."

"His spirit is always with us, Willow. Always." She stroked her daughter's arm.

Willow grabbed her mom's hand, squeezing it. "Thanks, Mom, for making this whole transition easier. If I didn't have you here, what would I have done?"

"Come here." Evelyn urged Willow to sit, encircling her tiny frame and cradling her in a hug. "I'm your mother and will always be here for you, no matter what. You will figure things out one way or another. I have faith in you." She sat back, brushing a strand away from Willow's face. "You're stronger than you think."

Willow couldn't ignore the moisture gathering in her eyes. "Thanks for believing in me, even when I sometimes don't believe in myself." She wiped a tear before it rolled down her cheek.

"Believing in you is part of my job, sweet pea."

Willow forced a smile, then pecked a kiss on her mom's cheek. "I've got to run, Mom. Love you."

"Love you, too, dear."

Willow rested both hands on the steering wheel of her aging car, her heart basking in the warmth of her mom's unconditional love. Returning to Cedar Hill had been the right choice—hopefully, one of many more to come.

****

Zach dashed out the door and, like second nature now, took Willow's grocery bag.

"I stopped by Mom's and saw all the lumber you dropped off. Thank you. Should be plenty." She smiled and followed him into the kitchen.

"No problem. We found plenty of scraps, and Dad enjoyed the outing. If you need them, then Liam will set aside more boards. The store always has extra."

Willow wasn't used to such kindness without strings attached. She liked Zach more and more each day—on a deeper level. A quiver fluttered across her belly, but she didn't flinch. *I'll sit with my feelings and not let fear intimidate me.* "Okay, great." She lowered her head and became absorbed in chopping vegetables for the salad.

"What kind of pizza do you like? How about pepperoni and mushrooms?" Zach leaned against the counter with one hand stuffed into the front pocket of his jeans.

He was close enough that she could smell the faint musk of his aftershave still lingering on his skin. "My favorite."

"Good, because that's what I ordered." His

ringtone blasted from his back pocket. "I've got to take this." He swung around. "Hey, Trent. What's up?" He hurried outside.

Willow could hear part of the conversation through the screen on the window.

"Should work. I'll get a flight on Tuesday. We can rehearse later at your place and record Wednesday. Okay. I'll text you my flight info. Can't wait." Zach chuckled aloud before ending the call.

Is he leaving for Nashville already? She bit her bottom lip, and a chill washed over her, stinging her skin with an icy apprehension. "Is everything all right?"

"Yeah, I'm psyched. One of my buddies wants me to record a song with him." He rubbed his hands together, swaying his body back and forth with a big grin on his face. "I'm hoping this will give me some breathing room for my writing."

"Are you coming back?" *Look down. Can't let him see my disappointment.*

"After the session is finished. I'm not done here yet, Mason." He tilted his head. "Are you going to miss me?"

She shook her head, suppressing a verbal response, and grabbed tongs from the drawer. "Salad's almost done." She gripped the metal utensil, and her knuckles whitened. She forced an exhale, thrusting the emotions out of her body. Forget this man. A relationship would never work. She slammed the drawer shut with her hip. *I'm getting too attached. Not good.*

The doorbell rang. "I'll get it. Must be the delivery guy." Zach traipsed through the living room toward the front door.

Fifteen minutes later, George devoured the pizza.

"Darn, this is good." Tomato sauce smeared on one cheek, but he wiped it with a napkin before making a mess.

Willow made a mental note for future dinners on nights when she was tired.

"Did we get you enough lumber?" he asked.

"Should be plenty. I appreciate your help." She swatted at a wisp of hair drifting into her face.

"No problem. We always have scraps at the store." George poured dressing onto his salad.

"I picked up two electric sanders, too. On Sunday, we can tackle the steps and anything else that needs sanding." Zach reached for another slice of pizza.

"I have one in the garage. I don't want to take up more of your time." Willow sipped her iced tea.

"Nonsense. He's happy to help." George grinned and jabbed some lettuce with his fork.

"Besides, I want to do as much as possible before I jet off to Nashville. But I am coming back." His gaze darted toward her.

"Okay. Thank you." Willow grabbed her plate, stood, and broke his penetrating glance. She reminded herself the sooner she finished the apartment, the sooner she could move in and avoid these daily evening encounters.

****

Later, Willow kneeled on the wooden floor, taping the walls in the kitchen. Beads of sweat formed on her brow, and she swiped the wetness with her sleeve.

Feet stomped on the outside steps, and Zach bounded into the apartment through the open door, his head twisting in her direction.

"Almost finished here." She returned her attention

on the project in front of her.

"I'll mix the paint and set up." Without hesitation, he strode to the supplies and prepped for the evening's work.

As Willow stood, she slumped her shoulders but eased into working with Zach. *I'm not much company tonight.* The phone call with her lawyer weighed heavy on her heart, and she couldn't shake the feelings of doom surrounding her. If she talked about it with Zach, would she feel better? No, not a good idea. Too much shame. *I need to focus on getting this work done.* "I love this color. It brightens up the teeny space." She didn't want to be a downer all the time.

"I agree. Good choice, Mason." He stopped painting. "Hey, are you okay?"

Before she could answer, her ringtone sounded—Tim. "Sorry, I need to take this." She dropped her brush and retreated outside to the stairs for privacy.

A few minutes passed, and Zach lifted his head. "What's that noise?" He wiped both hands on a towel and headed toward the steps.

Halfway down the stairs, Willow sat with her head in both hands, her body shaking with rolling sobs.

He tiptoed along the steps and sat close. "Hey, hey. What's wrong?" He put an arm around her and handed her a clean cloth. "Here."

She couldn't stop crying. Tim confirmed she needed to come to New York, which wouldn't be pleasant. The devastation consumed her. Once again, she would be smack-dab in the middle of Charles's mess. She wanted that painful part of her life to be over—for good. She took the rag and wiped her runny nose, but the tears flowed.

"Come here." Zach grasped her with firm hands, enveloping her into his chest and scooting nearer.

Willow sank into his comforting embrace. The musky scent of the man seeped into her nostrils, washing over her like a gentle rain. God, how she needed this and cried some more.

Zach gently rubbed her back with one hand while rocking her back and forth.

She wailed, letting it all go. She didn't care if she had worked hard at keeping her defenses up with Zach. Too much time had passed since a man had held her. The heat of his body merged with hers, and she melted into him, safe and secure. Her bawling slowly morphed into sniffling.

A cardinal warbled on the nearby fence.

She slowed her breath, listening. She rested in his arms for another minute—she couldn't budge.

Zach remained silent.

Wiping smeared mascara off her face, she eventually slipped out of his grasp and blew her nose on the rag. *No pride here.*

"Wanna talk about it?"

She shook her head. "I'm too embarrassed."

"Okay." He grasped a hand. "I'm here if you change your mind."

She dipped her head in response.

He released his grasp and stood. "I'll finish my wall. Take as much time as you need." He bent his elbow, wiped sweat off his temples with his forearm, and returned to the apartment.

Willow sat, focusing on the stairs below her. She couldn't believe she lost it in front of Zach. *What am I doing?* But she was tired of keeping her feelings inside.

Should I talk to him? Their friendship was evolving, and he had already seen her most vulnerable self. Or perhaps sweep it under the rug and pretend it didn't happen. Denial was something she could do. Either way, back to painting and keeping her mind off New York and the future. But she couldn't keep her mind off the memory of being held and comforted. She wanted to return to that moment and stay there—until dusk became night.

As Willow entered the room, she stole a quick glance at Zach. She witnessed a faint lifting on the edge of his lips, but he didn't say a word. She appreciated his respect for her privacy and lost herself in the back-and-forth motion of the rollers and brushes.

An hour passed, and Zach dropped his brush into the metal tray with a *clunk.* "We're about done. Check it out."

She took one last swipe at the wall and stepped back. "All done." She cast a sheepish grin in his direction. "Thanks for helping me. I'll find a way to make it up to you."

"No need. My pleasure. Besides, I'm very grateful to you for caring for my father. He likes you, and you make this transition much easier. Your gentle caring is priceless."

Her gaze lingered on him, and butterflies fluttered freely in her belly. She didn't resist the feelings and let them fly.

"Are you coming to Rosie's birthday party tomorrow?"

"Wouldn't miss it." She wiped the excess paint from her brush on the edge of the can.

"Let's clean up." He picked up a rag. "And,

Willow, I meant what I said about being a good listener if you need it. I hate to see you tortured like this." His focus didn't waver from the fix it had on her.

"Thanks, but I want to forget about it for now. I'm very good at denying things and pretending they don't exist. Might be what got me into this mess." *Oh, God. Too much sharing.*

"I understand."

The two gathered the dirty tools and washed at the spigot.

When Zach stood, he leaned over and brushed an unruly curl from flopping over her eyes.

Willow didn't flinch. She stood very still. What would it be like to have him kiss her? She was so drained that she struggled to keep her wall up.

"See you tomorrow." And he left.

As dusk rolled into the Ohio hills surrounding her, she inhaled a deep breath and trailed her fingers down the side of her face where he had touched her. She wanted more with this man but could never allow anything to happen. *Never.*

Chapter Nine

The next day at work, Willow tied a glittery pink ribbon on Rosie's present and stuck her birthday card under the taut sash encircling the box. She put it on the shelf in the store's storage room until she left for the party at noon. Twiddling with her pen, she glanced over the books on the shelves. She was grateful for this easy job, but it didn't stir her with passion like the art gallery position in New York.

There, she had a fast-paced and exciting role in discovering new artists and took exceptional care of those with special exhibits. If she was honest, she didn't pursue her photography career when married. Charles always kept her busy with his social calendar, helping to secure his place in the financial world and high society circles. *When did he start to slip?* She racked her brain for clues but couldn't come up with any. A text pinged from Leah.

—*Can you pick up the cake? I'm swamped over here. Please*—

—*Sure*—

—*You're a lifesaver. See you soon xo*—

Willow smiled, daydreaming about an afternoon of no responsibility and a chance to relax. *If I can.* She massaged her shoulders, forcing them to let go. *I'm putting my troubles on the back burner and spoiling myself with burgers and cake.* And having Zach at the party was a bonus.

****

As Willow maneuvered her vehicle into Leah's driveway, she tightened her grip on the steering wheel. A ripple of uneasiness circulated throughout her body. She would have to deal with the undeniable chemistry brewing with Zach, but she was ready—at least, she hoped. She wore a yellow dress, its fabric flowing around her slender legs. A matching sweater, in case the air was cool, and her best summer sandals completed the outfit. At least, she'd kept some stylish clothes from her New York closets, but the expensive jewelry Charles had given her—gone. Everything was confiscated before she could hide them. *Too bad. I could have sold them.* She entered the patio, holding the cake.

Zach stood next to Liam at the grill and stared as she approached.

Is he gawking? She tilted her face toward him on her way to the house, then stepped into the kitchen. "Need any help?" Despite everything going on, she tossed back her chestnut curls, feeling attractive today. *I should dress up more often.*

"You're a lifesaver." Leah, deep in work mode for the party, took the bakery box from Willow's hands. "Get ready for an onslaught of seven-year-olds!"

"No problem. What can I do?"

Leah slid the cake onto the counter and stopped to look at her friend. "Aren't you gorgeous!"

Willow brushed her fingers over the skirt's material, adjusting it at the waist. "Just because you haven't seen me in a dress for a while doesn't mean I've forgotten how to wear one."

"Well, you're stunning. Help me take the food to the tables. I already see people mingling in the yard." Leah scooped up bags of hamburger and hot dog buns, condiments, and extra napkins.

Willow followed her outside and helped arrange the food and drinks. Afterward, she strolled over to say hello to Mr. Hayes.

George sat in a chair near the grill, holding a glass of iced tea with his legs stretched out.

"Hi, George. Ready for a party?" The sweet, caramelized aroma of barbecued chicken and the smoky smell of grilling hamburgers filled the air, making Willow's stomach rumble.

"I can't wait to see Rosie's face when she opens presents and blows out the candles on the cake. Those are precious moments." He swished ice cubes around in his glass, then drank it.

"Yeah, I brought my camera to capture some of the magic."

Zach snuck up behind her and whistled. "Very pretty."

Willow watched his gaze scan her and felt heat spread across her flushed cheeks. "Thank you." An explosive paralysis invaded her limbs, leaving her frozen in place. After last night's encounter, she fought against a surging vulnerability, which scared her. "I'll grab my camera from my car."

"I want to get my guitars out of the truck, so I'll walk with you."

Great. "Okay."

Zach came closer, skimming her elbow with an arm. "I'm glad to see you're feeling better today."

"I decided to put my worries on the back burner—

at least, for the weekend." She grinned but kept her gaze focused straight ahead.

"Yes, I find denial works wonders sometimes." Zach raked his fingers through his hair, eyeing her.

"Yes, it does." She pivoted and opened the trunk of her car, removing her camera and bag.

Zach grabbed two guitars from his truck.

"Is someone else playing with you today?" Willow readjusted the strap on her shoulder.

"I was hoping Dad might join me for some oldies, like the ones we used to play together when I was a kid. I'm not sure he'll remember how to play, but I wanted to give it a try. If the timing is right."

"I understand." As she walked by his side, she was silent and grateful he didn't pressure any more conversation.

Soon, the party was in full swing, with kids frolicking, screaming, and romping about in a bouncy house, while parents ate and drank as they watched.

As Willow meandered around taking pictures, she smiled, her spirit overflowing. She found the best shots, and her art came alive, transforming captured emotions into artistic inspiration and visual storytelling on paper. *God, how I need this creative outlet.* She had waited too long to pursue photography again. *Gotta finish my darkroom.*

"Hey, everyone. Time for cake!" Leah carried out the cake and placed it on a center table. Within moments, she was surrounded by a swarm of screaming children.

When Rosie saw the candles, her expression radiated the pure joy and excitement of a child on their birthday.

Willow circled the group and snapped photos, her smile beaming. She bent her head, focusing on the camera.

Zach leaned over to Liam. "Willow has a knack with kids, doesn't she? Rosie loves getting her picture taken."

"She's adorable. And she loves Willow." Liam pointed to his guitar case. "Are you playing that thing or what?" He smacked him on the back.

"Hey, Dad. How about we play a few together?" Zach grasped his dad's old guitar and handed it over. "We could start with a couple easy ballads we used to do."

George readily took the guitar. "If I forget the chords, I'll watch you and try to play along."

Zach grinned, strumming and singing, while the rest of his friends joined in on the choruses.

Willow stood on the outskirts of the circle, taking pictures. She wanted to get some of Zach and his dad. Zach's mellow, deep voice resonated in the air, and she listened, her chest tightening. The camera was a good decoy since she could hide behind it and still be close. She watched George sing with his son, and her heart melted. Their differences were healing, and their bond was strengthening again. In the late afternoon, most guests left, and Willow did her best to help Leah clean up the mess.

Rosie was content to play with all her new toys. She even wore the pink tutu skirt Willow bought— definitely a hit.

After Willow washed the last dish, she strolled to the back porch and sat beside Leah. Sipping iced tea and resting her feet on a wicker coffee table, she released a soft sigh. "Ah. Success, my friend."

"Thanks to you and everyone who helped." Leah lifted her glass.

Zach walked over. "Hello, ladies. Great party, sis."

Leah grinned. "Thanks."

He faced Willow. "Did you get some good photos today?"

"I hope so." She swayed back and forth in the rocker, feeling lighter. She glimpsed a future where she could finally pursue photography and nurture her artistic spirit. It felt darn good.

"Can't wait to see the prints." He placed a hand on Leah's arm. "I'll take Pops home. I can see he's tired, but I'm happy he stuck it out all afternoon."

"Me, too. I packed a bag with leftovers, so Willow doesn't have to cook dinner." She winked. "Let me get it."

Zach sat in the empty chair, inches from Willow. "What's the plan for your apartment restoration? Are you working tonight?"

"I hoped to organize my dark room. I need to sand my wooden table and contemplate paint colors for the steps—perhaps a gray to match Mom's window trims." If she stuck to work conversation, she was fine.

"Perfect. After I get Pops settled, I'll text you." He rubbed a hand on his jeans. "Dad did pretty good today. He even remembered some of the songs we used to play."

She toyed with a thread on her dress before looking up. "And he had the biggest grin. You coming home has helped him deal with his diagnosis better."

"I hope so. I'm not doing much but being here." He scraped his boot along the porch's wooden floor.

"Which is all he needed, Zach."

"I hope my returning to Nashville won't upset him." He turned his gaze outward, looking at his father in the distance.

"You must *always* live your life, Zach. Everything else will work out."

He shifted his attention, touching her. "I could say the same thing to you."

A tingle ran up her arm while heat spread across her neck.

Leah appeared with a large paper bag filled with leftovers. "Here you go. Those goodies should hold you over for a bit." She handed a smaller bag to Willow. "For your mom."

"Thanks." She took the food, grateful for her best friend's care.

"I'll say goodbye to Dad. Be right back." Leah left them alone.

The screen door flew open, and Rosie ran out, still wearing her pink tutu skirt. "Aunt Wiwwow, see my Bawbie. She has a new dwess." She jumped into the large wicker chair with Willow.

"The dress is beautiful, but not as beautiful and gorgeous as you." Willow put an arm around Rosie and squeezed her.

Rosie picked up the side of the skirt with her other hand. "I wuv it."

"Good. I hoped you did."

"Unca thack, are you playing more songs?"

"Not tonight, sweetheart. Another day, okay?"

Rosie ran her fingers across her new ballet skirt, picking at the sparkling material. "Okay." Then, she jumped out of the chair and ran to George and her mom.

"She's a darling. I've missed too much of her growing up." Zach's vision held steadfast to his niece across the yard. "Guess I'd better leave. Talk later?"

"Sure. I'm glad you played today." She raised her gaze upward, her heart pounding.

"Me, too." He stepped away, heading toward his dad.

Willow stood, grabbed her camera, and shot casual, spontaneous pictures of Zach and his family. She peeked at the photos through the viewfinder and grinned.

Zach got into his truck and waved goodbye from the open window.

She returned his gesture, flickering her fingers in the wind, taking him in. She shook her head. *I'm a goner.*

****

Thirty minutes later, Willow stepped into her mom's kitchen after the celebration. "Hey, Mom. Leah sent you some goodies." She placed the food on the counter.

"How was the party?"

"Wonderful. Leah outdid herself, as usual. I'll show you the pictures I took." She grabbed her camera and snuggled in beside her mom on the couch. "You need to view them on my camera since they aren't developed. Tell me what you think—honestly."

Evelyn scrolled through the photos. "These are marvelous, dear. You have exceptional talent. Get your darkroom ready."

Willow examined them with her mom, her confidence growing with each one. Did Zach have

93

anything to do with her new inspiration? "Want me to heat up something before I get to work?"

"No, I can do it myself. I'm not handicapped, but in the afternoon, I get tired. Hence, the sofa." Mom inched the corners of her lips upward.

"If you need anything, text me. I need to change my clothes."

"Will do."

Willow couldn't ignore the rapid pounding of her heartbeat against her ribcage as she bounded up the stairs. Was she finding her muse again?

****

Willow dressed in jeans and a T-shirt before heading outside. She opened the door to the darkroom, flipped the light switch, and took in a sharp breath. Even after cleaning it, the space was still a mess and a long way from operational. A musty smell still hung in the air. *Might as well dig in.* She put on her safety goggles and plugged in the sander, taking inventory of what was left to do. Hooks and some shelves would come in handy. Her phone pinged several minutes later. Zach.

—Be over in ten. Dad all settled—

—Thanks. Smiley emoji—

—Thumbs-up emoji—

Another evening with Zach. She was getting used to his companionship and didn't want it to end. *Can I trust him?* Repeat your mantra. *Friend, friend, friend.* She pressed a palm to her quivering belly, but she couldn't control the smile spreading across her face.

"Anyone in here?" Zach had arrived and stood outside the open garage door.

Whirring and *buzzing* blasted from inside. She

unplugged the sander. "In here!"

He peered inside. "Ahh. *This* is your darkroom."

"Yes. Well, eventually, it will be. Come in." A tight squeeze, but she could now take his nearness in short doses. "It needs work, but I'm excited to get it up and running. I'm sanding this main table and want to repaint it. I need to get some hooks and other hardware for the walls, and if I have enough lumber left, I would like to put a couple of shelves on top. Could you do it?" Willow stood inches away and felt his breath skimming her face. Her senses faltered from the smell of a faint scent mixed with citrus and sandalwood. Before swooning sideways, she tightened her grasp on the tool's handle.

"Piece of cake. What do you want me to do?"

The closeness was intoxicating, and she wanted him to kiss her. She couldn't speak.

"Willow?"

She shook her head. "Yes, yes. How about if you measure for shelves and see if any of the boards will fit? I'll keep sanding. The measuring tape is on the table."

He picked up the tape, measured, and hastened outside.

He's so darn likeable. When Willow finished sanding the table, she turned off the machine and ran a hand over the wood. "Oww!" She clutched her palm as pain shot through it.

Zach rushed to the doorway. "Are you okay? What did you do?" He grabbed her left hand, flipping it over to reveal a large, protruding splinter in her skin. "Not good. I've got tweezers in my first aid kit. Wait a second." He left her standing while he darted to his truck.

Willow squeezed her wrist. *What a klutz.*

A moment later, he appeared and took hold of her unsteady hand. He bent forward, removed the splinter with expertise, and wiped it with an alcohol wipe. He wrapped a bandage around the wound, then gave it a soft pat. "Good as new." He stepped back and grinned.

"Thank you. I should have been more careful." Words stuck in her throat after experiencing his gallant efforts.

"Don't beat yourself up. Happens to all of us. When I first started working with Pops, I had cuts and bruises all over my hands—still have scars. It comes with remodeling. Be sure you clean it good tonight."

"Okay." She gently ran her slender fingers over the covered injury.

"I measured the shelves, but we need a good saw. I'll take them to Dad's workshop tonight and cut them tomorrow."

"Great, thank you. I need to go to the hardware store tomorrow, but I promised Mom I'd take her to church in the morning."

"How about I pick you up around one? We'll go to the store and buy what you need. I'll see if Dad wants to come, too. He could work on sanding the lower steps while I handle the higher ones."

"If you guys want to. This has become more than a painting project, and I don't want to interfere with your writing process."

"No problem. I'll write in the morning and some tonight. I'm almost done with one song. If I finish it, I'll play it for you tomorrow. You can be my first critic."

She was struck at how open he was with her. She wished she could be as free with her emotions, but she wasn't ready. No matter how much chemistry existed, she couldn't let her heart be broken again. And he had *danger* written all over him. "I would be honored."

"All right then. See you tomorrow."

Willow nodded, then waved as he drove away. *Friend, friend, friend,* she repeated in her head. *He's only a friend.*

Chapter Ten

The next day, Willow tapped an upbeat rhythm on her steering wheel while listening to the car's radio and bobbed her head up and down. Arriving home, she jumped out and couldn't suppress a smile. She was nearing the completion of work on her apartment and darkroom, and she savored elation cascading like a fountain of warm water over her body. She had left Mom with friends from church and had an hour alone before Zach picked her up. Time passed, and she finished sanding the darkroom table, now ready for paint. Brakes squeaked outside, skidding to a stop, and she shot up her head. She peeked around the garage door.

Zach hopped out, grabbed his guitar from the back of the truck, and strolled toward her.

"Hey. Where's your dad?"

"He wanted to stay home. The party exhausted him yesterday, but he's quietly content, working away on birdhouses in the garage. I told him we'd be home for dinner. You are cooking tonight, right?" He stopped, readjusting his grasp on the case's handle and eyeing her.

We. He said *we'd* be home. She daydreamed about Zach's words, fantasizing about the *we.* She jerked her head, plummeting back to the moment at hand. "Of course. How's spaghetti? I made meatballs and put them in your freezer last week."

"You're spoiling me. What will I do in Nashville?"

"Take-out meals." She chuckled. "Let me get my wallet."

"Can I put my guitar in your house? I'll play my song later. I finished it this morning."

"Sure. Follow me." She showed him where to put his guitar in the living room and ran upstairs for her purse. When she came downstairs, she observed him holding a family photo in his right hand.

"This is your dad, isn't it?"

"Yes. After he died, I was leaving for college the next year. The loss stayed with me for a long time, and his death impacted my decision to marry so young. Guess I wanted a male figure to care about me." She paused, wrapping a loose strand of hair around her ear. "And I made a poor choice." Warmth crept along her neck and up her face. *Oh, God. I'm blushing.* She rested her fingers on the heat. *How embarrassing.*

He touched her right arm. "Now, you have a chance for a whole new life. I'm excited to see what you do."

She shivered, his innocent touch teasing her desire. She placed a hand over his. "Thanks."

Zach's ringtone chimed. "Sorry, I've got to take this." He darted outside.

Willow's heart palpitated like a ticking time bomb, ready to explode any minute. She didn't want to fall in love with him. She couldn't.

Zach ended his call and returned.

She shoved a hand into her pocket. "Everything okay?"

"Yep. My recording date got pushed back a day.

No problem. It will give me an extra day to work with you, so everything is good."

She'd take an extra day with this man anytime.

"Let's go." He opened the wide truck door. "Ladies first."

She shook her head. His delivery of charm never stopped. As she passed him, she inhaled a whiff of his herbal shampoo, lingering in his damp hair, breezing through her nostrils, and she slid onto the seat before her knees buckled.

Zach found the supplies at the store and loaded the truck, including extra wood from the lumber area Liam saved for Willow. When he returned to the house, he hauled the cut shelves into the darkroom.

"Let's start here." Willow pointed toward a wall.

Zach drilled holes for the support systems.

She helped steady the wood but couldn't hide a slight tremor in her fingers. Heat crawled up her spine, and sweat dripped down her face. "Hot in here."

He brushed his damp face with his sleeve. "Sure is."

She secured the hooks needed for developing and drying film. One slipped out of her right hand. "Darn." She reached to grab it.

Zach made the same movement, his firm right hand cupping over hers.

She tilted her head sideways. "I got it."

When finished, his muscular body brushed hers as he grabbed the screwdriver and hammer.

She darted to the side. A touch she could handle, but his entire body pressed against her, she couldn't. *Air. Now.* "I'll be right back." She rushed out the door.

In the late afternoon, Evelyn delivered a pitcher of

iced cold lemonade and snacks. "Here you go." She placed them on a picnic table next to the garage. "You two have been working hard. Time for a break." She peeked inside the darkroom.

"Thanks, Mom. Plumbing is still a problem."

"You'll figure it out. You always do." She came back and poured the drinks.

Zach took a glass. "Thanks, Mrs. Mason."

"Please, call me Evelyn. You've been around here long enough, Zach."

"Yes, I have." He sipped his drink, throwing Willow a quick side-eye.

Her mom left, and Willow, eager to redirect the conversation, pointed to two chairs under a spreading maple tree in the side yard, which offered plenty of shade. "Let's sit and take a break."

Zach picked up the snack tray, carried it to a side table by the chairs, and plopped onto a seat. "Great job, Mason. We're a good team."

"Yes, we are." She stretched her legs out in front and grinned.

"How long before you can use your darkroom?"

"When I get the plumbing fixed." She stared into her glass.

"I might be able to assess the situation and give you an idea of how big the job might be."

"If you have time, I'd appreciate it. I want to finish the steps today, or at least, the sanding and primer. And tomorrow, paint them." She tasted her lemonade and plucked a cookie from the platter. She held it up in front of Zach. "Sustenance." She chuckled.

"Wonderful to see you laugh, Mason."

Willow scuffed her sneakers on the grass beneath

her, conscious of heat inching toward her cheeks.

"Do you want to hear my new song called, 'Lit Like an Angel'?"

"I'd love to." *Anything you want.*

Zach walked inside the house, grabbed his guitar, and returned to the chairs. "Here goes. She was lit like an angel, bright as they come…"

Willow leaned back into the chair and closed her eyes, allowing his smooth, melodic voice to wash over her. The song was enchanting—stirring to the soul. A ballad and love song to a woman he loved. *Is this about his last relationship?* She was in awe of how he could craft something so moving.

He strummed the last chord and exhaled a long breath. "Well?"

She opened her eyes, leveling her sight on him. "Beau…beautiful." She stammered on the words, barely able to speak.

"I wrote about how when you least expect it, love can find you." He rubbed the guitar pick between his thumb and fingers, then tilted his head.

She flitted her gaze downward, her insides trembling at the meaning of the words slipping out of his mouth. She nodded, then flicked her eyelids upward. "You might have another hit on your hands."

"Thanks. I'm loving it, so I guess it's a good sign." He grinned, then cast his gaze on her with laser intensity. "You were the muse for the song." He stroked the side of his guitar, still staring. "When you smile, which isn't often, you light up like an angel."

She lowered her head, picking at dry paint on her jeans and couldn't speak. *What is going on?* Did he have feelings for her, or was this just a song—nothing more? *Get a grip.* She raised her chin. "Were the lyrics about your old girlfriend?"

"No, you inspired the hook, but then I fantasized about the woman and relationship in the song since I'm not in one right now."

"Oh, I see." A twinge of disappointment flooded her emotions. Her imagination had gotten the best of her for a moment. "Your label will love it. I did."

"I hope so." He put his guitar back in the case. "How about we finish the sanding and primer before I leave?"

"Sure." She stood, took his glass and the tray, and strode toward the kitchen. "Be right back." When she returned, she fell into an easy pattern of working. She handled the bottom of the stairs, leaving enough distance between them to breathe and relax. After cleaning up, Willow circled to face him. "I'll be over in an hour. Hope your dad can wait to eat."

"I'm sure he's still capable of grabbing a snack in the kitchen, if hungry." Zach picked up his guitar and climbed into his truck. He waved and left.

Standing on the porch, she tucked a stray hair behind her ear as he drove away. *Why does life have to be so difficult?* Too many emotions. Too many feelings. She should be honored to have been his muse for the song, but it made her want more with him. More than friends, but too dangerous in so many ways.

****

After dinner, Zach scratched his day-old beard, standing by the kitchen window. Willow had darted out of the house as soon as the last dish was washed and put away. She withdrew after hearing the song earlier and was difficult to read—a complex woman with unspoken words. She was processing something, and he had no idea what it could be. *Does she have feelings for me?* Yes, he wanted her, but he needed to respect her boundaries. The never-ending perplexity of women—they were a complicated breed. Zach walked into the living room, and he widened his eyes.

Dad was bent over his guitar, picking out a tune. He was humming, and a serene look emanated from his eyes.

"Hey, Pops. What's this song?"

"Something I wrote for your mom years ago. I can't quite remember the lyrics except for part of the chorus. I called it 'Forever Kind of Love' but never finished it."

"Play what you remember, Pops."

Dad crooned louder, catching a phrase now and then, but the melody rang out strong.

Electrical impulses charged Zach's spine, making his nerves vibrate. The composition was both haunting and inspiring. "Keep going, Pops. I'll get my guitar and a piece of paper." Zach spent the next hour hammering out lyrics and refining the song's chords with his dad. When he was done, Zach sat back in his chair. "Do you mind if I put this on my new album? You'll get a credit as a songwriter." He felt his chest swell with pride. He never dreamed he could write a song with his dad in this lifetime, not after the last ten years.

Dad tossed his head back, and a gleeful sound escaped his throat. "Of course, you can record it. I'd be honored." He pointed to the heavens. "And your mama would love to hear it again."

Zach rubbed both hands together, studying the lyric sheet. When he returned to Nashville, he'd have two songs to play for his manager. Maybe then, Mike would ease the pressure. "I have another favor to ask you."

"Shoot."

"Willow needs new plumbing in her apartment and darkroom. Do you mind riding with me tomorrow and checking it out while she's at work? You're more skilled, and I'd like to help her while I'm here."

"Of course." Dad paused. "You've been spending a lot of time with her this last week. Do you feel anything more than friendship on your end?"

Zach lifted his eyebrows. "You're probing me about a woman?"

"Yes, when the woman is special like Willow."

He bowed his head, staring at the floor. "She's amazing. And smart. And gorgeous." He wiped his palms back and forth on his jeans. "But I can't have a relationship when I live in Nashville, and she lives here. Wouldn't be fair."

"Keep listening to your heart, son. Sometimes, these roadblocks aren't meant to stop us but rather make us dig deeper into ourselves to discover what we need in our life."

Zach took a deep breath, contemplating his father's advice. "When did you get so wise?"

Dad snickered. "I've been around longer than you." He put the guitar back in its case and stood. "I'm headed to bed. See you in the morning."

Zach stood and hugged his dad. "I love you, Pops."

"I love you, too, son."

Sitting in his chair, he stared straight ahead. In some moments, his dad seemed normal, and at other times, he saw him drift away, which scared him. He sighed and wished he could do something to change the inevitable outcome.

The phone pinged—Leah.

—Call me when you're free—

—Calling—

He stretched both legs, then headed outside for privacy. "What's up?"

"I checked my work calendar and realized I can't take Dad to his doctor's appointment on Tuesday. You're not leaving until Wednesday now, right?"

"Yeah. I can take him. No worries. I want to chat with his doctor anyway."

"Oh, good. Tuesday and Thursday are my busiest days with clients, and I don't want to cancel any appointments. Thanks, Zach. How's he doing?"

"Pretty great. We wrote a song together for my new album. He partially wrote an old one for Mom, and we finished it." Zach felt his heart mushroom with emotion, musing over the last hour.

"Wow. Very cool. Now aren't you glad you came home?"

"Yeah, yeah. You were right. How many times do I have to say it?" Leah teased him every chance she could.

"I like hearing it, bro. Listen, gotta go. See you tomorrow. I'll stop by on my way to work."

"See ya then." Zach ended the call, his gaze gravitating to the stars in the evening sky. Writing a song with his dad felt like a gift from beyond— something he had never imagined possible. *Do I want a forever kind of love?* He combed his fingers through his hair. *Willow.* She was the kind of woman who worth such depth of love. *But what do I want?* Digging deeper into his soul was the only way he would ever find the answer—like it or not.

Chapter Eleven

Willow gift wrapped several novels for a customer, her skilled hands manipulating the ribbon before bagging them. If she was honest, this job fulfilled no passionate desire in her. Yes, she was grateful Marcy hired her without hesitation, but compared to the gallery job in New York, she needed to proceed forward, not backward.

And Zach. *Oy.* Good thing they were almost finished with her apartment. She was not only crushing on him but liking him. His confidence, charm, and generosity were all qualities she would have wanted in a man—at least, before Charles.

Her phone's ringtone broke the silence. *Tim.* A knot squeezed hard in her gut. "Hi, Tim."

"Hello, Willow. Can you talk?"

"Yes."

"The trial begins next week, and jury selection starts tomorrow. They haven't told me which day they will need you yet, but they will notify me in a couple of days. Are you driving or flying?"

"Driving or taking a train." She bit her nail. "My car is old—not so reliable."

"Do you have a place to stay?"

"I have one friend from college I could call. The other friends I made with Charles want nothing to do with me."

"I'm sorry."

"Is he still in jail?" She switched to digging her fingers into her palms.

"Yes, the judge believed he was a flight risk and might have money stashed somewhere, so bail was denied. You will have to see him in court."

"I figured." She unclenched her fists and twisted a loose hair around her finger.

The bells dangling from the door chimed, and two women entered the store.

"I have to go, Tim."

"I'll keep you posted. Don't worry, Willow. This will be over soon."

"Thanks, Tim." She ended the call and focused her attention on the ladies browsing the aisles, ignoring the ripples of nausea twisting her gut.

****

"Hey, Pops. Are you ready?" Zach jingled his truck keys against a leg and paced the living room floor.

Dad appeared. "Here I am."

His shirt was on inside out. "Um. New shirt?"

He examined his clothes and discovered the mistake. "Well, well. Guess I need to wear my glasses when I dress in the morning, huh?"

"Yeah, I guess so." Zach tightened his grip on the keys, stopping the clatter.

"Give me a minute." Dad returned to the bedroom and came out shortly afterward.

Zach guided his truck along the familiar streets and explained to his dad what he had seen when he assessed the pipes. Arriving at the house, he got out of the truck. "I want to tell Mrs. Mason we're here. Coming?"

"Of course. I always like saying hello to Evelyn."

George climbed out, slammed the truck door, and followed.

Evelyn opened the door, wearing an apron dusted with flour, her hair and hands speckled with it. "Isn't this a surprise! Come in."

Zach shuffled his casual stance. "No need. We're checking out Willow's plumbing issues."

"You're so wonderful to help her. Willow does appreciate it. She's been through a rough patch lately and needs her friends in Cedar Hill. Lord, not a single so-called friend supported her in New York. I never trusted Charles. Her father would have seen through his façade but sadly, was already gone when Willow got engaged."

Zach took in the information, and his heart ached. He read as much as he could find on the Internet about the scandal but yearned to hear it from her lips. But he guessed it was a subject she wasn't ready to share. "I'm sorry those things happened." He pointed to the garage. "We're going to check the darkroom first. I'll let you know when we're leaving."

"Okay. I'll be here." She turned, closing the door.

"Come on, Pops. The darkroom will take less work. She needs water for the large sink." Entering the space, Zach crouched with a flashlight, showing his dad the drain and underpinnings of the structure.

"With some new pipes and adjustments in the darkroom, Willow could be up and running in a day." George side-puckered his lips, stood, then followed Zach to inspect the apartment. "All these pipes are rusted in the bathroom, and the installation in the kitchen is incomplete." Dad shook his head. "This job would take several days, if not a week."

"I was afraid the upstairs would take more time." Zach shifted his weight, scratching his head.

"But we can fix the darkroom today. Come on, let's go to the hardware store and get the supplies." George motioned toward the truck.

Zach knew Willow didn't have the money for the materials, but he was fine paying until she did. He hoped she wouldn't be upset with him for doing so. "Okay, Pops. Let's get this done." Zach picked up everything he needed at the hardware store and returned to the Masons' home. He fixed it in two hours with his dad's help, smiling at his success. Willow now owned a *functional* darkroom to pursue her passion. After wiping sweat from his forehead with a clean towel, Zach loaded the tools back into the truck.

Evelyn exited the house with a pie in one hand. "This is for you two. Willow will be thrilled. Are you surprising her tonight?"

Zach shrugged. *Should I?* At least, he'd see her face if she was elated or defend his decision if she was angry for overstepping. "Good idea. Don't tell her we were here, okay?"

"Mum's the word." Evelyn pantomimed zipping her lips shut with her fingers.

Zach pulled into the driveway at home before Willow arrived.

Dad entered the kitchen and patted Zach's arm. "We make a pretty good team, don't we?"

"For sure, Pops."

"Thanks for including me. I need to keep busy." He brushed off his tattered baseball cap with his store's logo and hung it on a hook by the door.

Zach studied his dad, agonizing over his dad's

illness. Pops was aware of what was happening, and Zach imagined he must be scared—anyone would be. "Couldn't have done it without you. The job was above my skill level, and I didn't want to admit it."

Dad nodded. "Good to admit when you need help."

Is he talking about me or himself? "Yep, guess so." Zach looked out the window. "Willow's here, Dad."

"Good. I'll wash up." He turned and headed for the bathroom.

Zach flew out the door to grab the grocery bags. "What's for dinner?"

She glanced at him. "Sloppy joes, salad, and brownies for your sweet tooth."

"Yum. Need any help?"

"No, thank you. I've got it covered." She focused on the tasks in front of her. *Forget about that infectious smile, all perky and adorable.*

When he finished the evening meal, Zach approached Willow in the kitchen. "What's on our agenda for the evening?"

"The kitchen could use a second coat, and then we're done." She smiled.

"Sounds like a plan. I'll come after Dad is situated for the evening."

After the last pot was washed, Willow placed the dish towel on its hook. "See you soon." She waved goodbye to George and left.

Zach strolled into the living room to check on his dad. "I'll be back in a couple of hours. Do you need anything?"

"No, son. I wish I could see Willow's face when you turn on the faucet in the darkroom." He chuckled. "You'll have to tell me about it when you get home."

"I will." He hurried out the door and hopped into his truck.

****

Willow slammed the car door shut and retrieved the developing supplies she had picked up earlier. She was anxious to process the pictures from Rosie's party and imagined she could carry buckets of water to the sink and tray as needed until she secured the money for a plumber. After dropping the items inside, she stepped away from the darkroom and waved to Zach, pulling into the driveway.

He stepped out of the truck. "Everything okay?"

"Yeah. I picked up some developing supplies on my lunch break and wanted to put them away. The paint is inside the garage. Can you get the cans, and I'll grab the brushes?" Willow was used to spending every evening with Zach. By now, she was comfortable except when he exuded his irresistible charm. Then, she wigged out—emotionally and physically.

After Zach set up in the apartment, he turned. "To be more efficient, I'll paint high if you paint low."

"Good idea." She poured some paint into a tray. Willow started at the floor and thrust the thick-pile roller over the textured walls. She wrinkled her nose at the paint's metallic smell, the odor teasing a faint sense of wooziness. She zoned out, making *W* patterns and daydreaming about the man next to her. *I can't help it.*

He whisked down without looking, and *splat!* He bumped her in the middle and jumped back, slinging microdots of color everywhere. Zach squinted, his face speckled with paint, and grinned. "Okay, this high-low thing wasn't such a great idea."

"You're right." She chuckled, grabbing a towel to

wipe her face, then threw it in his direction to do the same. After finishing the last wall, she brushed against him, inspecting the work. At the touch, she hopped back, feeling a spark of energy igniting within her. "Done."

"Fine job, Miss Mason." Sweat dripped across his forehead, and he wiped it with his sleeve.

His gaze softened when he looked at her, and she didn't stop the corners of her mouth from lifting. "Let's clean up."

"Yes, boss." Zach took the brushes to the outdoor spigot and crouched down, his shoulder skimming hers. With a quick flick of a hand, he sent water arcing through the air.

The sudden wetness landed smack on her cheek, sending her stumbling back with a squeal.

He chuckled. "Couldn't help myself."

"Oh, that's how you want to play, huh?"

Zach darted forward, putting both hands under the water in a cup formation.

His eyes lit up with a mischievous expression. "Don't you dare!" But she was too late to escape.

Zach tossed another stream on her face and jumped away from any retaliation.

"Two can play at this game, Hayes." Willow grabbed a cup nearby, filled it, and chased him around the yard until she got a good hit on his chest.

Zach threw both hands up. "Truce!"

"Okay, but I'm keeping my eye on you." She swiveled two fingers in a *V*-shape from her eyes outward and lifted the corners of her lips.

"I'm keeping my eyes on you, too, Mason." He imitated her gesture.

Uh-oh. I'm playing with fire. Turning away, she entered the garage, juggling the extra can and brushes, and set them down with a *thud* on the cupboard shelf.

Zach softly touched her left arm. "Let's inspect the darkroom again and ensure you don't need anything else."

"Okay. Maybe you'll see something I didn't."

He followed her into the room, running a hand over the new shelves. "These seem to be sturdy enough."

She edged closer to the sink. "The only thing not working is this." Grasping the faucet handle, she rotated it. A gush of water spewed out, splashing her clothes, and she shrieked. "What the…?" She swung around.

Zach leaned against the table, both hands in his pockets and a roguish smirk popping his dimples. He shrugged. "Magic?"

She widened her eyes. "You fixed it?"

"Pops and I did." He wrinkled his forehead. "You aren't mad, are you?"

Willow leaped and threw both arms around him, squeezing hard. "Thank you! No, I'm not mad." She shuddered, struggling to keep her emotions in check. "But I don't have the money to pay you back yet." She released her grasp on his body, the heat of him radiating through her skin and leaving her dizzy.

"No problem. The pipes weren't expensive, and Dad was happy to help. In fact, the work was very therapeutic for both of us." He brushed a hair from her face, then slid his palm along her cheek. "I want to help you, Willow. Please. Let me."

She felt her body pulse, just inches away, and her breath catching in her throat. She craved to let him kiss her. *He wants it, too.*

Zach leaned in nearer, dangling his lips near hers, but his phone's ringer stopped him.

She jolted back, catching her balance on the table. *No, I can't kiss him.* Not now. Not ever.

He tugged the phone out of his pocket. "Sorry, I've got to take this. It's Trent."

She nodded.

He crossed the door's threshold, chatting away outside.

Deep breaths, Willow. Deep breaths. She closed the darkroom door behind her and the possibility of their first kiss with it. She was shaken but in a reflective way. *Is Zach going to kiss me? What does he want?* She pressed her lips together, keeping herself busy by picking up a loose tarp and folding it. He was still talking, standing in the yard, so she settled on the front porch to wait—and compose herself.

When he finished, he slipped his phone into his back pocket, then joined her. "Sorry. We worked out some details for our rehearsal on Wednesday."

"No problem." She stood, anxious to get away. "Thanks again. I couldn't be more thrilled."

"If you haven't got a plumber for the inside, then we can talk about it when I return."

"Are you sure you're coming back? Nashville might lure you away." She swayed side to side, one hand in her pocket while studying his expression.

"I'm coming back but not sure for how long, though. Depends on what we decide to do for Pops. I'm taking him to the doctor tomorrow, so I'll get a clearer picture."

"Good luck. Guess I'll see you later." Willow took a deep breath, calming the jitters in her belly.

"I would like to take you and my family out to dinner tomorrow night. Give you a break and give me a chance to spend time with all of you together. What do you say?"

A night off cooking was always welcome. "Are you sure you don't want to take *just* your family?"

"I want you to come, too. To thank you for everything you do for my dad." He stopped. "And because I want you to." His attention latched onto her gaze and didn't waver.

She held his focus, a chill running through her entire body. This intense chemistry wasn't going away. "Okay." She was rendered speechless by the alluring energy, its force overwhelming her. No use discussing the *near* kiss.

He grinned, then left.

Zach leaving was a good thing. Although her lips never touched his, he still bent in to kiss her—undeniably. She needed a break from all the emotions swirling inside her every time they were together. She felt her heart straining to break free from the wall she had built. She couldn't ignore her feelings, no matter how hard she tried, but with love comes pain—and loss. No way was she enduring such a miserable road again. The ink on her divorce papers was barely dry. She needed to find herself again and move on—alone.

Chapter Twelve

The next day, Zach navigated his truck into the doctor's office parking lot, clenching the steering wheel. He wiped the sweat on his brow, glancing at his dad. *Is he nervous?* Who wouldn't be? The doctor might paint a grim picture of reality, or at the least, remind them of a challenging future ahead. But his dad was strong and resilient. Zach drew a deep breath, grateful for the abundance of funds in his bank account—enough to hire help and keep Dad at home for the remainder of his days.

As he sat in the waiting room, Zach skimmed through the magazines. He could always tell when people recognized him. He would see them whisper in their husband's or friend's ear, point, or boldly ask for his autograph. He didn't mind. Being famous was part of the gig—and success, a gratifying perk.

The nurse called George's name and gestured for him to follow her into the office.

Dr. Macintosh, a slim, distinguished-looking man dressed in a white lab coat, stood to greet him. He had graying hair at the temples, wire-rimmed glasses, and crystal-blue eyes. "Nice to see you again, George. Have a seat." He pointed to the chairs in front of his desk and returned to his seat.

George briefly lowered his head in response and rubbed his palms together before he sat.

The doctor addressed Zach. "I need to do a battery of cognitive tests, so if you don't mind sitting here while we do them, I'm fine with it."

"I'll sit right here. Won't make a peep." Zach sensed the doctor could easily calm a patient's nerves. He studied his dad, whose lips were pressed tight, and his forehead held a wrinkled brow.

For the next half hour, his dad answered various questions and took a written test. His memory was weaker, and he struggled with some cognitive items.

Zach felt a lead weight settling in his gut, its heaviness steeped with dread. He hated seeing his dad this way and kicked himself again for taking so long to return to Cedar Hill. His career didn't seem as important now as the time spent with his dad while he had him. He needed to make these home visits more frequent and longer between touring. Thank God, he'd finished an extensive tour and wouldn't be going out on the road again until the spring of next year. Unless some other single gigs came his way, which they would.

When the doctor finished, he motioned for Zach to slide his chair closer. Dr. Macintosh leaned forward in George's direction. "The testing wasn't so bad, was it?"

"I guess not. Not sure I got an A, though."

Zach laughed with the doctor. Dad still had his humor intact.

"Here's the gist of it. You received the diagnosis after the MRI, but these tests tell me more about how your memory and judgment skills are doing. You're strong in some areas, but your memory is mildly impaired now. We can't be sure of how long this disease will take to weaken you further, but I'm sorry to say, it will happen. The important thing is to keep you safe. You will need more care at some point, and as I understand, you will stay home. You can start taking medication, and as research shows, it helps to slow down the process. I would like to see you again in three months, and we'll keep adjusting the prescription as we need to. But from your medical records, I see you're in good health otherwise, which should also help. Keep getting exercise every day, eat a healthy diet, and do things to stimulate your brain, like crosswords and word games. I'll be here if you have any questions."

Zach was grateful for Dr. Macintosh's sincere, kind gaze oozing compassion out to his dad. "Thanks, Doc."

George stared at the doctor's desk for a moment, fiddling with his hat in his lap. "Yeah, thanks."

Zach stood, ready to get out of the office. He wiped the sweat dripping down his neck, his lungs needing fresh air. "Come on, Pops. Let's go home."

George shook the doctor's hand and followed Zach out of the door and into the parking lot.

Zach sat briefly before starting the ignition, then turned his head. "Are you okay?"

"Yeah. Not the news I want to hear from a doctor, but I recognize what's coming. My buddy's mother had it later in life, and I saw what happened to his family. I don't want you and Leah to worry about me, so let's set up this care thing right away. I will cooperate and agree to let a stranger into my house. Willow must live her life and doesn't need to take care of an old man."

"Willow enjoys your company, Dad, and she needs the money. I'll see if she wants to continue the dinner shift. She might surprise you."

"Whatever you say, son." George glanced out his

window. "Let's go."

Zach guided the truck out of the parking lot, still feeling a massive weight in the pit of his gut and heart. He couldn't fix this, but he would make sure his dad had the best care ever. Securing his financial future, he could do.

****

Willow stood in front of the mirror, turning side to side, as she studied her body and dress at every angle. Even though she was having dinner with her closest friends, she still felt nervous around Zach—especially after their almost-kiss in the darkroom. Her pale-blue dress hugged her slender body, accentuating her elegant curves, while her curly dark hair draped past her shoulders. She stepped closer to the mirror, applied a soft, pink gloss to her lips, grabbed her purse, and headed to the living room. She skipped off the last step and twirled in front of her mom.

"Aren't you beautiful!" Evelyn clapped her hands together, her palms landing in prayer formation.

"Thanks, Mom. Not too much, is it?" She didn't want to appear overdressed, but she was thrilled to be going out to dinner. Sometimes, she missed the glamorous part of her old life in New York.

"Absolutely not. A certain country cowboy might take notice."

"Stop, Mom. I don't need to impress Zach, but I will indulge in an evening away from the kitchen. Do you want me to bring anything back?"

"No, dear. I have plenty of leftovers from my lunch with the girls. Enjoy yourself."

Willow strolled with a lilt in her step, her mind consumed by thoughts of Zach. The night before, he had awakened a desire within her—a yearning for passion she had long forgotten. She was positive he was going to kiss her before his phone blasted. She wasn't clueless. She set her boundaries for a good reason, and cautiousness paid off so far. *But did it?*

Arriving at the restaurant, Willow caught sight of Zach's truck and Leah's SUV. She opened her compact mirror, touched up her lipstick, and headed toward the front door.

Once inside, Zach motioned for her to join them at a table in the back and pointed to the adjacent chair. "I saved you a seat."

Great. She had hoped to sit far away. *Not in the plan tonight.* "Thanks."

The lively group discussed Rosie's return to school, George's birdhouses, and Willow's apartment.

"I can't believe I haven't seen it yet. I'm coming over this weekend, for sure." Leah grinned.

Willow sipped her wine, then swirled the burgundy liquid in the glass while staring at it.

"Wait until she gets some furniture." Zach smiled, his gaze aimed in her direction while toying with his beer bottle.

He's being supportive. "Even better when I get the plumbing put in." She laughed, making light of her fiscal situation preventing the apartment's completion.

Zach leaned over. "Good to see you smile and be happy, Mason."

She tipped the merlot, savoring the dark-fruity taste with a hint of toffee, and ignored the heat crawling up the back of her neck, aiming for her cheeks—and a full-on flush.

"Yeah, Dad has some ideas, right, Pops?"

George described what Willow needed and suggested a plumber.

Willow angled her head, taking in his advice, but conceded she couldn't do anything about it until she had more money. Listening to the conversation, Willow stretched for a tortilla chip at the same time Zach did, and her hand brushed against his. A tingle rushed through her veins with the innocent touch. *Does he feel it, too?* How much longer could she refrain from the chemistry enticing her?

When finished, Zach grabbed the check, and everyone thanked him. "My pleasure." Out in the parking lot, Zach leaned into his dad. "I need to talk with Willow. Be right back." He pivoted, offering an outstretched right arm to Willow and grinned. "After you, mademoiselle."

As Willow strode across the parking lot, she shivered in the nippy, dusk air of approaching autumn.

Zach took off his jean jacket and draped it over her shoulders. "Here. Don't want you getting sick." Both hands lingered for a fleeting second.

Her wall was crumbling. This man was genuine, kind, and caring. She had seen it time after time over the last two weeks. Country star or not, Zach had a heart—a heart she yearned for. He made her forget her problems and inspired her to pursue her dreams. She intertwined her gaze with his and held steady. "Thanks."

Approaching the car, he pivoted his stance, keeping his steady view on her face. "I'll miss you, Willow."

"I'll miss you, too." Her heart pounded. *Will he really miss me?*

He flexed his brawny arms and embraced her, not

letting go. One hand slid up her neck, drawing her closer.

She let herself sink into his grasp, her knees weakening but held up by his strength. His gentle breath seeped through her hair, warming her skin, and his muscular chest molded into her body. After a few moments, a reluctant Willow stepped away. "Take care of yourself, cowboy."

"I'll be back. Don't worry."

She took off his jacket and dangled it in front of him. "Thanks, and good luck in your recording session with Trent."

"Thanks." He grabbed his coat, tipped his hat toward her, then left.

Willow stood still, watching him drive away. Part of her heart was in that truck, and she could do nothing about it. Nothing at all.

****

The next day, Willow returned home from work and entered the kitchen.

Evelyn twisted her head. "Hi, honey. A bunch of mail for you is on the counter. How's George?"

"He's okay. He kept asking me about Zach. He forgets why his son isn't here." She rolled her head in a half-circle, working out a kink refusing to go away. Being in the Hayeses' house without Zach was weird—some of the magic had been missing in her day.

"I feel for him."

"Yeah. Me, too." Willow grabbed her pile of mail and plopped onto the couch in the living room with her mom. Most of the envelopes were bills. "Oh, my God."

Mom snapped her head up. "What's wrong?"

"These credit bills are for over a hundred thousand

dollars! Charles took cash advances out on *all* our cards. What will I do?" The anger inside of her kept the tears at bay. "He's ruined me."

Evelyn put an arm around Willow. "You'll get through this. Talk to your lawyer about getting exonerated from this—make it part of your upcoming divorce agreement. And some agencies negotiate with the credit card companies."

Willow blinked back the wetness behind her eyes. Just as she was picking up the pieces and rebuilding her life, she sensed another catastrophe on the horizon.

Evelyn kissed her forehead. "Ask for help, Willow. Prayer always comforts me, and inevitably, I find a clear path. Have a little faith." She squeezed her again, then stood, walking over to a rosewood hutch pressed against the wall, and removed a box from the top drawer. "I have a gift for you, sweetheart. I've been saving it for the right time." She returned, sitting next to Willow.

"Mom, you didn't have to buy me a gift. You've already given me so much. Without you, I'd be homeless—and miserable."

"This is a keepsake to help you remember your true essence whenever you doubt yourself. Go ahead. Open it." She placed the present in Willow's hand.

Willow unhooked the delicate latch on the velvet box. She opened the top, widening her eyes at the sight of a gold necklace with a charm that spelled the word, *Faith.* "Oh, Mom. How elegant! I love it." She threw both arms around her mother, her head resting on her chest momentarily. "Thank you."

"You're welcome. Whenever you worry or stress about any situation you are in, touch this and be reminded of your faith. Faith, everything will work out for you in the best possible way. Stay connected, Willow. Your connection to a higher power will keep you at peace, even in the darkest times."

"Here, help me put it on." She twisted her body for a better angle.

Evelyn adjusted the clasp on the back of Willow's neck and leaned back, admiring the jewelry. "Exquisite, if I must say so myself."

Willow touched the word embellished in gold, resting her fingers on the coolness of the metal. "I love it."

"Me, too."

Willow breathed deeply, her right hand clutching the charm. She blew a lengthy stream of air through her puckered lips. "Now back to this." Willow picked up the envelopes, continuing to sift through the mail, and stopped at a letter from the Sterling Center for Photographic Arts in New York. She forgot she had submitted a photo for their annual juried exhibition. *Probably a rejection letter.* As she read the contents, she lifted the corners of her mouth. "Oh, my God."

"Now what?" Evelyn lowered the magazine she had been reading.

"You'll never believe this. My photo was selected as a finalist! This was mailed a couple of weeks ago, but because of the move, I'm getting it now." She handed her the letter.

Mom perused the letter. "Oh, darling. See, the universe is lifting your spirits and guiding you already. This is wonderful. I'm so proud."

"I won't get it, but to be a finalist is a big deal." Willow took the letter from her mother.

"Don't say you won't get it. No negativity. See yourself winning it, dear. At least, I will." Her mother tilted her head, studying Willow with intense focus. "I have faith."

Willow let a faint, gravelly laugh tumble out of her throat. "Very funny, Mom. I get it." She continued reading. "The winners are being announced next week and will participate in a gallery exhibition in New York in November, in addition to receiving a hefty cash prize." Willow couldn't believe something good happened—she had been under a dark cloud for too long. "I need to get my portfolio together. If chosen, I will get the exposure I've needed for work and to make a career for myself—*finally*."

"I have no doubt you will. I'm glad your darkroom is up and running."

Willow daydreamed of Zach and the almost-kiss. *Thank God he left for Nashville.* She needed a break from the undeniable chemistry driving her crazy. "Yeah, I'll work on my computer before bed. Not so tired anymore." She scooped her hair into a scrunchy. "And by the way, I'll leave for New York on Friday. I testify on Monday, and my lawyer set up a prison visit with Charles on Sunday. I've got to face the situation and discuss these financial disasters. I'm nervous about the whole thing, but I need to tie up loose ends to move on with my life."

"Spoken like a wise woman." Evelyn curled her feet under her on the couch and picked up the television remote.

"Thanks again for the gift, Mom." Willow pecked her mom on the cheek before heading upstairs. After tossing the mail onto the oak desk in her bedroom, she opened her computer and emailed Zach the picture she had taken of him and his dad. The black-and-white photo, taken from behind, showed them walking side by side—Zach's arm around him—and both carrying a guitar case with their other hand. She wrote a quick note. *Thought you'd appreciate this. Good luck with recording. Willow*

Later, as she lay in bed, she pressed a palm to her chest, her heart racing with excitement at being a finalist. *Finally, some validation in my sagging career.* And Zach. His life was all about fun and the next gal— not her style. Despite the pressures of court and the looming dread of seeing Charles again, Willow gained confidence at receiving the finalist letter. She felt her courage growing—enough to face her affairs in New York and to keep Zachary Hayes far away from her heart.

****

The following day, Willow asked Marcy to cover the store for a couple of hours so she could take her car in for a tune-up before the New York trip. She tried the ignition. *Ping-ping-ping.* Metal ground against metal, and Willow dropped her head to the steering wheel. *Great. Just what I need.*

Evelyn stepped outside and tapped on the car door. "I heard a clanking sound drift through the kitchen window." She cocked her head. "You need a tow, dear. I'll get my auto service card and call."

Willow grabbed her purse from the passenger seat. Was this a sign she shouldn't go? No, would only be wishful thinking. She forced an optimistic expression. "Thanks, Mom."

Sitting at the repair shop later, Willow flipped

through magazines and found an article about country music stars. Zachary Hayes flashed in front of her—adorable and sexy as ever, with an arm around a woman at some awards show last year. *She's beautiful.* Willow considered herself somewhat attractive, but she didn't compare to the striking, radiant woman in the picture, all glammed up for an event.

"Miss Mason?"

She raised her head to see the service technician standing in front of her. "Yes?"

"Afraid I have bad news. You need a new premium carburetor and a new steel gasket for the transmission, in addition to a new battery."

Am I cursed? "Can you finish it today?"

"Unfortunately, one of the parts won't come in until Monday. We can keep the car here, of course."

A sinking feeling in her gut told her she wasn't driving to New York. Train? The only way left. "Okay, thanks. I won't be back until Tuesday, so go ahead and fix it at your leisure." *If only I had purchased a new car last year when money was in my bank account.* She shook her head, picked up her phone, and called her mom for a ride.

Ten minutes later, she arrived.

"Thanks, Mom." She informed her of the ill-fated woes of the car.

"Darling, I have plenty of miles accumulated on my airline's account from every summer I took all those trips. Let me give some to you, and you can fly. Much easier."

"But what if you need them?"

"Forget it. They're yours. My gift is the least I can do for you while you go through this horrific ordeal.

Don't argue with your mother." Evelyn teased her daughter.

Willow didn't have the strength to argue. She forced a smile, accepting another gift, but would also do something special for her mother. She deserved it. "Okay, Mom. Thank you. When I return to the office, I'll work on getting a flight. Can you drop me off at the bookstore?"

Evelyn patted her daughter's hand. "Sure thing. You'll get through this, Willow."

Willow stared out the window at the trees, their autumn leaves transforming into colors of crimson and gold. A change of seasons lurked around the corner. She rubbed her palm back and forth across her chest, praying the next season of her life would evolve for the better. Her fingertip caressed the dangling charm settled on her breastbone. *Faith. Can I find it again?*

Chapter Thirteen

Zach opened his weary eyes and readjusted to his whereabouts, skimming his gaze over familiar items in his bedroom. *Ahh, my firm mattress*. Major improvement from his old one in Ohio. He lay still, reflecting on the previous night with Trent's family and rehearsing in his studio—*what a blast*. He and Trent worked out the harmonies, and his wife cooked a big meal afterward. She was six months pregnant with their first child, and they couldn't be happier. Would he ever be ready for such a lifestyle? He rubbed his chest, the tightness making it hard to breathe. *Not anytime soon.*

His phone's ringtone blared, and he glanced at the caller. *Leah.* "Hey, sis. Miss me already?"

"Ha, ha. Very funny. How was your rehearsal?"

"Awesome. We're recording this afternoon. What's up? Dad okay?"

"Yes. Everything's fine. Listen, I'm trying one of those caregiving agencies to help me out this weekend since Willow will be gone."

"Where's Willow going?"

"Didn't she tell you? She needs to go to New York. She's visiting Charles in prison on Sunday and testifying at the trial on Monday. Not fun stuff."

Zach was silent. Did she cry on the steps because of the trial? "I had no idea. Is she okay?"

"She's as good as she can be. Her mom gave her

miles to fly, and she's staying with her one friend left in New York from college. I'm sure it won't be easy." Leah let out a gentle puff of air. "Now, back to Dad. Are you okay with me hiring someone?"

"Of course. I trust you, but when I get back, let's interview people together."

"Thanks, Zach. I've gotta go. A new client's here. When are you coming back?"

"Sunday or Monday. Depends on how the session goes today and if we need to go in again. I'll keep you posted."

"See you, then." Leah ended the call.

He shuffled into the kitchen to make coffee but couldn't keep his mind off Willow. His heart ached, visualizing what she was going through. *How can I help her?* He had grown fonder of her and fantasized about touching her skin without hesitancy, kissing her soft lips without a boundary, and holding her without fear he was crossing a line. Yes, he had it bad for Willow Mason, but he couldn't offer her what she deserved—commitment.

He grabbed a cup of coffee and sat at his computer. He discovered the photo Willow sent, and he smiled, goose bumps pouring over his body. The image displayed everything he ever wanted with his dad—love, camaraderie, and the shared joy of music. He had an idea of what he wanted to do with it, but he would wait to discuss it with Mike later. As he strolled into the kitchen, he whistled and gathered the breakfast ingredients from the refrigerator. He dipped his head, then raised it, humming and pleased with himself and his new plan to help Willow.

****

Later, Zach entered the studio, greeting all the players. Most were in Trent's band, but one new musician had arrived since Trent's bass player became ill with the flu the night before. He put down his guitar case, and as he stood, he widened his eyes—Marissa Peyton. His old girlfriend. He hadn't seen her in over a year.

"Zachary Hayes. Where have you been hiding?" Marissa sauntered over, hugging him while rubbing her body against his for a lingering second.

He held on to the hug, feeling all her curves in the right places and reflected on sultry evenings alone. *Yes, the chemistry is still there.* "Are you singing backup today?"

"Yep, along with two others who should be here any minute. What a coincidence, huh?"

"I guess so. You do have a fabulous voice." He was unable to control his lilting smile.

"Thanks, Zach. Let's chat later, okay?"

"Sure." He wanted to stay focused on the recording, so he returned to the guys to review the final arrangement. As he worked out the background harmonies with everyone, he couldn't stay away from Marissa in such an enclosed space and found himself standing beside her. As he caught a whiff of her floral scent, he felt his testosterone kick up, and past images of them together invaded his mind.

After an hour of rehearsal, Zach entered his separate recording booth, confident he was ready. His effortless voice flowed together with Trent's, and the song took on its own captivating force as the afternoon propelled on. When finished, Zach huddled with others in the mixing booth to listen. As the song ended, he cheered and high-fived others over the magic of the creation—a possible hit in the making.

Trent widened his blue eyes, running his fingers through his dirty-blond hair and stood. Not quite as tall as Zach, but he commanded a room. "Thanks for all your hard work today. Great job, and dinner is on me tonight—Valentino's at seven."

Clapping sounded throughout the studio for a well-deserved celebration.

Trent pivoted to Zach. "Can you stay for some of the mixing?"

"Would love to." Zach sat at the soundboard and waited for people to leave.

Marissa touched him on the shoulder. "I guess I'll see you tonight."

"I guess you will." He wondered if she was seeing anyone. *A little fantasizing can't hurt.* It might take his mind off a certain woman in Ohio. He sat next to Trent in the booth and helped to fine-tune the tracks after everyone left except for the engineer. As Zach listened, he welcomed the goose bumps rolling over his body and exchanged a glance with Trent—the song was better than good.

Trent put a hand on Zach's upper arm. "Thanks, man, for coming back to town to do this. I couldn't think of anyone else I'd rather be singing with than you."

"I should be thanking you, Trent. You gave me an opportunity to get my voice on the local radio stations with something new."

"After what you played me last night, you won't have to worry about radio play."

Zach had played "Lit Like an Angel" for him at his

house, and the undeniable response was positive. "Yeah, I'm excited about my new album coming together."

"Can't wait to hear the new stuff. Let's finish and go celebrate."

"I'm all yours." Zach bent over the audio console, joining him to make final tweaks to the song. Thank God he was getting something on the airwaves.

****

Zach climbed out of his hired car, admiring the twinkling white lights displayed along the front window of the Italian eatery. Valentino's, an upscale restaurant in business for years, was a favorite of many local country recording artists—photos of famous stars, including himself, scattered the walls. Greeted by the maître d', he was escorted to a private room in the back where the crew celebrated, and the alcohol flowed. He waved at Trent, then caught Marissa's gaze, who approached him.

"Come on. We saved you a seat next to Trent and me."

He scanned her snug top and skintight jeans that outlined her perfect body and lingered his gaze on her fluttering eyelashes as she talked. He noticed a desire bubble up inside him, overwhelming his senses. *How about a little fun this weekend?* He couldn't help himself. "Thanks."

Trent slapped Zach on the back and handed him a beer. He raised his drink. "Here's to a successful recording session today and a special thanks to Zachary Hayes for joining me!"

Everyone tipped their glasses or bottles in the air, toasting to success.

"Now, let's eat!" Trent laughed, his baritone voice echoing out into the room.

Zach took a large gulp of his drink and checked out Marissa. "So, how have you been?"

"I'm great. Been getting a lot of recording gigs, some demos, some records. I can't complain." She placed a hand on his shoulder. "What about you? And your dad? Sorry you and Leah are dealing with such a tough illness."

Zach held his attention on her sapphire-blue eyes and was reminded of her sensual appeal. "Thanks, appreciate your concern. I'm glad I returned home and plan on going back after this weekend. I've had some luck writing new songs in my hometown. I'm even writing one with Dad called 'Forever Kind of Love'."

"I can't wait to hear it. If you're staying in town, why don't we get together this weekend? I'm free."

Do I want to spend time with her? After weeks of testosterone teasing around Willow, he might not control himself. "Let me check my schedule, and I'll text you tomorrow." He perused the menu. "Are you seeing anyone?"

"No. I have a bad habit of comparing men to you. Frankly, none measure up to Zachary Hayes." She swept her fingers across his upper arm and quietly chuckled.

He twisted his body, adjusting his posture and feeling a new temptation itching in his gut. "Hopefully, you'll find a man who wants to tie the knot. You've always said marriage was important."

"Still the free bird, huh?" She toyed with a strand dangling by her neck.

"I guess so." Spending time with Marissa could

soothe some of the forbidden angst he had accumulated being close to Willow.

"If you want to have some fun this weekend, no strings attached, text me." Marissa squeezed his hand.

Heck, yeah. "Will do."

After dinner, the crew mingled a bit longer, then headed to their cars or trucks.

As Zach exited the door, he put an arm around Marissa, but word had gotten out to the paparazzi that two megastars were dining in the restaurant. *Click-click-click.* Multiple flashbulbs blasted in a burst of bright light.

"Zachary! Over here! Is that your new girlfriend?" a cameraman yelled in his direction.

Zach maneuvered Marissa away from the chaos and hurried her into the waiting car. He slammed the door shut and instructed the driver to take off. "Are you okay? Sorry about the nuisance."

"No problem. Now I can remember what happens when I'm with you in public."

"Let me give you a ride home."

"Thanks. I'd appreciate it."

Sitting in the backseat, he breathed in a waft of spice and floral as her warm body cuddled against his side—enticing, stirring his desires. Zach rubbed the stubble on his jawline and drew in a deep breath. He could cross the line at any second.

A short time later, she turned as the car idled in front of her apartment. "Do you want to come up?"

Aaargh. This is tough. He tightened one fist. "I'll head home tonight, but I'll text you tomorrow. Good seeing you again."

Marissa leaned over and kissed him on the cheek.

"See you soon, I hope." She hopped out of the car.

Zach threw his head back against the seat. What was wrong with him? Why couldn't he pull the trigger and make it a night with Marissa? He flashed thoughts of Willow and shook his head. *Is she the reason?* Had she gotten under his skin? Tomorrow was another day, and he was determined to take a little break with Marissa, no matter what tormented him inside.

****

The next day, Zach leaned back in his chair next to Trent, listening to what he hoped was the last mix of the song. He had spent the afternoon in the studio and was satisfied with the final cut. He hoped Trent felt the same way.

As the song ended, Trent slapped the mixing board, his energy high. "And that's a wrap!"

Zach threw his fists in the air. "Woo-hoo!" Then he fist-bumped Trent. "Thanks again for asking me to do this." He smiled, aware of a chill rushing through his veins and another idea for a song percolating in his brain. He wanted to get home before he lost the melody in his head.

"No, Zach, thank you for traveling down here. I'll keep you posted about the song's release date. And when you come back to town, give me a call so we can get together."

"Will do." Zach stood at the same time as Trent and hugged his friend. Then, he headed out the door.

Back at his house, Zach grabbed his guitar and eased onto his patio chair overlooking wooded hills and flowering shrubs. Different from his backyard in Ohio, but still green and luscious. *I need to call Leah.* "Hey, sis. How's it going?"

"Busy. I have a new woman starting today at four. Fingers crossed Dad will let her in the house," Leah murmured through a rushed breath.

"I'm sure he will. After the doctor's appointment, we talked about caregivers. I'll check on him later. Is Willow gone?"

"She flew out this afternoon. Keep her in your prayers, Zach. She needs all the strength she can get."

"Yeah, I will." Zach daydreamed for a moment about the dark-eyed woman.

"Zach?"

"Yeah, sorry. I'll be home on Monday. I want to do some things while I'm here before I come back."

"Okay. Love, ya."

After the phone call, Zach scanned the Tennessee hills and reflected on his time with Willow while painting her apartment. *She would like it here in Nashville.* Then he shook his head. *What am I thinking?* His phone pinged. *Marissa.* Thank God—saved from his self-torture.

—*Are we still on for tonight*—

—*Pick you up at six*—

—*Perfect. See you then*—

—Thumbs-up emoji—

Zach remembered when their texting had a spicier flair, but this was about being friends. *But if a little mischief happens along the way?*

****

Benito's, a popular restaurant, often drew a celebrity crowd and was hopping on a Friday night. Zach stepped out of his luxury car at the valet, and one paparazzo waited in the wings. He opened the door for Marissa and heard *click-click-click* as he was showered by light flashes. He hurried her into the building, where the maître d' guided them to a booth toward the back of the restaurant, securing privacy.

"This is a pleasant surprise. A date at our favorite restaurant." She slipped a hand over his. "Were you feeling nostalgic?" She slowly dragged her fingers across his skin.

As he felt Marissa's touch caressing him, he stared at her blonde hair tumbling past her shoulders and her enticing blue eyes. *Is this a date?* "Yeah, I love the food, and you did, too, right?"

She tilted her head back, lifting her eyelashes. "Yes, I do."

As the evening stretched on, Zach fell into an easy pace of chatting and catching up on their lives. He enjoyed himself with the noncommittal flirting and teasing with Marissa. He guessed he needed a release from all the pent-up energy he'd built up while spending days with Willow—trying hard to maintain boundaries with his sister's best friend, who was gorgeous and impossible to forget.

After dinner and wine, Marissa stroked his forearm. "What do you say we go back to my place for dessert?"

Hell, yeah, he should take advantage of this opportunity. Remind himself of why he loved his freedom. "Let me get the check."

When the restaurant front door opened, he was blinded by flashing lightbulbs again. *Click- click-click. Word spreads fast around here.* The valet had his car, and with a hand pressed against Marissa's back, he guided her into the front seat, avoiding reporters snapping photos. Zach hopped in and took off as fast as he could go. *Ahh, the calmness of Ohio—no paparazzi follows me in the buckeye state.* He missed the obscurity. Steering into the driveway, he sat for a moment. *Am I doing this?*

She caressed his right hand. "Come on. I'll make us a nightcap or a cup of tea, whichever you want."

"Okay." A drink sounded good. He wasn't sure what would happen next but was surprised by the hesitation in his gut. *Come on. This is Marissa, not a one-night stand.* He had a history with her, and a little fooling around might be well deserved, *if* she had no expectations of anything permanent.

Chapter Fourteen

The morning after arriving in New York, Willow stretched both legs under the covers, her muscles aching from the stress of travel. The sounds of the city streets below blasted through the window—taxi horns blaring, sirens wailing in the distance, and tires screeching to a halt at red lights or to avoid an accident. Thank God, she had one friend left here—Betsy Silvers. They roomed together their first year at college and stayed in touch as much as possible after Willow married. Willow had been sucked into a whole new circle of friends and how quickly they disappeared after Charles's scandal.

Betsy worked as a nurse at a nearby hospital. She wasn't married yet, but she told Willow an engagement to her boyfriend might be on the horizon.

Willow didn't want to put a damper on her friend's excitement but warned her about getting a prenup. After Charles, she couldn't help but give some to-be-heeded advice about taking the plunge into marriage. She zipped up her jacket, skipped onto the sidewalk, and tilted her head, scanning the signs for a good diner serving coffee and breakfast. Willow breathed into the awakening odors of Manhattan—bacon wafting from a nearby diner, gasoline exhausts from the cars and taxis, and fall dampness circulating the air among the multitudes of people scurrying along the sidewalk. *Ahh,*

New York. If Charles weren't in the picture, then she would have stayed.

As she ambled past the newsstand, she grabbed a newspaper but stopped when she glimpsed the front page of a gossip paper. *Zachary Hayes reunites with a local singer in Nashville.* Several photos of Zach and this attractive blonde-haired woman were on the front page. She pressed down a wave of nausea curdling in her stomach. Of course, he would return to his player ways. He couldn't help himself. *Yes, he almost kissed me, but it meant nothing.* He's not capable of real love or caring for a woman. *I don't need a man who would just hurt or humiliate me again.*

She bought the paper to read the article later and stuffed it into her backpack. *Not letting this ruin my day.* She strode toward the park, striking her feet against the pavement with determined force. She skipped along, reveling in the goose bumps tingling up and down her spine, and beamed a smile at those she passed. She was eager to explore the city with her camera—no distractions. *Forget about Zach. My muse awaits.*

After breakfast, she headed toward Central Park, one of her favorite places to shoot. Every person she witnessed had a story, and she loved to capture those imagined stories in one photograph. The bright sun shone on an early autumn day, and people embraced the last warmth before winter struck. She inhaled the earthy smell of the first fallen leaves and the sweet scent of damp foliage. She fought off the image of Zach's photo with the woman as it floated in and out of her mind, letting it go each time it did. She didn't have time for such foolish pondering over a guy who didn't want a relationship. They were friends—who almost crossed a line. Nothing more.

On the way back to Betsy's, she stopped by the old gallery where she'd worked—or at least, peeked through the window. She twisted her head, and she scanned the surrounding area for familiar faces, making sure no one recognized her—the humiliation still too fresh. She stood on her tiptoes, viewing the latest photo in the window display.

Suddenly, a man rushed around the corner without warning, nearly colliding with her. His feet skidded to a halt. "Willow! Is that you?" Rupert Morgan, a stocky man and her former boss, hovered nearby, gawking through his designer sunglasses.

"Hi, Rupert." Willow gripped the straps tighter on her backpack, her body shuddering.

"What are you doing here? Aren't you in Ohio?"

"Yes, I'm here for the weekend. Still living in Ohio." She didn't want to share her personal affairs. The media already caused enough damage.

Rupert frowned. "I hoped you'd moved back. We miss you here. You were the best-qualified salesperson and assistant I ever hired. I'm ready to fire your replacement. He's clueless about fine art photography. If you ever come back to the city, your job will be available."

Did the passing of time make people forget about the scandal? "Thanks." She debated whether to tell him one of her photos had been selected as a finalist for the Sterling Center's jury exhibit in November but decided against it. He never believed in her as an artist, and she wanted to keep it a secret until the results were announced.

"Keep me posted." Rupert hurried into the gallery.

What just happened? Rupert offered her job back as an overqualified saleslady. Downsizing in Ohio had given her the time to seriously consider becoming a full-time, fine arts photographer—not as a hobby or a distant dream, but as a profession. Even with the trial and the upcoming visit to see Charles weighing on her, Willow expanded her chest with the next breath and fantasized about new possibilities in the future. She picked up her pace, rushing to return to the apartment and upload her new pictures onto the computer. Yes, this is what a day of being an artist would feel like— excitement, inspiration, and determination. She was digging it and even forgot about Zach for a whole hour—progress.

****

Zach stood on his front porch, scanning his property and breathing in the warm air of a sunny Tennessee day. He turned, twisted the key into his door's lock, and strolled into the kitchen. He had spent a leisurely morning hanging out with Marissa and appreciated her cooking breakfast. Last night was cool, but he had no desire to spend the entire weekend with her. He wanted to spend the day writing and, later, having dinner with Mike and his family.

Tomorrow, he was hanging out with the guys, watching football, and he would head home on Monday. *Home.* Although he lived and breathed the Nashville scene, Zach felt like Ohio was his home again. His love for his hometown, Cedar Hill, was reemerging in his soul. He picked up his phone and hit his dad's number. "Hey, Pops. How's it going?"

"Fine, fine. When are you coming home?"

"Monday. I'll call you later about the time."

"Where's Willow?"

"She's in New York, Dad. She had to go for an awful court case concerning her husband."

"Husband? She has a husband? Where is he?"

"He's in prison, Dad. Don't worry, she's divorcing him. When I see you, I'll tell you the details, but she's very private about the matter."

"Okay, but you two should get married. You need a good woman like her, son."

Zach rocked back on his heels, feeling a shock wave of surprise surge through his heart. *What did Dad say? Marry Willow?* "Dad, we're friends. Nothing else."

"I see the way you look at her, and she looks at you the same way. I might be losing my marbles, but I recognize love."

Zach wiped the sweat from his forehead, as a tightness in his throat restricted his breath. *Where did this come from?* "Okay, Dad. I believe you, but let's not discuss this in front of her, okay?" Or anywhere. He felt his skin crawl at the thought of marriage.

"All right. When are you coming home?"

"Monday. I'll call you. Love you, Pops."

"Love you, too."

Zach tapped *End* on his cellphone and paced the floor, dwelling on Willow. He had witnessed a sadness in her chocolate-brown eyes, but when he saw her laugh, they lit up, glimmering like the light of an angel. He was inspired by her gentle caring with his father, her determination to rebuild her life, and her talent as an artist. He had forgotten those feelings a few days back in Nashville, but they still plagued him. He shook his head, then his phone pinged—Marissa.

—*Last night was fun. Let's do it again before you leave.* Heart emoji—

—*Thanks for your hospitality. Not tonight but I'll text you tomorrow*—

—*Be sure you do.* Wink emoji—

He drove out a harsh sigh, then typed nothing. He didn't want her to get the wrong impression they were a *thing* again. He wanted to play and nothing more. *Why don't I feel better about it?* He hung his head, laid his phone on the table, and shuffled to the shower. Something was changing inside, and he wasn't sure if he was ready for the shift. Or wanted it.

****

Later in the day, Zach arrived at Mike's house, eager to share his new material before dinner, but first, he couldn't resist drinking a beer on the back patio.

Mike's two boys, ages six and seven, passed a football back and forth in the spacious yard, their voices screeching and hollering as they played.

"Those two are getting bigger every day." Zach tossed back a misfired ball.

"Tell me about it. I never have a peaceful moment around here anymore. I'll have to wait until they go to college." Mike snickered and held up his bottle. "Here's to you, man. The new single might be a hit. I can feel it in my bones. Trent's manager sent me the rough cut earlier."

Zach joined in on the toast, and he couldn't ignore the shiver running up his spine. "Yep, you're right. Recording with him was a blast. Can't wait to get back in the studio with my upcoming album. Want to hear a new tune?"

"Are you kidding? Hell, yeah." Mike tipped back his beer bottle.

Zach grabbed his guitar, trailing his fingers over the neck until he found the beginning chord. As he sang his new song, "She Was Lit Like an Angel," he reverberated a velvety tone in his voice, its melody mesmerizing the listener. When finished, he latched his gaze onto Mike. "What do you think?"

"Awesome, man. Who was the inspiration for this one?"

"A woman back home who's helping to care for my dad. She's experienced a rough patch in her life, so laughter and joy have been minimal these days. But when she does smile, her eyes light up like an angel—at least, in my imagination they do. Thus, the song."

"Glad you found your muse in Ohio. You needed to recalibrate your spirit and love for music again. Stay as long as you want." Mike grinned and grabbed a chip from the side table.

"I will." Zach exhaled a long breath through puckered lips. With a likely hit on the horizon with Trent and a promising start on his new album, visiting to Ohio had proven to be the right decision in more ways than one.

Chapter Fifteen

On Sunday morning, Willow felt a knot tighten in her stomach, and she pushed her unfinished coffee aside. The few bites of toast she'd eaten were threatening to spew back up her throat. After an excruciating discussion with her lawyer the night before about the trial and her prison visit with Charles, she couldn't stop the tremors in her hands. She squeezed her fingers back and forth, forcing the shaking to cease. *It will all be over tomorrow. Please God, help me through this.*

She traveled to one subway stop and then got on a metro bus, which took her a short distance from town. Tomorrow, he would be transported into the city for the trial. As Manhattan left her view, Willow chewed a nail, a nasty habit she picked up since her world was upended weeks ago. Visiting hours in the prison started at one o'clock.

Upon arriving, she clasped both hands together, digging her nails into her skin as she stood in line, waiting to go through security.

In front of her, a weary mother struggled with a fidgeting young boy, most likely seeing her husband or boyfriend.

Willow stared at the woman. Was she visiting someone she loved—or had loved—like Willow was? *Mine is a lost love.* She shook her head, turned over her purse and valuables, and was guided into another room, waiting for her name to be called. She eased onto the stiff, plastic chair, fiddling with a loose thread on her shirt. She kept her gaze lowered, avoiding any eye contact. The air in the room smelled like an old sneaker—musty, almost putrid.

Fifteen minutes later, a guard called out her name. "Willow Barton!"

Willow raised her right hand and stood.

He motioned toward himself. "Follow me."

Because it was a low-security prison, she was allowed to see Charles in a large room with small tables, where she could sit directly in front of him. Willow waited, as the rancid smell of body odor reeked in the air, churning her stomach.

Then he appeared—shuffling toward her.

Willow flew a hand up, covering her mouth for an instant, and she caught her breath in her throat. His hair was cut short, his face shaven, and dark circles lodged under his eyes. Somewhat disheveled, he was dressed in a faded blue jumpsuit, almost gray, with handcuffs on his wrists. *Who is this man?*

Charles lowered himself on the other side of the worn table. "Thank you for coming. This must be hard seeing me in here."

Moisture welled up in her eyes. Seeing him was too much to handle. Memories flooded in, and nausea rose from her belly, the threat of vomit rising in her throat. She blinked and kept the tears from falling. "Yes, this whole thing has been hard."

"I didn't want you to see me in here or to have to come to the trial. But I couldn't stop it once the prosecution requested you." He stretched his fingers toward her.

Willow jerked both hands away, placing them on her lap. She did not want to touch him or be touched. "Well, I'm here now. Do you have anything you want to say? Or discuss about our finances?"

Charles took a breath. "I screwed up, Willow. When I started making money, I got greedy and wanted more. The money couldn't come quick enough, and I started gambling. Some days I scored, others I didn't. When I needed more cash, I started tinkering with my client's accounts. I was going to borrow and pay them back. No one would find out. But the expenses got out of hand, and my debts grew. Then, my boss discovered the mistakes and deception in the ledgers at our office. I was too ashamed to tell you what was happening."

The stale ventilation in the room irritated her lungs, its suffocating odor choking her words. "Charles, I loved you. We didn't have to live in such an expensive apartment, drive fancy cars, or take exotic trips. I would have settled for a small apartment in Brooklyn or New Jersey. But the fact you ruined my life, along with yours, is unforgivable." *There, I said it.* She couldn't forgive him.

Charles bowed his head, rubbing his left hand clenched in a fist in silence for a minute. *Cling-cling.* The handcuffs jiggled against the table's surface. "I understand. The outcome of this trial is uncertain, but my lawyer predicts my jail sentence won't be more than five years since this is my first offense—could be less on good behavior. I've had time to evaluate my life in here, Willow, and I hoped you might give me a second chance once I get out. I still love you."

A second chance? Are you kidding me? Willow

shook her head. "Charles, you are a selfish man, and I want this divorce. I will never trust you again. I'm moving on." Anger propelled her clarity. *Time to leave.* Her lawyer could figure out the financial mess he left behind. She no longer wanted to discuss it with him.

Charles sat silent for a moment, then spoke. "I hope one day you can forgive me, Willow." He shifted his body weight, sliding on the chair back and forth. "Will you write?"

"I can't forgive you now, and I doubt I will write." Willow stood. "My lawyer will be in touch with yours. Goodbye, Charles." She waved at the guard, signaling she was ready to leave. She forced herself to look away from the tears falling down Charles's face, struggling to hold back her own. *When does the suffering end?*

****

Later in the evening, Willow collapsed on the pull-out bed in Betsy's living room and stared at the ceiling, going over the visit with Charles in her mind. Feeling a sharp pang, she laid her palm on her chest. When they first got married, how she loved him—all the dreams and possibilities. She would have done anything for him and had. She settled for mediocre jobs so she could be at his beck and call when needed. She made him the priority in her life, not herself. Thus, when the rug was pulled out from under her, she suffered, and the grief kept rolling in and out without warning. *How can I ever trust in love again?*

Her phone pinged. *Zach.*

—*Good luck tomorrow. Leah told me about the trial. Don't be mad*—

—*Thanks*—

—Smiley emoji—

She sent nothing back, put the phone on the side table, and shut off the light. She had no bandwidth left to deal with anyone—not even Zach.

****

The following morning, Willow ached throughout her entire body as she climbed the steps to the courthouse. Seeing Charles yesterday unnerved her in more ways than one. He tugged on her old feelings of sincere caring for the man and agitated her anger. She was still consumed by his betrayal and stupidity. Today, she would have to see him again in the courtroom and relive the agony of what they once had and lost. She writhed in pain, her neck muscles spasming— unrelenting, unforgiving, and merciless. This day could not end soon enough.

Her lawyer met her inside and took her to a small conference room in the corridor to wait until she was called to testify. He confirmed that the judge had honored her request to only come into the courtroom when called. Tim reviewed the questions with her again, then left to talk to Charles's lawyer before the trial began. Fifteen minutes later, Tim waltzed through the door. "You'll never believe this. Charles took a plea deal. You don't have to testify."

Willow widened her eyes and stood. "I don't have to speak in front of everyone? The trial is over?"

"Yes, you can go home. And his lawyer asked me to give you this." Tim handed her a folded note.

A message from Charles? As she took the note, she couldn't control the quivering in her fingers.

Tim glanced at the note she held. "I'll leave you alone and contact you in Ohio regarding the paperwork for your divorce. You're almost done, Willow. Life will get better—you'll see." He side hugged her, picked up his briefcase, and exited into the hall.

Willow tightened her grasp on the note, hands trembling, and dropped to the chair. With jagged breath, she unfolded it to see Charles's writing.

Dear Willow,

I'm so sorry. I know this has been terrible for you. After seeing you yesterday, I decided to take a plea deal. You were right. I am selfish, and I want to change. I took the deal, so you wouldn't have to testify and could get on with your life. I will always love you and hope someday you can forgive me. Take care of yourself. All my love, Charles

As her eyes filled with wetness, she sat frozen in her chair. She reread the letter and let the tears trickle down her cheek, the salty drops gliding over her lips. For the first time in their marriage, he considered her and not himself. She folded the note and dug into her purse for a tissue. She wiped her eyes, blew her nose, and tucked the letter inside of her pocket. Time to go home—back to Ohio and her new life.

****

On Monday morning, Zach zipped his bag and waited for his car to arrive, taking him to the airport. He reflected on how Marissa had shown up at his door with breakfast and a failed attempt for a sultry send-off in the bedroom this morning. He excused himself, saying he needed to make phone calls—and then ignored her flirtatious plea. What was wrong with him? What happened to the wild, carefree Zachary Hayes?

Nashville had been a blast, but he wanted to return to Cedar Hill, his family, and Willow. He noticed that she wasn't very communicative in her text last night, but he figured she was nervous and wanted space. He understood but was curious about the trial. His feelings for her had intensified, but he wrestled with reality, dousing his desires. He lived in Nashville, and she was rebuilding her life in Cedar Hill. Long-distance relationships rarely worked. Somehow, other women weren't as appealing anymore. Even a little fun with Marissa had left him feeling empty. *What the hell?*

****

The plane ride was smooth, and Willow headed toward baggage claim upon arrival. As she made her way through a forest of people, she bumped into a man, causing her to trip, but she regained her balance. She lifted her head and found herself staring into Zach's eyes.

"Willow Mason!" He spread a grin across his face.

Willow felt her stomach flip-flop, as if she were plunging down a monstrous rollercoaster drop. "Zach." She could only say his name.

"Are you coming back from New York?" He adjusted his grip on his luggage.

"Yes. And you, Nashville?"

"Yep. What a coincidence. Do you have a ride home?"

"No. I planned on ordering a car." Waves of trepidation, circling like a cyclone in her gut, were wreaking havoc on her fragile emotions. She wasn't ready to see Zachary Hayes. Not today.

"I've got a car. Let me give you a ride."

"Okay." She'd be stupid not to accept.

"Come on, follow me."

She fell into step while peering at the floor until she arrived outside the terminal, where his driver took her suitcase and computer bag.

He opened the door. "After you." He motioned with a hand.

She forced the sides of her lips to lift. "Thanks."

The drive home was forty minutes, and Willow was not much for conversation. She let her mind drift as she observed the passing trees, filled with orange and reddish hues, shedding their summer growth and preparing for winter—a new season. *God, how I need a new season.*

Zach peered out his window. His phone rested on the leather seat and rang with Marissa's name flashing.

Willow recognized the name from the gossip article. "Go ahead. Take it, if you want."

He picked it up and sent it to voicemail. "I can call her back later." He tossed a glance to Willow. "Are you okay? If you want to talk about anything, I'm a good listener, despite what Leah says."

She grinned at his joke. "I'm okay, thanks. I'm glad this trip is over. I don't have to return for anything else."

"Good. I imagine the trial was difficult."

She took a deep breath and exhaled with a labored sigh. "I didn't have to testify. At the last minute, Charles took a plea deal, and they settled his case. Thus, the earlier flight today."

"Not going to the trial must have made things easier."

She nodded. "Seeing him in prison yesterday wasn't easy, though." She rotated her head and resumed viewing the colorful spectacle in front of her, indicating the conversation was over.

"Yeah, I get it." Zach stayed quiet and picked up

his phone.

Willow's ringtone broke the silence. Mrs. Jordan's name, her mother's neighbor, flashed across the screen. "I've got to take this." She picked up her phone. "Hello?"

"Oh, honey, I'm glad I caught you. Now, don't worry, but your mom is in the hospital. She had a flare-up with her lupus, and her doctor wanted her to come in for tests and treatment."

"What hospital is she in?" Willow shook as she held the phone.

"Cedar General. Maureen, her good friend from church, is with her. Don't worry, dear. She's not alone."

"Thank you, Mrs. Jordan. I'm almost home and can get there soon." She ended the call and glimpsed at Zach, blinking back restrained tears.

He grasped a hand. "I heard the word *hospital.* What's going on?"

"I guess Mom had a bad flare-up from the lupus."

"We'll go straight to the hospital. Don't worry." Zach informed his driver of the change in destination but kept Willow's hand in his, not letting it go.

She could feel the warmth of Zach's hand radiating up her arm, giving comfort. She didn't resist and let him hold it for the remainder of the ride. *Oh, how I need to be touched in this way.*

****

When he arrived at the hospital, Zach insisted on staying and hired the driver to wait as long as needed. "I'm not leaving you."

She hurried through the corridor, rushing to be at her mother's bedside. After entering the room, she dropped her purse and enveloped her mother in both arms. "Mom! Are you all right?"

Evelyn was hooked up to an IV and other monitors but smiled. "I didn't want you to fret. I had some swelling and joint pain along with a mild fever. My doctor ordered me here as a precaution. He's always concerned about infections leading to organ damage. I'll be here overnight. No big deal."

Mom was protecting her, but Willow wasn't budging. "Well, I'm here now, and I'm staying until after dinner."

Evelyn eyed Zach hovering by the door. "Hi, Zach. How did you two end up together?"

"We bumped into each other at the airport. Can we get you anything?" He came closer.

We. He used the word *we*. Willow didn't want him to leave, but asking him to stay would be unfair.

"No, thank you, dear." Evelyn straightened her pillow. "How was your trip to Nashville? Willow told me you were recording a new song with Trent Adler."

"The whole experience was awesome. If you want to listen, I've got a rough cut."

Willow watched Zach and her mother converse, his kindness again pulling her heart in his direction. Spending four or five days away from the man had put her attraction on the back burner. But now, face-to-face with him, she couldn't ignore it. "Listen, Zach. You don't have to stay. I'll arrange a ride later." Willow wrung her hands.

He adjusted his watchband. "Why don't you and I grab something in the cafeteria for dinner and keep your mom company while she eats?"

"Sounds perfect, dear." Evelyn adjusted her pillow in the bed. "Then, you two can leave. I'm a little tired and will go to sleep early. What do you say?"

What could she say? She watched her mother and Zach orchestrate the next activity, and she had no strength to argue. "Fine."

"Settled. Go see what you can find. I ordered a turkey sandwich earlier, but if you see a good dessert, buy it. Can't resist my sweet tooth." She chuckled.

Zach motioned to Willow. "Come on. You heard your mother." He held the door open.

"Okay." How did she end up here?

Zach patted her shoulder as he walked next to her, heading toward the cafeteria. "Try not to worry. She's in good spirits, and I imagine this is something common with lupus." Then, he rubbed her back between the shoulder blades. "She'll be all right."

"Thanks for staying. I guess I could use the company." She tucked a loose strand behind her ear.

"I didn't want you to go through this alone. From what I've seen, you've struggled on your own too much in your life." He draped an arm around her, giving a gentle side hug.

All she wanted to do was to fall into his smothering embrace and let him hold her while she sobbed out all the pain wracking her body for weeks. But she'd settle for a hug.

****

Willow leaned back against the seat on the short ride home from the hospital. After a tense day, she gradually loosened her shoulder muscles. She viewed Zach scrolling on his phone and texting. *Thank God he was with me today.* Yes, she was a strong woman, but his support had been a welcomed relief.

The driver angled into her driveway.

The house was dark, and Willow fumbled for her keys in her purse.

"I'll go to the door with you." Zach jumped out, grabbed her suitcase, and followed her.

After she put the key in the door, she twisted her body to face him, tilting her chin upward. "Thank you for the ride and staying with me today. Made things easier. See you later." She took her travel bag from him, then turned toward the house.

"Hey, come here." He grabbed an arm and enveloped her body.

Surprised, she allowed herself to sink into his grasp, her petite frame snuggling into his chest, cradled in his warmth. She needed a hug, and nothing felt more right on this rough day. Heck, a rough year, if she was honest.

As he edged away, he brushed a hair from her eyes. "Call me if you need anything." He stood still. "Will I see you tomorrow?"

"Yes. Mom's best friend will want to pick her up, if she gets out."

"Text me if you can't. We'll order pizza." He squeezed her right hand, then let it go.

"Okay." She waved goodbye, then dragged her luggage into the house. As she shut the front door, she slumped against it, hand over her heart, and slid to the floor. The relentless tears fell nonstop. She let all the fear and anxiety of the last few months gush out, flooding her hands, her shirt, and the floor. She hung her head, weeping uncontrollably, until she could no longer breathe without grabbing a tissue from her purse. She stared blankly ahead into the darkness, wiping her face until the crying ceased.

The *tick-tick-tick* of the clock in the entrance hall broke the silence, and Willow expelled a breathy groan. Ten minutes later, she hoisted her butt, groped for her suitcase, and trudged up the creaky steps—completely exhausted. *When will it all be over?*

Chapter Sixteen

The next day, Willow flopped on the floor, sorting out a box of new books ready to be shelved in the bookstore. Thank God her mother was coming home this afternoon and would be fine. The doctor changed her medication and would continue to monitor her symptoms, if they flared again.

The bells on the door jingled, and Marcy waltzed into the store, heading straight for Willow, and hugged her. "I've been worried about you. Are you okay? How did it go?"

"A mixed bag of emotions, but I got through it." *Not going into details, especially after last night's meltdown.* This part of her life was private, and she was determined to keep it so.

"I missed you around here. Deedee did all right, though." She sneezed, then snagged a tissue from the box on the counter. "Listen, the town council meeting is Thursday night. Robert Matthews is quite the shark and has a battalion of lawyers in his pocket. Your job might end. I want to be straight with you." Marcy cocked her head with her attention aimed straight at Willow.

"I figured." *Don't need this stress.* "No worries. I'll find another job if you decide to close shop." *If I can find one.*

"Thanks for understanding. If the council meeting approves the proposal, I'll crunch the numbers with my accountant and keep you posted."

"Thanks, appreciate it."

Marcy readjusted her purse strap, waved to Willow, and hurried out the door.

Willow rested her head in her right hand, her elbow propped on the table. *Am I losing my job?* Most likely. *Should I take the job in New York?* Maybe. *Keep working on my portfolio?* Absolutely. She lifted her head. *Clarity at last.*

****

Willow bounded up the steps to the Hayeses' back door with groceries in both arms, unprepared to see Zach again. Yesterday's encounter aroused a hidden intimacy, and it scared her. She sensed a closeness that stirred emotions of the heart—more affection than lust. She needed to focus on her portfolio. *And don't forget those tabloid pictures.*

Zach opened the door and took the groceries out of Willow's hands, exchanging a glance.

"Thank you." Then she stepped away, hurrying into the house.

"I've missed your cooking. My dad did, too." He set the bags on the kitchen counter.

"You're sweet, but you both will get used to Mrs. Felding's ways."

He edged nearer. "Are you going somewhere?"

"Eventually. But you won't be here, so why do you care?"

"I do care, and I am sticking around for a while—at least, until I finish writing songs for my new album." He stayed, angling his head, and stuffed a hand in his back pocket.

She pulled out a cutting board, utensils, and

vegetables, then stepped to a different work surface. She squeezed the end of the knife, suppressing the tremors in her hand, but kept chopping items for the salad.

Zach backed away. "I'll go out to the garage and check on Dad."

Willow nodded and took a breath in and out, settling her nerves. When finished with food prep, she set the table and took out two bottles of dressing from the refrigerator.

Later, George meandered into the kitchen. "Smells good." He side hugged her. "And boy, am I glad to see you, Willow Mason."

"Well, I missed you, too, George. Pizza night, one of your favorites."

"Terrific! I'll wash up." He pointed at Zach. "You better wash those dirty hands."

"Right behind ya, Dad." He turned and followed.

She bent over, opening the oven. The aroma of bubbling cheese and overflowing marinara sauce filled her nostrils, and she gave in to George's insistence to sit and eat with them. She was hungry but also anxious to develop the film she had taken in New York in her darkroom. A few would be perfect for her portfolio.

After dinner, Willow glanced at Zach as he cleared the table, silently slinking around her like a Siamese cat. *He's giving me space.* When finished, she wiped both wet hands on the dishtowel. "Thanks for your help. I'll help your dad with his remote before I leave."

"Any house projects tonight? I'm free labor, if needed." Zach pressed his dimples upward.

Willow recognized a mischievous light emanating from his eyes. "I'm working in my darkroom tonight. I want to see what I captured in New York with my camera."

"Do you mind if I stop by?" He leaned against the counter, crossing his arms against his chest.

She did enjoy his company as a friend—even with the festering chemistry. *I can sweep it under the rug. No problem.* "If you want to. You know where to find me." *What am I doing?* She couldn't stop an invisible force hijacking the words from her mouth.

"I have to make a call, then I'll be over."

"Okay." *He's probably calling his old girlfriend. Remember.*

****

Standing in the darkroom, Willow heard Zach's truck tires grind over the gravel outside. She took several deep breaths, calming herself. She replayed the almost-kiss before leaving for New York in her mind. *Can't happen again.*

"Anybody home?" Zach's voice echoed from outside.

"In here." Before she could take another breath, she spotted Zach's frame spread across the doorway.

He scanned the room, staring at her photos hanging to dry and others still in solution.

"Please, shut the door. I'm doing a process where I can't have light in here." She blew at a strangling hair over her eye, unable to brush it away with gloved hands covered in a chemical solution.

Zach obeyed and inched closer. "These are amazing, Willow."

"Thanks." She struggled to focus on her work. She could hear his breathing and smell the faint musk scent of his aftershave. *What was I thinking?* She couldn't handle this kind of intimacy. Not now. "Here's one of Rosie from the party. I'm framing it for Leah."

He took a step and leaned in, his arm grazing hers. "Awesome."

She plucked the last photo from the bin and hung it to dry. She removed her gloves and used the sink, her body brushing against him. This time, she gazed into his eyes—big mistake.

He swept a dangling curl away from her face. "Better. Now, you can see."

She froze, tilting her head upward and inviting him in. She wanted him to kiss her, but she was playing with fire. Would he interpret her stillness as permission to kiss her?

Zach lowered his head, then his lips to hers, gliding his mouth across the moistness and grazing the tip of his tongue over her lips.

She didn't flinch. She slid both hands up his chest, grasping his shirt, and met him halfway with an intensity bursting inside. Then, she flashed the photo of Marissa in her mind. *I can't kiss this man.* He's taken— by Marissa and every other woman who wants him in Nashville. She released the kiss and nudged him away. "I can't do this, Zach. You're with Marissa. I saw the tabloids in New York." She rushed past him, sprinting to the lawn outside, and landed next to the garage. Willow steadied herself against the back of the building, hand over her heart, panting.

He followed, and when he stood in front, he reached for a hand.

She yanked it away.

"I'm sorry, Willow. I thought you wanted me to kiss you. I'm sorry."

She shook her head. "No worries. I let you kiss me. If I'm honest, I wanted you to. But being together would never work. We live different lives and want different things for ourselves. You're here temporarily. I can't be a fling, and you still have those, so we need to remain friends only." Her heart twisted inside.

Zach shifted his weight, scratching his head. "You're right. I'm not ready for the kind of relationship you deserve, Willow. I can't be the man responsible for hurting you more than you've already been. Please, let's go back to being just friends."

She blinked, forcing the moisture to stay in place. Just friends. But in her heart, she faced the cruel reality she had fallen for this man. "Yes, friends."

He extended a hand to shake hers. "Deal?"

She slid her right hand into his, feeling the warmth radiating up her arm. *This is the last touch we will have.* "Deal."

"Are you okay?"

"Yes, I'm fine." She mustered a smile to hide the turbulent storm inside. Anything to make him leave.

Zach exhaled a heavy breath. "Okay. That's a relief. Guess I'll leave then. See you tomorrow?"

"Yes."

He circled, hopped into his truck, and drove off.

She wiped the wetness in her eyes with her shirt and viewed the empty road. Oh, dear God, why was this happening? She needed steadiness in her life, not another disaster, and Zach was an explosion waiting to happen.

Chapter Seventeen

Late the next afternoon, Willow counted the money in the register and tidied up before closing. A text pinged. *Zach.*

—I'm sorry if I crossed a boundary last night and upset you—

—I'm not upset—

—I don't want any weird vibes between us. Your friendship is important—

Zachary Hayes wanted *only* friendship. She'd better accept it.

—No worries. See you tonight—

—Thanks. I want to make things right between us again—

—Everything is good. Thumbs-up emoji—

—Smiley emoji—

What was she doing? She forced air out through pursed lips, berating herself for encouraging the kiss last night. *Forget about it. Move on.*

Marcy waltzed through the door. "Hi. I wanted to catch you before you head to the Hayeses' house and remind you about the council meeting tomorrow, if you want to go. Should be interesting."

Willow wasn't sure she wanted to attend a meeting deciding the fate of her job in this town. "It depends on when I finish with George. Text me the address. If I don't show, text me the outcome, okay?"

"You've got it. Some store owners are nervous about selling, but others are willing to take a big check. I'm on the fence. After Chet's death, I could use the extra money, but since you've been running the store, I'm out of the red. You're an amazing saleswoman, Willow."

Saleswoman. *Great. What I always wanted.* She couldn't get away from it. "Thanks."

After Marcy left, Willow closed the shop and hurried to the grocery store for supplies. She had a sinking feeling the council would approve the building permit, and she would soon be out of work—again.

****

As Willow drove into the driveway, she saw Zach strut from the garage. Seeing him sent a wave of uneasiness throughout her body—she feared any awkwardness.

He hurried toward her. "Let me help you." Zach reached for the groceries.

She surrendered a bag but kept her gaze lowered. "Thanks." Once inside, she busied herself, taking out items from the bags. "Dinner will be about an hour. I have more prep work to do tonight. How's George?"

"He's deep into birdhouse production." He paused, tapping his fingers on the counter. "Listen…are you sure you're okay about everything? Between us, I mean?"

She glanced up, noticing his scrunched forehead. "We're grown adults, Zach. No problem. We got caught up in the moment, then realized friendship is better for us. Right?"

He shuffled his feet on the linoleum floor, kicking the edge of the doormat. "Right."

"Go spend time with your dad, and I'll call you guys." She needed as much space as she could muster from this man. She couldn't wait until he returned to Nashville. After she checked the casserole in the oven, she peeked out the window to see a strange vehicle arriving at the house.

A tall woman with flowing blonde hair and a killer body, revealed in tight jeans and a vintage T-shirt, stepped out of the car.

Willow recognized her from the tabloids and gasped—Zach's girlfriend. *Marissa.* She pressed her palm against a heavy weight sinking to the bottom of her gut.

The doorbell rang, and Willow hurried to the front door to open it. "Hello."

"Hi. Is Zach here? I'm a friend from Nashville." She extended her right hand. "Marissa Peyton."

Willow shook it. "Come inside. He's out in the garage with his dad. Let me get him. Have a seat in the living room, and I'll be right back." Willow moved on autopilot, her blood racing through her veins at a furious pace. Seeing Marissa in person was a completely different experience compared to in a magazine. She hurried to the garage and curled her trembling fingers into a fist, hiding her nerves. *Will he be happy to see her?* "Hey, Zach. You have a visitor." She stood motionless, catching her breath.

"Yeah? Who?" He concentrated on painting a roof for his dad's collection.

"Marissa Peyton." Saying her name out loud sent a flutter through her stomach.

"Here?" He turned quickly, widening his eyes and lifting an eyebrow, then dropped the wet brush on the workbench.

"Yes. In the living room. And dinner's almost ready, so you can invite her to stay. We have plenty." She retreated to the house, contemplating his shocked reaction when she told him. *This should be interesting.*

"Hey, Pops. We might have a visitor joining us for lasagna. Okay?"

George nodded, then looked up. "Is it time to eat?"

"Yeah, come on. We can clean up the paint supplies afterward." Zach entered the kitchen first with his dad following.

Marissa stood in the doorway, chatting away to Willow. She threw her hands up in the air. "Surprise!" Then she walked closer and hugged Zach.

He returned the hug and kissed her on the cheek.

Willow studied his frazzled expression and swore discomfort hovered in the air.

He shifted his stance and gestured with his hand. "Dad, this is a friend of mine from Nashville. Marissa Peyton."

George sized up the woman and cocked his head. "I thought Willow was your girlfriend."

Zach dropped his jaw, and he froze, speechless.

Willow jumped in to save him. "We're friends, George. Good friends." She winked at Zach and watched as Marissa broadened her eyes and ping-ponged her gaze back and forth between herself and Zach. Willow couldn't stop the grin inching up her cheeks.

George eyed them again. "Okay. But Zach should marry *you*. But he never did what I wanted anyway. I'll get washed." He abruptly turned and headed toward the bathroom.

Willow flattened her lips hard, muffling a laugh that struggled to escape. She felt a tiny spark of amusement watching Zach squirm. *Is George a conspiring matchmaker?* The corners of her mouth rose.

Zach eyed Marissa. "Can we talk outside for a minute?" He guided her to the patio.

Willow peeked out the open window and witnessed Zach's furrowed brow and grim scowl. If Marissa was here this week, then Willow wouldn't have to worry about one-on-one encounters with him—which could be advantageous. After the kiss, she needed to secure her heart in a locked position and lose the key.

Zach kept his hands tucked inside his front pockets. "I wish you had called or warned me you were coming, Marissa."

"But then it wouldn't be a surprise, would it?" She grabbed his left hand from his jeans.

Still staring, Willow noticed that he didn't resist her touch.

"Where are you staying? You can't stay here because of my dad. Another human in the house would disturb his daily routine." Zach shifted his stance and let go of Marissa's hand.

"I found a hotel close by. No worries. I can only stay a day or two. I wanted to see your hometown and talk about *us*. But we can chat later." She reached, squeezed the hand again, then let go.

He bent his chin forward and wiped the sudden sweat forming on his forehead.

Willow yelled from the screen door. "Dinner's ready." Marissa was like padding between her and Zach, so she accepted the offer to eat with them.

Willow hoped the buffer would protect her heart from opening any more than it had already—even though seeing him with another woman caused a pang in her chest.

Marissa talked nonstop at dinner, asking questions and describing her recent experience in the studio with Zach in Nashville. Then, she turned to Willow. "What do you do? Have you always wanted to be a caregiver?"

Willow coughed, almost spitting out her food.

"Willow's an old family friend." Zach jumped in first. "She's helping to make dinners, and she's a talented photographer."

Was that an affectionate tone infused in his words? She smiled back, grateful for the explanation but touched by his faith in her as an artist. "I also manage the local bookstore on Main Street. If you have time, you should visit it while you're here." *Try to be civil to the competition. Wait. You have no competition because you have no relationship with Zach. Period.*

"I'm not a big reader, but I will." Marissa focused her attention on Zach, smiling, then buttered her bread.

Later, after Zach helped clear the table and was alone with Willow, he eased closer. "Listen, I'll spend time with Marissa tonight since she traveled all this way. I hope you didn't need any help with the apartment tonight."

She could smell his woodsy odor from the outdoor workshop mixed with her Italian cooking, its aroma comforting. "No problem. I'll spend time in my darkroom again, working on my portfolio."

He scratched the side of his head. "See you tomorrow?"

"Yes." She bit her bottom lip and returned to

scrubbing a pan. When finished, Willow retrieved the remote for George, waved to the others, and left.

****

Zach strode into the living room. "Pops, I'm getting Marissa settled at the Crestview Hotel. Don't wait up."

George nodded and was silent.

Zach motioned to Marissa. "Follow me in your car." As he entered the parking lot, he climbed out and carried her suitcase inside.

She checked in and found her room, with Zach right behind her. When the door closed, she threw her purse on the bed and sidled closer. "How about a little fun?"

"Nothing has changed on my end about not wanting a committed relationship." He studied her expression and saw no disagreement.

"No problem." She edged nearer.

He did have a mountain of stress he needed to release. He bent and kissed her, then guided her onto the bed. *Why not have a little fun?*

Chapter Eighteen

The next morning, Zach awoke to the smell of coffee. *Dad must be up already.* His time with Marissa had been a physical release, but no matter what he told her, he kept being hit by her questions about their relationship—as if they had one. He was far from committing to one woman, which was why he broke up before. Last night, she subtly suggested having a free, monogamous relationship. He could come and go as he pleased, if her bed was the only one he slept in. Sounded like a commitment—*not interested.* Marissa was gorgeous, talented, and lived the country music lifestyle in Nashville as he did. *Why don't I want to settle down with her?*

Whenever he had these contemplative debates in his head, images of Willow popped into his brain. *What is it about this woman who makes me question everything in my life?* The more Willow pushed him away, the more he wanted her. *Aargh.* He threw back the covers, grabbed a shirt and sweatpants, and padded across the floor to eat breakfast with his dad.

Pops was sitting on a chair, drinking coffee, and browsing through the paper on the patio.

Zach opened the screen door. "Morning. Want some eggs?"

"Sure. Are we going to the store?"

Zach noticed that his dad's eyes seemed glazed

over and not as bright as usual, which concerned him. "Later. I was hoping we could finish our song this morning. What do you say?"

"Song? Okay." He returned to drinking his coffee and staring at the newspaper.

Zach arranged the placemats on the table, and his phone pinged. He glimpsed at it. *Marissa.*

—*Breakfast?*—

—*Can't. With Dad. Sorry. Lunch?*—

—*Okay.* Kiss emoji—

—*I'll text you later*—

Zach wasn't making her a priority. She had surprised him. He was keeping to his schedule, and this album was number one. After breakfast, he lugged his guitar to the living room and sat beside his dad. He had written the chorus and two verses—just needed a bridge. If he could talk about Dad's relationship with his mom, maybe something might spring forth from the muses. "Pops, how did you know Mom was the one? A forever kind of love?"

"Easy, son. She was pure at heart. She had the kind of love and generosity within her that always placed others first. No games, no nonsense. She loved others with a fierce heart, and when I experienced her love, I couldn't resist her charm. I wanted a forever kind of love with her and no one else." He paused a minute. "Willow is pure at heart. I can see it."

Where did that come from? "Yes, she is special."

Dad lifted his gaze. "The bridge should be about a woman with a pure heart."

Goose bumps raced up and down his torso. "You're right, Pops."

"Well, write it then." He chuckled, then stood.

"I'm going out in the garage for a bit. Are we headed to the store soon?"

"Let's go to the diner for lunch. What do you say? And the store afterward?"

"Sure." He shuffled away, leaving the room.

Zach grabbed his pen and pad and scribbled out ideas for the bridge. Pure at heart. *Is this the thing pulling me toward Willow?*

****

Willow handed the receipt to the customer and bent to grab a bag from under the counter for the three purchased items. For some reason, the store was busy this morning. After the customer left, the bells jingled again, and she looked up.

Marissa waltzed into the shop.

Willow felt a sudden cramp grip her stomach, and her breath caught in the back of her throat.

"Hi." Marissa waved. "I wanted to check out your store since Zach is busy with his dad."

"Sure. Explore the shelves. I'm here if you need help." Willow fidgeted with papers on the counter, pretending to be busy. She couldn't help but steal an occasional glimpse at the woman.

As Marissa ran her fingertips across the books on display, she hummed. "Would Zach like this one? I want to get him a present." She held up a novel.

"I love that witty author's writing. He's one of my favorites. Zach might enjoy it." *Be nice.*

"Sometimes, he reads on the tour bus, if the trip is long and he's not tired." When she finished browsing, she placed the book on the counter. "I might be going on tour with Trent Adler, and if their duet hits the top ten, Zach will come to some of the gigs. Should be a blast touring with him."

Willow imagined Marissa told her this to lay her claim to the country music star—Zach. *She thinks I'm a threat.* George's statement about her being his girlfriend must have been a shock. "I'm sure it will." She rang her up, gift wrapped the novel, and handed it over, forcing a smile.

Marissa thanked her and left.

Willow slid her palm across her chest, her heart twitching in a spasm. *I have to let go of my job at the Hayeses'.* She needed distance from the charismatic, cocky player.

Her phone vibrated in her pocket, and she pulled it out. *Marcy.* "Hi, I was calling you later."

"I wanted to remind you about the council meeting tonight. Can you come?"

"I'll try. Seven?"

"Yes. Should be interesting. See you then."

Yes, should be interesting. *I might lose my job. Great.* Willow texted Zach.

—Have to do an easy dinner tonight. How about pizza and salad?—

—Who doesn't love pizza? Is everything all right—

—Yes. Need to go to the town council meeting at seven—

—Okay. Marissa will join us. She goes back tomorrow—

—Fine. We always have plenty. See you later—

—Thumbs-up emoji—

She rubbed her neck, kneading the knot lodged there weeks ago and not budging. Desperate for a massage or a spa day, Willow slumped her shoulders farther. *Not in my budget.* Another customer entered the store and distracted her long enough to forget any residual pondering about Zach. *Worrying about this man will get me nowhere.*

****

Later, on her lunch break, Willow waved to Leah while juggling sandwich bags and drinks in the other hand, her wobbling evident with the cardboard tray.

"Let me help you." Leah grabbed the drinks. "Thanks for buying lunch."

"No problem." Willow lowered onto the bench in front of the river. "I needed to get out and wanted to talk about something."

"I'm all ears. What's up?" Leah dug into a bag for her sandwich.

"What's going on with your caregiver search?" Although she needed the cash, she doubted being around Zach was a healthy choice.

"Zach and I are interviewing potential candidates tomorrow afternoon. Most workers want an eight-hour shift, and I don't blame them. We want someone for an eight-to-four shift, followed by a four-hour shift, four to eight. He's fine at night from what Zach can tell for now."

"One person could do a twelve-hour shift. Then your problem would be solved." Willow dug into the bag, pulling out her sandwich, and bit into it.

"But I don't want to take away your shift, Willow." Leah stopped eating. "What's going on?"

Willow paused before her next bite, staring at the tip of her shoe in the grass beneath the bench, and took a deep breath. "The problem is Zach."

"Is he being a brat? I'll kill him."

"No, no. He hasn't been a jerk since junior high

179

school." She let out a labored sigh. "I'm attracted to him and don't want to be."

Leah burst out laughing. "Is this why you wanted to meet? Girlfriend, I could see the sparks flying between you two ever since Rosie's birthday party. Even Liam mentioned the magnetic vibe between the two of you."

As she lifted her head, Willow flushed with heat. "Are you kidding me? Was it so obvious?"

Leah patted Willow's leg. "Don't worry. Your secret is good with me, but he *is* different around you. I haven't seen him much over the last ten years, but when I did, he was always this cocky, arrogant, check-me-out kind of guy. Whether the influence comes from Dad or you, I like my brother more these days."

Willow sipped her iced tea, the coolness soothing her throat as she took in Leah's words.

Leah reached into the food bag for a napkin and dabbed away the creamy, sweet tang of mayonnaise from her lips. "What's your opinion of Marissa?"

"She's a stunning woman, confident, and crazy about Zach. They seem like a good fit."

"We'll see. She might say she's fine with his free, independent ways, but it always comes back to commitment. Zach never makes a promise, and I doubt he will now. My brother loves his freedom too much. And in my honest opinion, he has some fear regarding love and loss after seeing our dad lose Mom. If I love, I'll be hurt kind of stuff. Just my shrink interpretation, so keep a hold of your heart, Willow. I don't trust him, and he's *my* brother. When you're around him, keep those thoughts in mind."

Willow brushed a hair dangling in her face, staring

at the water. "Will do." *Does Zach have a deep-seated fear of loving a woman?*

"After the interviews, you can decide what you want to do. Deal?"

Willow jerked back to reality. "Deal. You *are* my best friend."

"Yep." Leah flung her head, chuckling. "Thanks for lunch. I need to get back to work." She tossed her empty containers into the trash and squeezed Willow. "Love you."

"Love you, too." Willow meandered back to the store, pondering Leah's comments about trust. If she couldn't trust him, she couldn't be with him. End of story.

****

When George arrived downtown at Chuck's Diner, he insisted on joining his buddies at the corner table. The air conditioning blasted cool air through the dining room while he removed his cap and lifted his chin toward Zach. "Go eat with your friend. How often do I get to chat with these guys?" He aimed his thumb at a bunch of rowdy men encouraging him to sit.

"Sure thing, Pops." Zach grinned and walked to the other side of the diner. He eased into a red-leather booth and relented to being alone with Marissa. After last night's conversation, she wasn't pressuring him for commitment, but her demands were coming. People didn't change.

"Hey." Marissa swooped in, pecking Zach's cheek. "Where's your dad?"

"With his friends." Zach pointed to the other end of the diner.

"I've missed this—the two of us." She fixed her

view on him.

He picked up a napkin, avoiding her gaze. "Let's check out the menu. I'm starved." During lunch, he chatted about music, Nashville, and recording gigs. He did have a lot in common with her, but he wasn't interested in a long-term relationship. He was getting clearer every day. Afterward, he suggested browsing Main Street while his dad was content to hang with his friends.

George shooed them off.

Zach checked out the stores along the town's thoroughfare, with Marissa by his side, and stopped when he passed Readers Bookshop. "I want to say hello to Willow. Do you mind?"

Marissa shook her head, pressing her lips together.

Why am I always thinking about Willow? He shook his head. *What's up with that?*

****

As the door opened, Willow raised her head, squatting by a bottom shelf. She stood, duster in hand, and wiped the sweat from her temple with her forearm. *What is he doing here?*

"Surprise! We were in the neighborhood, and I wanted to check out the books again." Zach opened his eyes wide, his large frame moving toward Willow.

She dropped the rag and secured her hair in a bun with a scrunchy. "Sure. Help yourself. The new releases are by the window." She wasn't prepared for this encounter today. She wanted to decrease her time with this guy, not increase it. She acknowledged Marissa with a nod and headed back to the storeroom. Out of sight, she stood still, clutching a shelf, her breath ragged. She gathered her wits together, then returned to the register.

Zach tossed two new releases onto the counter. "I'll take these."

"Where's your dad?" Willow keyed in the sale at the register.

"At the diner with his friends. I'm going back after I buy these."

After the transaction, she placed them in a paper bag and handed it over. "Here you go." Her fingers grazed his while lifting the parcel, making her shudder.

"Thanks. See you later?"

"Yes, you will."

He lingered for a moment, locking his sight with hers, then waved goodbye and left.

Marissa stuck close to his side, heading toward the diner.

He's not so lovey-dovey with her. Could it just be a physical thing they had? Why even contemplate it? Whatever their relationship was didn't matter. He would soon be going back to Nashville, to bask in all his fame and glory. *Let it go, girl.*

****

Zach strolled into the restaurant, but when he didn't see his dad with his friends, he sucked a breath, his heart skipping a beat. "Where's George, guys?"

"He said he was joining up with you down the street. We thought he was with you."

Zach clenched his fist and frowned. "You let him go by himself?"

"He seemed fine. He told us where he was going—to find you."

The guys were clueless. Zach whipped around and raced out of the diner, glancing in both directions of

Main Street. He gestured to Marissa. "You head that way, and I'll go this way. We have to find him. Check all the side streets." He jogged along the street, scanning the shops and sidewalks with clenched fists. When he got to the bookstore, he barged through the front door, hoping Willow could help.

The bells jingled, and Willow jerked her head upward. "What's wrong?" She dropped the pen she was holding. "Your dad?"

"The guys let him go by himself. Idiots! Can you leave the store?" He paced back and forth, raking his fingers through his hair.

"Sure. Business has been slow. Let me lock up, and I'll join you. Don't worry. We'll find him." She grabbed her keys and sprinted out to the street. "Did you check those streets behind the diner?"

"No, let's go." Sweat rolled over his temples. "How could I have left him alone? The fact he wandered off is my fault and not his diner buddies'." As he jogged toward the restaurant, he heard a siren blast in the distance. Zach collided his gaze with Willow's, and he raced toward the sound, Willow following. Two blocks behind the diner, he met up with the ambulance.

George was sprawled out on the street with a nasty gash on his head, blood everywhere.

Zach arrived first. "Pops, are you all right? What happened?"

"Guess I tripped." George adjusted the bloody-soaked towel.

A middle-aged woman standing next to Zach spoke up. "I saw him fall, called 911, and brought him a clean rag to stop the bleeding."

"Thank you." Zach's hands shook as he cradled his father. Seeing the paramedics approach, he stood to let them tend to any injuries.

Willow stepped closer and placed a hand on Zach's arm. "He'll be all right. Don't worry."

He kept his gaze on the medic, then grasped Willow's hand, squeezing it and not letting go.

Marissa hurried across the street. She caught up with Zach and touched his arm. "I see you found him. Is he okay?"

"I hope so." He let go of Willow's hand but did not grab Marissa's.

Willow took a step back.

The medic stood. "We should take him to the hospital for a scan and to watch for any signs of neurological involvement. He might have a concussion, too." He strapped George onto the gurney.

"Yes. Can I ride with him?" Zach clenched a fist.

"Of course." The emergency team lifted George into the ambulance.

He turned to Willow. "Will you call Leah?"

"Yes, don't worry. Give me your keys and your bag, and I'll drive your truck. I'm going, too."

Zach tilted his chin toward Marissa. "I'll call you later."

Marissa frowned. "Do you want me to come, too?"

"No, but thank you." He threw his keys to Willow, handed her his bag, and vaulted into the back of the vehicle.

The paramedics shut the door and rushed off to the hospital.

Willow glanced at Marissa. "I'm glad we found him. Thanks for helping." *She's upset he left her.*

Marissa nodded, whisked around, and stomped off toward her car.

Willow dashed back to Main Street, where Zach had parked his vehicle. She texted Marcy about the early closure due to an emergency and called Leah from the truck.

"I knew this would happen again. Let me call Liam, so he can pick up Rosie. I'll meet you."

Willow tapped *End* on her phone and refocused her attention on driving Zach's mammoth truck. She struggled to reach the pedals but, somehow, maneuvered it through the neighborhoods and into the hospital parking lot. *Please God. Let George be all right.*

Chapter Nineteen

Willow sat for a moment, taking a deep breath before she opened the truck door. *I'm here to be with George. It has nothing to do with Zach.* Was she fooling herself? She felt a pinch in her heart, remembering his facial expression—frightened, vulnerable, and guilty for the incident. She yearned to comfort him. This was a new feeling beyond wanting to be kissed and touched. Something deeper. *Oh, no. This can't be happening.* She hopped out of the vehicle and hurried to the emergency room entrance. She quickly found Zach.

He leaned over the counter at the nurse's station— all six feet of him—with disheveled hair and a strained voice, conversing with a doctor.

Willow observed people recognizing one of Nashville's biggest stars, either ogling or whispering to each other. She tiptoed up behind him, touching his back.

He pivoted, quickly throwing both arms around her in a firm squeeze without hesitancy. "Thank you for coming."

Willow shuddered at his sudden gesture, her voice struggling to speak. "How is he?"

"He needs stitches and a scan, but they're taking him to a room soon. Then we can see him. Did you call Leah?" He stepped back, releasing her hands.

"She's on her way."

"She'll be angry, as right she should be. I can't believe I left him at the diner. He was okay before when I left him. I guess I can't take anything for granted anymore." He grasped and twisted both hands in a circular motion. "He was looking for me."

"Don't beat yourself up, Zach." Willow wrapped both arms around her waist, swaying back and forth. "This could have happened anytime. Even when he was healthier."

With his lips pressed together, he took a slow, measured breath and shook his head. "I should have known better."

He needs to berate himself a little longer. Hopefully, everything would work out, and George would have a minimally invasive scar on his forehead.

Leah burst into the emergency room, out of breath, and stopped at the nurses' station. "How is he? Where is he?"

"He'll be okay, Leah." Zach rubbed a hand in circles on his sister's back, explaining what happened.

A nurse approached, sharing George's room number. "You can wait there. He's getting a scan now, and they'll wheel him up. His cut is all stitched, and he's in a good mood, so don't worry." She patted Zach's arm.

"Thank God." Leah loosened the crease on her forehead and threaded an arm through Willow's. "Let's go."

Zach followed his sister to the room and caught her glare. "I'm sorry, Leah. This is my fault. I should never have left him at the diner with his friends."

"I understand why you did it. I guess we need to

watch him like a hawk from now on." Leah massaged the back of her neck, tilting her head forward.

Willow glanced at Leah, who was rubbing her tense muscles and letting out soft, raspy sighs. This whole ordeal had taken a toll. She patted her friend's shoulder. "You'll see. He'll be okay. And aren't you interviewing possible staff tomorrow?"

"Yeah."

Willow rested a hand on Leah's forearm. "You'll get this resolved." She caught Zach staring, locking gazes. She held his eye contact and didn't waver until the door opened.

An orderly wheeled George into the room.

"Dad!" Leah leaped, wrapping both arms around him in the wheelchair. "You had us worried."

George smiled and gave a thumbs-up. "The whole gang is here."

Zach edged closer. "I'm sorry, Pops. I should have never left you alone."

"Nonsense. How often do I get to visit with my friends?" He paused, then slouched. "I don't remember what happened. Do you?"

"The paramedics figured you must have tripped off the curb." Zach scratched at his day-old stubble.

"Oh." George nodded, then dropped his chin. "I'm tired."

"Let's get you into bed." Leah stood close. "You can rest. The doctor wants to keep you overnight for observation, but you should be able to go home tomorrow."

"Yeah, and I'll hang out with you here." Zach shifted his stance back and forth.

"Whatever you say."

The orderly helped George crawl into bed.

"Back in a jiff, Dad." Leah motioned to the other two to meet her in the hall.

Zach and Willow followed.

"I need to get home to Rosie, so Liam can return to the store. Are you all right staying?"

"Of course." Zach shifted his weight, scraping his boot on the linoleum floor.

"I'll stay, too." Willow touched him. "After all, you helped me with my mom. It makes the time pass quicker." More time with this man meant more anxiety, but she was drawn to support him. "I'd be at the house anyway."

Leah tilted her head. "What about your council meeting?"

"I'll text Marcy." Willow shrugged. "I don't need to hear all the rhetoric, and she can text me the results."

"Are you sure?" Leah narrowed her brow.

"I'm sure." She straightened, brushing a loose strand from her eyes.

Zach touched Willow's shoulder. "Thank you." He pivoted and walked back to the room.

Willow waved goodbye to Leah, then returned to the room, hesitating at the doorway.

George lay in bed, snoring with uneven rasps that filled the space with low, guttural growls, like an engine struggling to start.

Zach turned. "Want to grab some coffee or something to eat in the cafeteria?"

"Yeah. We can find a treat for your dad." She pressed a palm to her belly, her stomach rumbling.

His phone pinged. "Marissa. I feel bad leaving her stranded on her last night."

"Go ahead, if you like. I can stay here with your dad."

"No. I'm not leaving." He texted back. "Let's go."

Willow followed him through the hospital halls. She found a table in the corner of the cafeteria after getting food. She listened as Zach chatted about his dad, clearly still dwelling on the guilt he felt for leaving him.

During the conversation, a young woman walked up to the table. "I'm so sorry to interrupt, but you're Zachary Hayes, right? My boyfriend loves you, and he's in here getting a kidney transplant tomorrow. Can I have your autograph? This would brighten his day. Please?"

"Sure." Zach smiled, lowered his cup of coffee, and took the woman's pen. "Tell him good luck with his operation, and I hope he feels better soon."

"Thank you so much. I can't wait to show him!" The woman skipped out of the cafeteria, grasping the scrawled signature from one of her boyfriend's favorite singers.

Zach studied Willow. "You're grinning. What's so funny?"

"Sometimes, I forget you're a famous country music star. I guess I've been used to you being Leah's big brother who used to torture me."

"Oh, yeah? How so?" He lifted a brow and rested an elbow on the table, bringing his fist to his chin.

"Whizzing through the neighborhood on your bike with friends and getting pleasure by making us scream as you aimed to knock us over. Teasing me about being a book nerd. Calling me *skinny* Willow. Want me to go on?" Willow eyed him as she sipped her tea.

He leaned in. "Was I a bully to my sister's best friend? Would you forgive me if I said I was sorry now?"

She side-puckered her lips together, absorbing his plea. "Maybe."

He touched her left hand, his dimples jamming into his cheeks. "Please?"

She took a long, deep breath. "All right. You're forgiven." She laughed, her giddiness bubbling out into the air.

Zach kept a hand on hers.

The warmth of Zach's hand radiated up her left arm, its heat spreading across her chest and enveloping her heart. She didn't budge. She wanted his warmth all over her. She wanted Zachary Hayes, but she couldn't have him—too dangerous. An intimate relationship would destroy her. She inched her hand away, then picked at her salad, her fork circling an onion on the plate as the tangy scent from the dressing wafted to her nose.

His phone pinged again. "Marissa."

"You should call her."

"You're right. Give me a second." He stood and stepped into the hall.

Willow sliced a piece of tomato in half and brought it to her mouth, the juicy, sweet flavor filling her cheeks. She stared at the hallway door, then poked at a cucumber without eating it. She loved spending time with Zach but needed to stay focused on her life. Being with him sent turbulent ripples through the calm waters surrounding her, disturbing her inner peace.

When he returned, his facial expression had changed.

"Anything wrong?" She rested her fork on the plate.

"She's upset I didn't ask her to come to the hospital."

"Well, she is your girlfriend, so I can understand." Willow rubbed her fingers along the side of her mug.

"She's not my girlfriend." He tightened his lips.

Willow ignored his dampened mood from the call. "I'm buying a treat for your dad. Be right back." Standing at the register, Willow observed Zach rubbing the back of his neck and staring into his cup of coffee, his face marked with a worried frown.

Willow approached him, holding a paper bag, and lifted it. "Peach pie. His favorite."

"You know his favorite pie?" Zach slid his empty cup to the center. "Very considerate of you."

She noticed his grimace had softened. "Come on. Let's go."

He followed Willow to the elevator. Standing behind her in the crowded space, he edged closer. "You smell like roses."

She twisted, her dark curls swishing across her back. She wanted him to touch her, wrap his fingers around her ringlets, and embrace her. But it couldn't happen. "My favorite scent." As the elevator door opened, she lifted her lips in a gentle arc and strolled out. She turned to see if he was behind her. "Coming?"

"Right behind ya." He wiped perspiration off his forehead with his shirt sleeve.

Willow bounded into George's room, swinging her paper bag in the air. "Look what I brought you!"

George was sitting in bed with his dinner tray in front of him. "Oh, good. Much better than this junk."

He scowled, motioning to the food, and twisted his lips sideways. "Tomorrow, I want a large pepperoni pizza." He winked at Willow.

"Anything you desire, George." She patted him.

"You're my girl. Now get me a fork, please."

Zach straightened his posture, watching them. "Hey, Pops. If you're still hungry, we can go back to the cafeteria and grab a sandwich."

"No need, son. I'm fine." He glimpsed at Willow. "How about a game of gin rummy? Good for the brain. The nurses' station might have a deck of cards."

"Sure. I'll go check." Willow left the room on the hunt for cards.

George fixed his gaze on Zach. "Nice to see you two together. She's the kind of gal you need, Zach. Take it from me. I've lived longer. The other gal you invited to the house doesn't have the depth like this one. Just saying."

"I'll keep it in mind." He dragged his agile fingers through his messy hair.

Willow waltzed in, holding a deck of cards, and circled both arms in the air. "Ta-da!"

The three spent the next hour joking and playing, their voices echoing inside the room in a burst of competitive energy.

After a while, Zach glanced up. "Hey, Pops. You look tired. Maybe you should get some rest, and I'll be back tomorrow to pick you up. What do you say?"

"Yeah." He motioned to Willow. "Can you find my shows on the TV, hon?"

"Of course." Willow helped George get comfortable, then followed Zach to the parking lot.

He held the door, then hurried around, and slid into

the driver's seat. He squeezed the steering wheel and pushed out an audible breath. "Thanks for coming tonight. You were right. When you have someone with you, handling a crisis is much easier."

****

"No problem." Her phone pinged. *Marcy.* "Oh, dear. This is the news I've been dreading." She read the text.

—*Council approved construction. I'm selling. I'll swing by the store tomorrow morning and give you details*—

Willow shook her head, shutting her eyes. "Shoot."

"Bad news?"

"Yeah. I lost my job." She opened her eyes, pooling with wetness. She didn't want to cry, but one tear escaped down her cheek.

He leaned over and wiped it away with his thumb. "Don't worry. You'll find something else."

"Yeah. I hope so. I'll have to suck it up, get out of my comfort zone, and find a new job—all over again." She wiped another tear trickling down her cheek.

"Care to share? I can be a good listener." Zach started the truck.

Willow groaned, twisting in her seat. "Maybe the universe is telling me I need to get serious and pursue photography. But I'm not sure how to do it." She glanced over at his rugged stature, sitting tall, his muscular arms on the steering wheel, and his wavy hair hanging over his eyebrow. *He is one hunk of a man.*

"Listen, let's brainstorm different ways you could do it. Tomorrow, after dinner, we can sit and discuss a plan. What do you say?" He shot a quick glance toward her, then refocused on driving.

She swirled her fingers in a circle over her heart. "If you have time."

"I have time for you, Willow."

"Thanks." Warmth slid up her neck, spreading across her ears, and landed on her cheeks in a fiery blaze of heat.

Fifteen minutes later, he steered the truck into her driveway and stopped.

Willow grabbed the door handle to exit but felt his hand slide over her forearm.

"Wait." He vaulted out of the truck and darted around to open her door.

She stepped to the ground, her legs wobbling.

Zach closed the door. "Come here." He embraced her. "I wanted to hug you. We've had a long day."

She fell into his embrace without resistance and buried her face into his chest, her body molding into his.

After a few moments, he inched away, both hands resting on her shoulders. He fixed his gaze, then placed his palm on her cheek. "You're an impressive woman, Willow Mason."

She didn't stir, staring into his eyes, and felt warmth radiating along her jawbone.

"Thanks again for staying with me. See you tomorrow."

Breathless at this point, she nodded.

He released his hold, climbed back into his truck, and left in the night.

Willow floated her chin upward to the night sky, seeing stars shimmer in the distance, and prayed. She listened to her breath ease in and out and wiped away one last tear sliding down her cheek. *Please, God, give me guidance. How can I heal my heart?*

Chapter Twenty

The next morning, Willow counted money in the register, then perused the bookstore, resting her sight on one of her photographs. She studied it, visualizing her show in a gallery and clients hiring her to capture a feeling behind the lens, whether for personal or commercial reasons—a real lucrative business. *A girl can dream, can't I?*

Marcy called earlier and relayed details of the meeting with the town council—nothing new.

Outside the bookshop, cumulus clouds, swollen like cream puffs, floated by in the sky, and Willow sent another prayer asking for guidance, for both her professional and personal life. She wiped her clammy hands on her jeans before rearranging another book on the shelf. Her phone pinged on the counter, and she leaned over to see the name of the person texting. *Rupert Morgan.*

—Hello, Willow. Have you given any more thought to my offer—

—Thank you, Rupert. Not yet. Give me another week or two—

—Okay, but don't take too long. I need to fill this position and let this employee go. He's a waste of my money—

—Okay—

Going back to New York might not be the answer,

but at least, she had options. *But what do I want?*
****

Sitting at the dining room table, Zach cracked his knuckles, a bad habit he never relinquished, and sighed after the last candidate left the house. He eyed Leah. "Well?"

"I like the young man for the day shift. Dad would feel comfortable with him. And the first woman from the agency was energetic and willing to do shorter shifts. We could ask her to make dinner as Willow does—whenever she's ready to let go of this job."

"Doesn't Willow need the money?" He hated he couldn't help with her finances. She would never take a loan, so he would have to figure out another solution if he helped.

"Yes."

"She's losing her job at the store." Zach rubbed his day-old stubble on his jaw.

"Yeah, I thought so. I hope she doesn't move back to New York." Leah dipped her chin, writing a note on her legal pad.

"Why would she do such a thing?" Zach wrinkled his forehead.

"She ran into her old boss from the gallery in the city, and he offered her a job again. She hasn't decided yet."

A sharp twinge pinched Zach's heart. Willow moving out of Cedar Hill? Even if he was in Nashville, he could see her when he came home, and he planned to spend more time with Pops. "Oh." What more could he say?

"After Dad's settled at home, let's figure out a time for him to meet these two. I want him to have as much say in the selection while he can."

"Sounds like a plan." Zach adjusted his watch. "I best be leaving for the hospital. I'm sure he's chomping at the bit to get out."

"I'm glad nothing more serious happened." Leah stood and hugged Zach. "I'm so happy you're here."

"Me, too." He pecked her on the cheek. "I'll text you later."

"Okay." Leah checked her watch, then rushed out the door to work.

Zach sat for a moment, mulling over feelings about Willow. The connection was intensifying—its back-and-forth momentum driving him crazy. He wrestled with a gnawing disappointment, shrouding him like a dark veil. But he wasn't ready for the kind of relationship she deserved. *Why not?*

****

Arriving home, Zach sized up his dad. As suspected, he couldn't wait to get out of the joint. He had no concussion or injury to the brain—just a few stitches on the head, which could be removed in a week or so. "Home sweet home, Pops." He hopped out to help.

George shooed him away. "I'm fine. Just a bump on my noggin. Everyone needs to stop doting on me."

"Can't help myself." Zach raised his palms, facing him with a shrug.

Ambling toward the house, George halted. "You're a good son, Zach. I'm glad you're here."

"Thanks, Dad. I'm glad I'm here, too." Zach's heart ached again with regret for all the years he had missed with his father.

"Okay, enough of the mushy stuff. What's for

lunch? Bologna sandwiches?"

Zach snickered. "Of course—my specialty. But don't worry. Willow will be here later with pizza for dinner."

"She's a good one."

Zach nodded. *Don't I know it.*

****

Later in the afternoon, Willow shut the drawer and locked up the cash register. She was leaving early to buy groceries for George and run an errand for Mom, who was taking new medication. She had more energy to do things around the house now, like gardening and baking. At least one aspect of her life was on the right track. An hour later, she pulled into the Hayeses' driveway.

As usual, Zach hurried out the kitchen door to grab the groceries from the trunk of the car. "Here. Let me help."

"Thanks. How's your dad?"

"Happy to be home. He's in the living room, dozing in his chair. This whole ordeal wore him out, but he won't admit it." Zach opened the screen door and motioned for her to enter.

"I'm sure it did." She unpacked the groceries, then organized the ingredients for the salad and placed the pizza in the oven at a low temperature to keep it warm.

"I can help chop." He plucked a knife from the drawer.

"I've got it. I'm sure you have better things to attend to." Willow grasped a bowl from the cupboard.

His phone pinged. "Marissa. She's not too happy."

"Oh, yeah? Why?"

"She says I've got something going on with you,

and she wasn't thrilled."

Willow narrowed her eyebrows together for a second. "Us? Why would she say such a thing?"

"She grumbled about how much time we spent together, and she complained you were the one at the hospital with me, not her."

"But I work with your dad. I've known him all my life." She concentrated on chopping celery. *Does Zach have feelings for me?*

"Yeah, but…women. They get jealous." He stopped, then shifted his weight while scratching his head. "Um…you know what I mean."

She quit cutting. "I can't believe you said that."

Zach jerked a hand to his lips. "I realized it the second it flew out of my mouth."

Willow waved her knife at him. "Women are much more than you could ever understand, Zachary Hayes."

"Yeah, you're right." He shifted his body weight. "Guess I never had the right woman to teach me." Zach stared.

Amusement flickered across his face. *Is he flirting now?* "Guess you never did." She dropped her knife on the cutting board and strode into the living room. "Hey, George. Dinner will be ready in five minutes, if you want to wash up. How are you feeling?" Taking care of him centered her, and she needed to readjust her emotions.

"I'm fine. Did you buy pizza?"

"Of course, I did. By special request." She patted his shoulder, her smile spreading ear to ear. "A beautiful evening awaits us. Let's eat out on the patio. What do you say?"

"I'll be right out." George strolled toward the

bathroom.

She returned to the kitchen, took placemats out to the patio table, and checked on the pizza. She didn't refuse Zach's offer to help carry things out. *Put him to work, and he can't stand and talk in my face.* She poured iced tea and took a seat next to George.

The three jested about the escapades of the last twenty-four hours, making light of the situation.

"Dad, Leah and I selected a couple of staff members from the caregiving agency. They're coming to the house on Monday for your approval. Okay?" Zach set down his fork and turned his gaze to George.

"As long as Willow stays on for as long as she can, I'm happy." George patted her right hand. "You're a kind woman."

"I'm flattered, George, and yes, I will." She squeezed and released his nearby hand, then tossed her curly, chestnut hair away from her face.

George pointed his finger toward Zach. "And how long are you staying?"

"Not sure, Dad. I kind of like Ohio again. I want to finish my songs, and then I'll head back. But if something comes up, my manager will call me."

She caught his gaze but jerked her head back. Those eyes—too sexy. Droplets of sweat dribbled down her back, her body temperature rising.

His ringtone blared. "Trent Adler. Sorry, I've got to take this. Excuse me." He stood and hurried out on the lawn behind the house.

She could hear his animated voice on the phone and glanced up when he returned. "Well? Good news?" She welcomed his elated expression, making her melt.

"They're releasing our song as a single next

week—as a precursor to his album being released next month. Pretty exciting. We both have a good feeling about this one." He swayed side to side. "This calls for a celebration. Anyone up for a beer?"

"I'll take one." *A little alcohol might calm my jitters.*

"None for me. I'm ready for my shows. You two party away." George stood. "Congratulations, son. I can't wait to hear it. You need to finish 'Forever Kind of Love' soon. I have a good feeling about the song." He tossed his napkin onto the table and went inside the house.

Zach twisted his head in Willow's direction. "I'm amazed at how clear and cognizant he is at times. His encouragement is more precious than ever. I want to finish our song tomorrow."

"Better get on it." She chuckled and gathered the dishes on her way to the kitchen.

He helped clean up, then grabbed two beers. "Let's go outside. We need to talk about your career, too."

A tingle creeped up her spine. This might be what she needed—a beer and some planning for her new dream. She'd take Zach's help. After all, he wouldn't be here forever. "Okay. Lead the way." She helped drag chairs out on the lawn by an overflowing apple tree. Its branches hung heavy with ripe fruit ready for picking, and a sweet smell of fallen cores left by the squirrels wafted through her nose. She grabbed a writing pad and pen from her purse, kicked off her shoes, and was ready for business. The air was still warm, but when the sun set at night, a coolness surrounded them. Willow bit her bottom lip, holding her pen and waiting to scribe. "What are your ideas?"

"All serious, eh?" Zach stretched his legs and opened his beer.

"This is serious. If you don't want to help me, fine." She dropped her pen.

"I'm teasing you." He took a swig of the ale. "First, you need a website. You should start reviewing other photographers' sites to understand how to do yours and sketch your design flow. People need to see your work, Willow, and drafting an outline is something you could do right away without money."

She already had a million ideas racing through her head. She cocked her head, biting her lower lip again. "How much will the website cost to get up and running?"

"One to two thousand. I've got a guy, though, so I can get you a discount." He tipped his bottle again.

She gulped. This amount was too far a stretch for her right now. "Okay. I'll start with research and sketch out a plan."

He stroked her nearest arm. "Don't worry. I'll be a consultant if you need me, even if I'm in Nashville."

A pang gripped her heart. *Reality check—he's leaving.* "Okay. What else?"

"You need to explore ideas about building your brand. What gives you the most joy in photography? What kind of pictures do you want to take? We should examine your portfolio together and see if we can determine some ongoing theme in your photos."

"You do have good ideas." She jotted down his suggestions on her pad, then fidgeted with her pen, rocking it back and forth. "If you don't mind, I would appreciate it. I'm hoping I'm ready to reveal my work. If I'm not, I might as well throw in the towel on this career." She chuckled, wiggling her toes in the grass.

"Yep. You need to put yourself out in the public eye." He glanced down as his ringtone sounded. "It's Marissa."

"Take it if you need to."

"I'm sorry." He stood and swung his lofty figure away for privacy.

She stared as he spoke—his fingers pinching the skin above his nose, his head bowed, and his voice rose. She could trust him when he was plain, old Zach, a helpful friend, and neighbor. But when it came to women, well, his track record was a blatant display of his preferences. He was a player, and his desire to remain so was solid—and *not* changing.

"Sorry. Now, where were we?" He returned to his seat.

"Everything okay?"

"Yeah. Nothing new." He twiddled with his bottle, then tossed it back, his mouth taking a generous swallow. "Back to branding. Would you show me your portfolio this weekend? Between the two of us, we can figure out something." He eased back into the chair.

She wished he was the man she wanted him to be. "Sure." She took another sip of beer, slipped into her sandals, and stood. "I'll head home now. I have some things to do and want to check on Mom. Thanks for the ideas. You've given me a to-do list not costing a fortune." She tossed her pen inside her purse.

He stood. "I'll hang with Pops and work on our song."

" 'Forever Kind of Love'?"

"Yeah. Maybe someday I'll be ready for it." He narrowed his glance toward her.

"Maybe you will." She sauntered away before he got too close. She hung her loose limbs at her side. *Half a beer and I'm feeling it. Better leave.*

Once inside, Willow said her goodbyes to George and thanked Zach again. She dropped into the front seat of her car, gripping the steering wheel and staring at the house. *Pull away.* But she needed his help. After all, friends first. *Friends.* Keep the mantra going before she got into trouble again and succumbed to his touch or another kiss. *Not happening again.*

Chapter Twenty-One

The next morning, Zach's pen ran out of ink, so he tugged at drawers in his bedroom dresser, searching high and low for another one. A box he'd never seen sat on the top shelf of his closet. Curious, he grabbed it, forgetting about the pen search. Zach opened the lid to reveal various items of his mother's scattered inside— some pictures, one of Zach's high school medals, a story Leah wrote in sixth grade, and an envelope. He grasped the last item and took out a letter, crumpled and yellowed. As he read it, he blinked against burning tears. Dad had written a love letter to his mom.

Dear Adelyn,

You are the most valuable treasure in my life. Your beauty and caring astound me. When you laugh, you light up the entire room, and I feel so blessed you love me. My love is endless and will remain so forever. You have my heart, Addie, and always will.

I look forward to our wedding day and can't wait to call you my wife. Oh, the adventures we will have! With a forever kind of love like ours, no challenge will be too great, and no amount of joy will be too much.

I love you, darling, forever and beyond.

George XO

Zach sat on the floor, leaning against the bedpost. He recalled sweet images of his mom and felt his chest tighten with sorrow for Pops and all he had endured when he lost her. And yet, somehow, he carried on. *I should have been more sensitive.* But Zach needed to move past the regret and be thankful for every day he still had with him. *A forever kind of love.* All he had to do was dive into his parents' relationship, and he could finish the song. He reread the letter, smoothing out the wrinkles in the paper, and brooded about Willow.

She was the kind of woman who deserved a forever kind of love. *Can I change and be the kind of man she deserves? Not sure.* His history with women was questionable, and he could never hurt her—*and* he didn't trust himself. When the front door opened, Zach jumped, hearing Leah's voice resonate in the foyer. It must be time for the new caretakers' interviews with Dad. He folded the letter and set it on his nightstand to show Leah and Pops later, then ambled toward his sister's voice.

Leah stood beside her father at his old, rolltop desk in the living room, watching him shuffle through some documents.

Zach stepped closer. "Whatcha got?"

"I'm sorting through some of these papers while I still have half a brain." George chuckled, ruffling through old bills and manila envelopes.

Zach smiled—grateful Pops' easy humor remained intact.

"The staff should be here any minute, Dad. Want some iced tea or lemonade?" Leah hovered nearby.

"Tea would be great." He arranged several envelopes into a pile and shoved them aside just as the doorbell rang, then sat on the couch next to Leah. He met the caregivers, chatted briefly with each one, and approved the choices. He turned to Leah. "I'm not ready to let go of Willow yet, so can you check with her about future employment?"

"Sure, Dad." She smiled. "She enjoys your company." When finished with the interviews, Leah turned to Zach. "I need to pick up Rosie at her friend's house, but we'll be back at five for a barbecue. Right?"

"Yep. Willow found Mom's recipe for the sauce in a drawer." Zach grinned.

"Yum. I'm sure she can do it." She pecked her dad on the cheek and rushed out the door.

George stood. "Time for bologna sandwiches?"

"You got it. After lunch, I want to show you something I found in the closet." Zach rose from the chair, arching his back in a side-to-side stretch.

"Oh, yeah? What?" George cocked his head and arched an eyebrow.

"A love letter you wrote to Mom before you got married."

"Heck, let's look at it now."

Zach retrieved the letter, handed it to his dad, and sat on the couch beside him. He watched his facial expression brighten at the mention of his beloved wife.

As George read it, a single tear rolled down his cheek. He brushed it away with several fingers and let the letter drop to his lap. "See. This is what I was talking about. We had a forever kind of love, lasting an eternity. And this is the kind of love I want for you. When it comes, I hope one day you'll be ready. Your Marissa gal—she's not forever material. You know who I think is, but you need to live your life, not me. Thanks for finding this." He touched Zach on the shoulder.

Overwhelmed with emotion, Zach enfolded him in

a solid hug. "Thanks, Dad, for everything you've done for me." Tears trickled down Zach's cheeks, their wetness falling to his shirt. "I'm sorry I stayed away for so long. I'm so sorry."

George patted him on the back. "You had to find your way. Let's enjoy the time we have together. I love you."

Zach leaned back, wiping his face with the back of his right hand. "I love you, too." He expanded his chest with the next breath. "And Dad...how did you get over losing Mom?"

"You never get over it, but with time, you heal." George paused. "Grief has a funny way of showing you a road, and you have to walk it—no matter how difficult it might be. But Addie is with me every day. I feel her, I talk to her, and the love never dies."

Zach scratched his head. *Am I afraid of falling in love? Afraid of loss and pain?*

George stood. "How about those tasty sandwiches now?"

Zach relinquished his introspection. "I'm on it, Pops." After lunch, he would finish the song. He now had the understanding to put his heart and soul into it. Reading Dad's love letter gave him insight in more ways than one, and a new vision for himself was coming into focus—if he dared to follow it.

****

When Zach saw Willow arrive at the house for dinner, he put his guitar into its case and met her with open arms, ready to carry groceries.

"Here you go." She handed him two bags. "I have something else I want to carry in."

He stepped aside, holding the bags.

She hoisted two hefty frames wrapped in brown paper out of the trunk.

"What are those?" He shifted the weight of the bags he clutched in his arms.

"A surprise for George and Leah. No peeking." She twirled in a semicircle, determination evident in her stride.

He nodded, following her into the kitchen. "Need help?"

"No thanks. Where's your dad? In the garage?"

"Yep."

Willow placed the frames in the living room, then returned to the kitchen. "How's his head?" She rummaged through one of the bags, pulling out items.

"Healing without any problems, so far." He watched, hands hanging from his back pockets.

Willow lifted his mom's recipe from a side drawer, then reached toward the cupboard to take out ingredients, bowls, and utensils.

"I'll be outside if you need anything." He dropped both hands to his sides.

"Did you finish your *forever* song?"

"Almost." He bent his elbow, scratching his head. "It might be done."

"You can play it after dinner." She returned her focus to preparing the barbecue sauce.

"Yeah. I could." He peered through the screen door. "Pops is coming out of the garage. Be right back."

A few minutes later, she peeked out the window at the two men sitting on the patio. Their bond had strengthened since Zach's first night home. Home. She wished Cedar Hill was his home, not Nashville. But, at least, she knew he would spend more time here, since he had mended rifts with his dad, who needed him now more than ever. As Willow struggled to find a way to let go of this man and stop the growing attraction inside her, she let out a breathy murmur, her heart aching. Before she could stew over it, she was distracted by a high-pitched voice calling from the living room.

"Wiwwow. Wiwwow. Where are you?"

"In here, sweetheart." Willow sliced the last carrot.

Rosie ran into the kitchen and leaped toward Willow, crushing her in a fierce hold. "What are you doing?"

"Making the sauce. Want to help?"

"Yes!" She jumped, her bouncy ponytail swinging back and forth.

"Go wash your hands, and you can help with the salad." Willow prepped the vegetables earlier, so Rosie could pour the ingredients into a bowl and mix them.

Leah sauntered through the kitchen door. "I see she found you. She was very excited." She gave a quick side hug to Willow and placed another bag on the counter. "Dessert."

Willow shook her head, loosening the tension in her neck, and was relieved her best friend was here. Leah's presence helped widen the distance between her and Zach and was a good distraction. "I'm almost done. Want to set out the placemats and silverware? The chicken is in the fridge. You can bring it, too."

"Got it." Leah balanced everything in both arms, teetering in a near stumble out the door.

Willow stroked Rosie's back. "How's the salad coming?"

Rosie flipped the lettuce in the same motion, over and over, with a wide grin on her face. "Almost done."

"Let me see." Willow picked up the bowl. "I say you've tossed this salad like a pro. Great job."

Rosie hugged her again and hopped off the stool.

"Why don't you carry the napkins outside?"

"Okay." She grabbed them off the table and skipped out the door.

Zach entered the kitchen. "I see you have a helper." He hesitated behind her.

Willow sensed his body, the closeness sending a shiver up her neck. She inhaled his musky scent mixed with an earthy odor from hours spent in the woodshop, which didn't help either. "She did quite well. See?" Willow lifted the salad bowl. "Can you take it out? I'll get the sauce."

He lifted his fingers, tucking back a loose strand of hair hanging above her eyelid before grabbing the bowl. "Better. Now you can see."

"Thanks." A soft flutter stirred in her heart.

Zach stared, his dimples pressing into his cheeks, then left the kitchen.

His comical face was endearing yet maddening at the same time. With her whole being, she wanted his touch to linger. She yearned for it. She fantasized about it. She craved it. *I'm so done for.*

About twenty minutes later, Zach stood over the grill, turning the chicken breasts as wafts of sizzling barbecue sauce drifted through the air, while chatting to Liam. Sweat poured off Zach's brow as he flipped them over the hot coals.

Willow poured iced tea into glasses and passed the salad bowl around the table.

"Man, that smells good." George reached for a bottle of dressing.

"Almost done, guys." Zach reached for the platter, then removed the meat, one piece at a time. He carried the dish to the table. "Let's eat!"

George bit into the chicken and moaned. "Tastes just like Addie used to make. Excellent, Willow."

"Thanks, George." She could feel warmth wrapping around her cheeks.

"Yum." Leah dabbed sauce dribbling down her chin with her napkin, then smiled.

"You rock, Willow." Liam cracked a smile, then cut up a piece of chicken for Rosie.

Willow quietly ate, listening to everyone's chatter at the table and relishing the success of the meal. When finished, she glanced at Zach.

He caught her gaze, raising the corners of his mouth.

She held his stare until she couldn't stand it any longer. "When you're done, play your new song, Zach."

George perked up. "Did you finish it?"

"I did, Pops. I'll play it." He wiped his greasy hands on a towel, grabbed his guitar, and began strumming the chords to the ballad, his voice transporting listeners to an ethereal realm where hearts awakened.

"She was one step from heaven,

a shining star from above.

And I knew in my heart,

she was my forever kind of love."

When Zach finished, he stilled.

"You nailed it, son." George grinned.

Willow shivered with goose bumps at the sight of Zach's tear-filled eyes. The song emerged deep from his soul and, in the process, revealed himself to the core. *Forever kind of love.* She wanted the same kind of love again, but could she ever trust a man enough to find it? "I love it," she murmured, encouraging him.

Leah applauded. "Might be your best song yet, brother."

"Thanks, sis."

Seeing a reddish hue spread across Zach's cheeks, Willow grinned.

"Play it again!" Rosie clapped and giggled.

Everyone laughed at her earnest excitement.

"How about I play some more after dessert?" Zach tilted his head and smiled.

Dessert was a reasonable substitute.

"Okay." Rosie relented. "Wiwow, can I help?"

"Of course. Follow me." Willow grabbed a few plates and headed toward the house. She witnessed another depth of this man who pulled on her heartstrings. *Oh, why aren't circumstances different?*

Leah had ordered a chocolate cake, Rosie's favorite, with buttercream icing.

Willow removed it from the box and watched Rosie's brightened expression. "Let's cut it outside. Can you get those paper plates on the counter?"

Rosie skipped, grabbed the plates, and was out the door in an instant.

Willow searched for a platter in another cabinet, found one, and slid the cake onto its surface.

The screen door slammed, and Zach appeared. "Want me to carry the dessert?"

"Sure. If you drop it, you'll be responsible for the mess." She smiled.

"Thanks a lot." As he grasped the round edges of the large plate, he looked down, a chuckle escaping his throat.

Willow shook her head. *This chemistry is not going anywhere.* So long as Zach stayed in Cedar Hill, she'd be forced to confront her attraction, day after day. She let out a sigh, turned, fetched the two framed photographs from the living room, and carted them to the patio.

Leah cut the cake at the insistence of Rosie and smacked Zach when she caught him licking the frosting with his finger. "Get your own piece." She laughed.

"Quite tasty." Zach's focus drifted toward Willow. "Did you bake it?"

"No, Leah's treat from Crestview Bakery on Main Street."

"What's in your hands?" He stuffed another bite into his mouth, then wiped the sugary icing from his upper lip.

"Gifts for George and Leah—when their fingers are less sticky."

Leah leaped forward. "I cleaned mine. Let me see!" She grasped the package from Willow and untied the ribbon. As the paper fell away, she gasped at the photo of her and Rosie from the birthday party. "Oh, Willow. You captured our relationship and the joy in our eyes." She hurried to the other side of the table and hugged her friend. "Thank you."

"You're welcome." Willow felt a warm sensation wrapping around her chest. "And thank you for helping me readjust to living in Cedar Hill again."

"The photograph is quite exquisite, Willow." Liam leaned closer, staring at the image.

"Thanks." She grasped the other one and stepped next to George. "And this one is for you."

George carefully took the present and unwrapped it. He handed it to Willow to hold, so he could see it better. A tear escaped his eyelid. The black-and-white picture of Zach and him, strolling with their arms around each other and carrying guitar cases, had been taken from behind. George smiled at Willow. "Thank you. This is one of the best presents I've ever received. Let's hang this in the living room tonight. I want to see it every day."

Willow glanced at Zach, catching him blinking back the moisture in his eyes.

"Will do, Pops." He settled his gaze on Willow. "Your gift is meant to be seen, Mason. I'll help you with a plan like we discussed the other night. No refusing me, understand?"

She was jolted by his intensity, preparing her for the possibilities of a new dream. She nodded, unable to get another word out of her mouth.

"Listen to my brother, friend. He's smart about this stuff and has been a successful artist for ten years. Right, Dad?"

"Right." George lifted the frame again, admiring the photo.

"Okay. I will. Thanks, Zach." In a fervent flurry of movement, she began clearing the table.

Leah stood to help and threw the dirty paper plates into the garbage, leaving the men outside. She snuck behind Willow. "Are you nervous about spending more time with my brother?"

Willow billowed air through pursed lips. "If I'm honest, yes, but he's right. If I want this career, I've got to handle my fears. I'll wear protective armor around my heart while we're together—if I can." She grinned and turned on the sink faucet.

"He's returning to Nashville at some point, but I catch the way he studies you. Zach's desires might be for more than being friends, but I still don't trust his wild lifestyle. And neither should you. Stay strong and be friends. Period." Leah fixed her with a strong gaze, hands planted firmly on her hips.

"Well spoken, my friend." Willow washed the dirty pans and put away leftovers. She was flooded by a warm sensation throughout her body, making her heart mushroom. She loved this family. *What would it feel like to be Zach's wife?* She dropped the pan, shocked by her musing, and shook the thought away. With such ideas, she would create more trouble for herself, and she already had enough for a lifetime.

Leah crept behind her. "Are you okay?"

"Yeah. Daydreaming about something I shouldn't be."

Leah peeked over Willow's shoulder at the view outside of her family, then touched her. "I'm here if you need to talk."

Willow relinquished her sponge, wiped the runny suds on a towel, and hugged Leah. "Thanks."

"Liam needs to get back to the store, and I need to help Rosie with homework unless we procrastinate and wait until tomorrow. I'll see what her mood is. Talk to you later."

Willow nodded and finished cleaning the kitchen after packing a to-go bag for her mom.

Zach entered the kitchen, holding her photograph.

George followed. "We're hanging it right now. Come help us pick a good spot." He whizzed by Willow, heading toward the living room.

With a shrug and a raised brow, Zach flashed a lopsided grin.

Willow smiled at his amused facial expression, and she relented. "Okay. Then I need to go."

George pointed above the fireplace mantel. "Here. Remove the old painting we bought at a yard sale and put it on the floor. Then, I can admire this work of art from my chair."

Zach did as he was told. After measuring and securing the wire in the back of the picture, he hung it.

They all stepped back, admiring the piece.

"Thank you, Willow." George side hugged her.

She was surprised by his affection, but she welcomed it. Perhaps her art would heal her wound, still raw with emotion. She hoped so and grabbed her purse to leave.

"See you tomorrow?" Zach tilted his head, staring.

"Yes, text me. I take Mom to church, and then I'll be home in the afternoon, working in the darkroom or on my computer." Willow waved goodbye, climbed into her car, and sank her butt onto the front seat. She yawned, dead tired from shoving her feelings into her gut, hoping they'd disappear. But they didn't. She was so screwed.

Chapter Twenty-Two

The next afternoon, Willow plucked a rag out of her bucket. She scrubbed the laminate top on the old kitchen table and two worn-out cushioned chairs left by her dad in the garage apartment. Assembling an office space was important. She didn't want to create a tense situation where she was alone with Zach in tight quarters like the dimly lit darkroom again—too much temptation.

She bounded down the steps to retrieve her computer and waved at Zach pulling into the driveway. "I'll be right back. Let's work upstairs." She pointed to the apartment, then caught a glimpse of Zach ambling up the steps before she ran into the house. After tossing her work materials into a tote bag and gathering snacks, Willow clambered up the stairs, her feet stumbling on the last rung while holding her computer and a tray with drinks and cookies. "Oh!" She cried out as her foot caught on the last step and iced tea sloshed over the glasses.

Zach jumped forward. "I've got this." He slid the wooden tray out of her grasp. "Don't need to flood your computer." He inched the corners of his lips upward.

"Thanks. Mom sent us refreshments." Her heart rate mounted, avoiding a near disaster.

"Can't refuse food and drinks." He set the tray on the table.

Still shaking from the near fall, she sat on the chair, opened her computer, and took out her legal pad for notes. "Ready."

Zach leaned back into the stiff chair, stretching his long legs out under the table. "Let's start with your branding, and then we can design the website on paper. Could you show me your portfolio?"

She found the folder on her desktop, clicked it open, and swiveled the computer toward him.

"Come sit next to me so we can sort them out together." He straightened his posture.

She hesitated. *Is he flirting?*

Zach threw up both hands. "No funny stuff. Just work between friends."

She elevated the corners of her mouth, hinting a smile. "Okay." *He's respecting my boundaries. Good.* She remained silent as she sorted through the photos, content to listen to his hypnotic voice while he picked out his favorites from the portfolio. She welcomed his insightful comments, clarifying the questions in her head about her brand.

When he got to the last one, he reclined backward in his chair with elbows bent, holding the back of his head. "I've got an idea. What stands out is your gift for exposing people's hearts and souls with your lens. You capture a depth of spirit when you catch a look in their eyes or action in some subtle way. Not easy to do. You'd be wasting your time taking portraits at a department store. You're an artist, Willow, and a fine arts photographer. We need to get your work out to an audience and let the word spread. I guarantee your talent will do the rest."

Completely numb, she froze. He nailed it—the part

of her lying dormant but sometimes crying out to be heard—an artist's calling she could not ignore. She locked her sight with his, not wavering. The intensity of their chemistry was turning into something much more profound. His actions were caring, and he was helping her find a way to make her most sacred dream come true. "Thank you." She touched his forearm. "You put into words what has been in my heart for a long time." She trailed her fingers along his shirt, idling time, then dropped them to the table. "What's next?"

"Let's pick the best photos for the home page of the website and some others. The portfolio will be accessible with its own tab. Did you browse some other photographers' sites?"

"Let me show you the ones I liked." She took back control of the computer and discussed the layout for her site in-depth.

"I'll call my guy tomorrow and see what kind of deal I can arrange. He's very good at design, and once you tell him what you want, he'll take over. He's easy to work with."

"How can I ever repay you, Zach?" She circled a loose strand behind her ear, then twiddled with it before letting go.

"What are friends for, Willow?"

His goofy grin spread across his face. Her heart was so full—full of gratitude for this man.

His ringtone sounded. "Mike. Gotta answer it." He stood, walked outside, and sat on the steps, talking to his manager.

She picked up her phone, scrolled through her emails, and stopped on one from The Sterling Center. Her heart rate accelerated, but after she read the news, she puckered her lips in a frown. She didn't receive the spot. She was runner-up and wouldn't be displayed in New York. Achieving first-place recognition would have been the perfect opportunity to launch her career. Now she was back to square one again, an undiscovered artist living in Ohio without the cultural opportunities a fine arts photographer needs from the big cities.

When Zach returned, he slightly raised a brow. "Is anything wrong?"

Willow dug her nails into her palms. Should she tell him about her *almost* success? She trusted him while discussing her career, but only then. "Yeah, kind of."

"Want to talk about it?"

"One of my photos was selected as a finalist for the Sterling Center for Photographic Arts annual juried exhibition in New York some weeks ago. I found out I didn't win the spot—only runner-up. I was holding on to winning—the one thing giving me hope."

"Perhaps you're looking at it the wrong way." He leaned closer, fixing his gaze. "Runner-up *is* a big deal. We can use the selected photo on the website. Think about the other photographers who never made it onto the list. You've already succeeded, Willow." He touched her outstretched arm. "This is the artist's journey—up and down. Believe me, I've experienced it all, and I'll support you every step of the way." He dropped the hand.

"Thank you." A slight shiver went up her spine. *Does he really care about me?* She lowered her head, sliding her fingers across her phone screen, and read the email again.

"Listen, Mike informed me I need to be in

Nashville for the week. They're releasing Trent's song I did with him, 'Heart on the Homestead', and we're doing a bunch of radio interviews, press events, and whatever our label arranges. We're signed to the same label, so they're all over this release."

"Sounds exciting. I'm happy for you." She avoided his gaze in an instant, disguising her emotions about his sudden departure.

"We made progress today, and I'll be a phone call or text away. I'll talk to my website guy in Nashville and tell you what he says."

"Thanks. But it might be a while before I have the money."

"He might be open to a monthly pay plan. I'll see."

She gave a subtle tilt of her head and closed her computer. *He's anxious to go. Probably has a million things to do.* She rested her fingers on the edge of the table as she stood and lifted her gaze to meet his.

Zach inched closer, taking her other hand. "I don't have a date for when I'm coming back, but you've made these last few weeks extra special, Willow. I'm glad you're in my life."

She threw both arms around him and whispered in his ear, "Thank you."

He met her with a firm embrace, not letting go.

She released her grasp and stepped aside, feeling a weight settle in her gut. *He's not kissing me.* Was she disappointed *or* relieved? Either way, she would miss him.

"I'm grabbing takeout for Dad and me tonight, so no need to come. I want some private time with him, and I've got to discuss care issues with Leah."

"Yes, I understand. I'll eat my dinner with Mom.

She'll be thrilled." Suddenly, she was consumed by an ominous sense of dread. *Zach is leaving.* She gathered all her things and traipsed down the stairs with Zach at her heels. Willow's hands were full, so no chance of another hug or kiss—he was pulling away. "Thank you again for all your help. I appreciate it."

"Thanks for taking such good care of my dad. You're a good friend, Mason." He anchored his gaze on her.

Tears pooled in her eyes, and she didn't want him to see. "You're a good friend, too, Hayes. Safe travels." She turned and listened to his truck door slam before it pulled out of the driveway. She shuffled into the house, fighting the onslaught of a flood about to burst forth. *No more crying.* But she let one tear slip before the door shut behind her. *Nothing I can do about my aching heart.* She set the computer on a nearby table, pressed her palm against her chest, and shook her head at the reality of what was happening inside. *I couldn't help myself.* Zachary Hayes had inched his way into her heart, and she had let him—with no regrets. *Was it worth it?*

****

Zach called Leah on his way home, and she agreed to call the caregiver and arrange some hours during the day for George. She would continue to do early morning checks, and Willow would make dinner. Moments ago, he was excited about returning to Nashville. But now, confusion clouded his vision, and his heart ached at the thought of leaving Willow. He cared too much about her, so he pulled away. After grabbing dinner at a Thai restaurant, he arrived home.

George was out in the garage, working on his

birdhouses.

"Hey, Pops. I'm back." Walking into the shop, he examined the finished bird dwellings scattered on a workbench and picked up an almost-dry one. "Pretty good."

"Best one yet." He lowered his brush. "Where's Willow?"

"She's not coming tonight." He scratched his head. "I bought Thai food. Sound good?"

"Why isn't she coming?" George narrowed his brow.

"I got some news today. I need to leave tomorrow and wanted some private time to chat."

George dipped his head and continued working on the birdhouse roof.

"My manager called. They're releasing the song I did with Trent, and we need to do some promotion stuff all week." *Will he be upset?*

"Oh yeah? Good." He kept painting.

"Are you hungry? Don't want it to get cold." He shifted his stance.

George put down his brush, wiped both hands on a rag, and patted Zach's shoulder. "You need to return to Nashville. You have a thriving career, and you need to keep moving forward wherever it leads you. I'm so proud of you." He tossed the dirty cloth on the workbench. "Just wish you'd find a wife." He scoffed under his breath.

Zach shook his head. "Someday, Pops. But I'm not sure I'm ready to take the plunge into matrimony."

"Don't wait too long. Don't let love pass you by. If you do, then I guarantee it will be the one thing you'll regret growing older. I have no regrets. I found the love of my life, and my life became richer."

Zach nodded as he flashed an image of Willow in his mind. "Let's eat, Dad." He wanted to end this conversation. He needed to distance himself from ruminating about Willow Mason and settling down. Too confusing. Too haunting. Too terrifying.

****

The next day, Willow closed the cash register and placed the money into the safe in the storage room. The sale started tomorrow, and she had already placed *Going Out of Business Sale* signs in the window. Scores of customers would pour into the store over the next few weeks, and she was happy for the distraction. She missed Zach already. *No goofy smile at the Hayeses' house this evening.* A slight pang pinched her heart. *Will he come back to Cedar Hill? And if so, when?*

She motored into the driveway, and Zach's truck was gone. Her heart sank further. His stay in Nashville was more permanent. If the trip was a quick jaunt, he would have flown. As she carried the grocery bags into the kitchen, she felt the lilt in her step fade to a shuffle—no Zach to help.

George exited the garage and waved.

She curved her lips upward. "Hey, George. How are you?"

"Fine, fine." He strutted through the kitchen, then stopped. "What's for dinner?"

"How about spaghetti? I figured we needed some comfort food, right?"

"You miss him, too? I was getting used to his big, burly presence as he mulled through the house, strumming the same chords over and over while writing a new song." He chuckled and tossed his baseball cap onto a hook by the door.

"Did you like the new guy today?"

"He's a good cook. He made a healthy lunch and was interested in my workshop in the garage. I might teach him a thing or two. After lunch, he spent most of the time doing laundry and cleaning. I could get used to this homecare."

"I need one of those guys." She grinned, setting the bags on the counter.

"Don't we all? I'll be in the living room. Call me when dinner's ready."

"Will do." About an hour later, Willow scooped spaghetti onto dishes, letting the steaming marinara sauce drip over the noodles as the rich aroma of garlic and basil filled the air.

George sank into the chair cushion at the kitchen table, and his phone's ringtone went off. *Zach*. He accepted the call, putting it on speaker. "Hey, are you in Nashville yet?"

"Yep. Just made it. Everything all right? How was the new caregiver?"

"I'm fine. Jimmy made lunch and carefully cleaned the house in his four hours. He'll work out."

"Is Willow around?"

"Yep. We're having dinner. We miss you."

"Miss you, too. What are you eating?"

"Spaghetti."

"One of our favorites. Say hi to Willow, and I'll check in on you tomorrow. You're making me hungry, and I have nothing in my kitchen. I've gotta order something. Love you, Pops."

"I love you, too, son. Thanks for calling." After ending the call, George glimpsed at Willow. "He says 'hi'."

"Yes, I heard." She forced a smile. Being at the Hayeses' house every night would be rough, stirring up feelings about Zach. She needed to get a grip and forget about him. But he had seeped under her skin and into her heart—nothing she could do about it.

After dinner, she settled George with his remote and left. *What am I doing?* Her two jobs seemed meaningless and so far away from her dreams. Yes, planning a career path with Zach was thrilling, but launching a successful profession required money. As she absorbed the reality of her situation, she slumped over the steering wheel, took a deep breath, then drove home.

Willow entered the house, threw her keys on the counter, and put leftovers for her mom in the fridge. "Hey, Mom. Spaghetti's in the refrigerator whenever you want it."

"Thanks, honey. You received a letter in the mail today."

Curious, Willow browsed the table where her mom put her mail out. She picked it up, and she gasped, her gut squeezing at reading the return address. *Charles.* He wrote her a letter from prison. She dropped on the couch and turned it, front and back, saying nothing.

Evelyn tapped Willow's thigh. "Take your time. Could be another apology. Or he's lonely. You have a new life, darling. And you're moving forward, leaving the hurt and humiliation behind, which is exactly what I want for you. Focus on the future."

Willow leaned over, snuggling into her mother's side and rested her head on her shoulder. She released a loud sigh.

Evelyn put an arm around her, stroking her hair. "Everything will be all right, Willow. You'll see. Hearts are resilient."

Willow sank into her mother's loving touch, eyes closing as she loosened the knots in her neck. Her feelings about Charles were dissipating, and her feelings about Zach were escalating. *Is it a blessing he left? Before I fell too deep?* If she was honest, though, her heart had opened, no matter how hard she had tried to keep it closed.

Willow straightened her body. "I'm taking a long, hot bath, putting my jammies on, and then I'll read his letter. Thanks, Mom. Anything you need?"

"No, dear. You get some rest. I'm fine."

Willow hoisted herself to a stand, every muscle aching, then dragged herself up the stairs. Everything she had been through, her new endeavors, and the upheaval in her life all over again had finally taken its toll. After a bath, she slipped into her plush robe, its velvety texture caressing her skin, and climbed onto the four-post bed, collapsing in exhaustion. She removed the letter from the envelope and opened it, her stomach quivering.

Dear Willow,

Let me say one more time how very sorry I am for everything. As I ponder our relationship and what I did, I'm mortified at how I could ever do something as horrible. You were the love of my life, and I blew it big time. I can't even imagine what you went through as I was carted away to the police station— the trial, the newspapers, the humiliation. You did not deserve any of it. When I started tinkering with my client's accounts and gambling, I became greedy—especially after big wins. But things turned sideways, and I became an addict. I never thought about how my actions would impact you, and I am genuinely sorry. I hope you're moving on, and perhaps you can forgive me at some point. I realize you will never want to be with me again, and I'm saddened. I hope you are truly successful in whatever you do in the world. I will always love you.

Charles

She leaned back against the headboard of her bed as a single tear morphed into full-on sobbing. She rolled over, shoving her face into the feathery cushion of her pillow, and let it all out. She didn't want her mom to hear. As the tears flowed, so did the pain of losing a life which meant so much and was now gone. Her love for Charles had vanished, and in its place, a hole remained in her heart—a hole needing healing. *How can I ever love again?*

She gripped a tissue, wiped her face, and blew her nose. She shifted her body, lying still on her back, and contemplated forgiveness. *How can I forgive Charles?* He took everything, leaving her raw, exposed, and vulnerable to the world. Despite attempts at reorganizing her life, she continued to be met with obstacles and disappointments. Losing her job, not winning the coveted spot at the Sterling Center, lacking funds to start her photography career, and Zach coming in and out of her life—all too much. A gentle tap sounded at the door, and she lifted her head. *Oh, no. Busted.* "Come in."

Her mother waltzed in and offered her a steaming mug of cocoa. "Thought you might need something."

Willow sat, taking the hot chocolate, and wrapped her fingers around the cup. "Thanks, Mom."

"Do you want to talk?"

Willow picked up the letter. "Read this."

Evelyn settled on the bed near her daughter and read the letter. "*Can* you forgive him, Willow?"

She sipped the hot chocolate, staring into space. "I don't know."

"I always liked this quote from Mahatma Gandhi. It says, *Forgiveness is the attribute of the strong.* Perhaps, sweetheart, in the forgiving, you will find strength—strength to live the life you deserve."

Willow was silent for a moment, absorbing the words. She placed her mug on a side table and embraced her mother. "Mom, you always were the wise one. I love you so much."

"I love you, too." Evelyn stood, placing a hand on Willow's cheek. "Get some rest. Tomorrow is a new day of the rest of your life."

Willow grinned, warming her hands while gripping the mug. "Thanks, Mom." Alone again, she took her cup and sat on the chair by the window, gazing at the stars shining in the darkened sky. She contemplated her mother's words and prayed for the strength to forgive Charles. Offering forgiveness might be the solution to moving forward and having some success in her life. What else did she have to lose?

She closed her eyes and was swarmed by visions of Zach in her mind. She missed him, no denying. But she could no longer dwell on something not real. Willow lifted a hand, touching the charm hanging from the necklace. Such a simple word yet so powerful. *Faith.* If she was meant to be with Zach, it would happen. Until then, Willow Mason was her priority. *Forget about Zach.*

Chapter Twenty-Three

Customer after customer waltzed through the door at the cozy Readers Bookshop throughout the next day. Townsfolk saw the signs that announced they were closing, and people flocked in for last-minute deals. Willow dug into the cash register for a customer's change but glanced up when her mom entered. "To what do I owe this pleasant surprise?"

"I wanted to browse the sale, but a special delivery arrived from Nashville early this morning. It seemed important, so I brought it." She held out an express mail envelope.

Willow scrunched her eyebrows. The only person living in Nashville was Zach. Did he send her something?

"Well, open it!" Evelyn widened her eyes, her voice bursting forth.

Willow ripped the mailer apart, her fingers trembling. Inside was another envelope with the name of Zach's record label on the return address. She opened it and took out a check with a sticky note attached. After seeing the number, she gasped. The note read: *For the photograph becoming my album cover. Good work, Mason. Zach.* She stumbled toward the stool behind her to sit, gaping at the check. Could this be true? Had she sold her first professional photograph besides the ones hanging in the bookstore?

"Well?" Evelyn hovered, tapping her foot.

Willow handed her the check.

"My darling, this is wonderful news." Evelyn curled her lips up in a grin. "Congratulations. You will have to thank Zach later. He must have expedited the process, so you'd have money for your plumbing or the new website you want to do."

"I'm stunned. I never dreamed my work would pay this much." She quivered as goose bumps prickled the nape of her neck.

"The amount is proof of how much you are worth, Willow. You need to start believing in yourself." Evelyn held out the payment.

"Zach said the same thing." She took back the check, grinning as she stared at the amount.

"He would know. Look how far he's come. Why don't you call him? He's probably waiting to hear you received it."

"When I have a break, I'll text him." Recovering from the shock, she leaped off the chair, jumping up and down and waving the check in the air. "I did it! I did it!"

Evelyn clapped. "Let's celebrate this tonight. Why don't I cook, and you can invite George to our house?"

"I'd love to, Mom. Thanks for the night off." She kept looking at the total sum on the paper to make sure it was real.

"Okay, settled. I'll hurry and come back another day to browse. I need to run to the grocery store."

"Thanks, Mom." She side hugged her.

"Take this acknowledgment in, dear. Receiving the check is a big deal." She pecked Willow on the cheek and left.

Willow smiled. Yes, getting paid for her work *was* a big deal. She waited for Deedee to arrive for her part-time shift, then hurried to the river to text Zach. Sitting on her favorite bench, she drew out her phone. She exhaled slowly through pursed lips, her nerves firing inside like a swarm of bees.

—I got the check! I'm excited. Thank you so much. Woman-dancing emoji—

She waited as the bubbles emerged.

—You deserve it, Willow. I'm psyched the photo will be my album cover—

—You're my biggest supporter. Now I can start on my website. Plumbing can come later—

—Thumbs-up emoji—

She didn't want to stop.

—How are things going in Nashville?—

—Been a whirlwind but a blast. I love working with Trent—

—Have fun and thank you again—

—No problem—

And he was gone. She was excited she would be a part of his next adventure—their connection wasn't over yet. Would the universe surprise her? She lifted her gaze toward the azure sky. "Thank you, God." After one last view of the Crestview River, she headed back to the bookstore with a swing in her step, smiling at all she passed. *Is my life finally changing?*

****

Willow had called George earlier, who was thrilled to be invited to the Mason home for dinner. She arrived at the Hayeses' house, still wishing Zach's truck was parked on the gravel, but the longing in her heart had been appeased by her earlier interaction. She hopped out to check that the house was secured, but she couldn't stop the upward tilt of a hard-earned smile.

George was on the front porch, ready to go.

"Hi, George. Let me check the doors."

"Believe it or not, I locked both." He stood waiting, both hands stuffed into the front pockets of his baggy jeans, his body swaying back and forth.

"I believe you, but I left my house once or twice before thinking I did, but I didn't." She allowed a playful snicker to slip out.

"No problem. I'm getting used to this care thing."

He doesn't seem to mind my double-checking him. She did find the back door unlocked but kept it to herself. *No need to upset him.* "Let's go, George." She climbed into the front seat, made sure he fastened his seatbelt, then drove the short distance to her house.

Evelyn was on the porch, waiting, and waved.

George got out of the car and smiled while removing his baseball hat. "Thanks for the invite."

"Anytime. We need to celebrate Willow's first photography deal." Evelyn wiped her hands on her apron.

"Oh, yeah?" George craned his neck, looking at Willow.

"Zach's record label sent me a significant payment for the photo I took of the two of you—the one on your wall. Zach wants it for his album cover, and they paid me."

"Zach has good taste." George traipsed up the porch steps and into the house. He followed Evelyn to the dining room, then pulled out a chair, lowering himself onto the seat.

Mom set the dining room table and prepared most

of the meal. She seemed like her old self, full of vigor and vitality tonight. Willow's heart warmed over, watching her throw a little dinner party.

George's ringtone blared out. "Sorry." He yanked it out of his back pocket. "Zach."

"Answer it!" Evelyn sprang to her feet.

"Hey. You'll never guess where I am. Put me on the camera thing." In an instant, Zach appeared on the screen, and George motioned for Willow to come closer.

Willow looked at his eyes, and a bolt of energy rocked her belly, shooting currents of electrical impulses throughout her nerve endings. "Hi."

"Hi. Where are you guys?" Zach squinted, bringing his face closer to the phone.

"We're at Mom's. She made dinner to celebrate the check you sent me."

"You should be proud, Willow. I am."

Evelyn squeezed her face into view on the phone. "We're all proud."

"Wish I was with you, guys." Zach grinned into the screen.

"Yeah, I wish you were here, too." Willow felt a melancholy warmth seep into her chest, missing him.

"I've got to run." Zach looked away from the phone, then back. "But I'll call you tomorrow, Pops. I can see you're in good hands."

"Okay." George handed the phone to Willow.

"Thanks, again." Willow couldn't take her gaze off him.

"You're welcome. You're off to a good start. I talked to my website guy, so call him tomorrow."

"Will do."

"Have a good evening, Willow."

"You, too." She waved, then hit the *End* button. She stared ahead, pondering the tone of his voice. *Was it softer?* She shook her head, then lifted her gaze, catching George and Evelyn exchanging a look. "What?"

"How long will it take you two to realize your feelings for each other? I can see it written all over your faces." George darted his gaze from Willow back to Evelyn.

Evelyn puckered her lips together and raised an eyebrow.

Willow's cheeks burned hot, her palms sweating. "Zach doesn't want a permanent relationship, and I'm not ready to open my heart to someone again after all I went through in New York."

"My dear, you can't control love." George reached for a glass of water, chuckling. "Love comes when it wants to. Make sure you don't close the door on something you might not get back."

"Wise words indeed. Now, let's eat." Evelyn placed serving spoons in several bowls and dished out the meal.

Willow contemplated the full impact of what George had said. What if closing her heart wasn't the answer to healing her pain? She ignored the tightening in her chest and shook off the feeling. *Time to enjoy a win.* She chatted, feasted, and devoured her mom's homemade cake which had the word, *Congratulations,* swirled on the top in chocolate icing. She tried to push the images from the phone call out of her mind, but forgetting Zach wasn't easy. After eating the cake, Willow could see George was tired, and her mom was, too. "Are you ready to go home, George?"

"Yes." He glanced in her direction, his glassy gaze meeting hers.

She dipped her head in silent response. "I'll be back to help do the dishes, Mom. Don't do everything until I return."

"I'll start, and you can finish later." Evelyn said goodnight to George, then scooped up two serving bowls and headed for the kitchen.

Willow stood, made sure George had his phone and jacket, and took him home. But she couldn't help thinking about what George had said about love. Could she control falling in love with Zach? Probably not. *Oh, dear. I'm in trouble.*

****

Willow couldn't stop her hands from shaking as she unfolded Charles's letter again. She showered after dinner cleanup and stretched out on her childhood bed, pondering forgiveness. *Is it the key to healing my heart?* She reread it, then hopped out of bed, searching for a pen and paper in her old desk in the corner. She grabbed a notebook to write on, then returned to the bed again, leaning against the headboard and wrote.

Dear Charles,

Thank you for your letter. Yes, your actions devastated me and tore a hole in my heart. Ever since the night you were arrested, I have closed my heart tight in fear of being hurt again. But I now realize my true healing might come from forgiving you. As awful and humiliating as your crimes and betrayal were for me, your punishment might be as bad. We will never be together again, but I do forgive you. I forgive you because we all have flaws. I forgive you because I need to let go of you and release this darkness in my heart. Then I can truly move on. Take care of yourself, and I pray you find peace someday.

Willow

There. I did it. She felt the heaviness in her heart float upward. She took a deep breath, stood while grasping the letter, and padded toward the window. She spread the lace curtains apart to see the stars coming out and lifted the window, her skin cooling in the night air. She inhaled and prayed. *Please God, let my heart be healed.* Willow opened her eyes as a chilly breeze washed over her, its freshness awakening every cell in her body and reenergizing her. After shutting the window, she folded her letter and put it in an envelope, ready for tomorrow's mail. She collapsed onto her mattress and sighed with relief. "I'll get through this." *Hopefully.*

****

The next day, Willow rearranged the hardback novels on display in front of the store. With the constant flow of customers each day, the shelves were growing emptier. Willow was grateful for Marcy's help, glad that she now puttered in the back storage room, checking on the inventory.

Marcy strolled into the checkout area. "At this rate, we might sell everything. I hope someone else opens a bookstore in town. God knows, they're important. I feel guilty closing this one."

"I understand." Willow propped more hardcover copies onto their stands in the window showcase.

"Did you find another job?" Marcy rummaged through a drawer near the register.

"Not yet, but I'm not worried. I'm giving my

photography more attention and hope to make it my full-time career someday." Willow stood back, assessing the layout of her display.

"Yes, you sold all your pieces here."

Willow had saved the money for her website. She bent to pick up another crime novel and felt her phone vibrating in her back pocket. She yanked it out. *Zach.* She flinched, pressing a hand to the flip-flopping in her stomach.

—Call me later when you're at Pops's. I might have another gig for you. Smiley emoji—

—Sure. I'll text you—

—Thumbs-up emoji—

Questions flooded Willow's mind, swirling in chaos—uncontrolled, yet anchored to a growing confidence in herself. Her right hand shook as she slid her phone into her jeans and returned to work. *Another photography job? Where?*

Later, Willow juggled a pizza in one hand and a grocery bag in the other, when she entered the Hayeses' kitchen. She couldn't stop her restless thoughts. *What does he mean, another gig?* The garage door was open, so she trekked through the backyard to find George, then approached the side entrance. "Hello! Anybody in here?" She walked through the doorway.

"Hi, Willow." George stood next to the bench with a paintbrush in a hand.

"Hi. I have pizza for dinner, and I'll make a salad. Sound good?"

"Perfect. I'll be a minute. I want to finish painting this tiny gem." He lifted a birdhouse, smaller than the rest, to show her. "For the little ones."

"Perfect." She brushed a hair from her face. "Zach

texted me earlier, and he wanted me to call him when I got here. He has some news. Can we do it before dinner?"

"Of course, dear." He returned to guiding his paintbrush in delicate strokes against the wood.

She hurried into the kitchen, commotion wreaking havoc in her gut, and focused on slicing vegetables for the salad. A million ideas tossed about in her brain like a pinball machine. *What does Zach's text mean?*

The screen door opened, and George waltzed into the kitchen. "Let's call him."

She texted first.

—*Your dad and I are both here. Is it a good time to talk?*—

—*Calling*—

"Hi. Do you want me to put you on speaker, so your dad can hear?" Willow fidgeted in her chair, then placed the phone on the table.

"Sure. Hey, Pops. How are you feeling today?"

"Pretty good, son. Don't worry about me. I'm getting used to Jimmy coming midday to help. My house has never been so clean." He let out a soft chortle.

"Glad to hear it. So, Willow, I wanted you to call because I showed your photograph for my album to Trent. He would like you to do a photo shoot for him— for a possible album cover like mine. He wants some casual pictures taken on his farm with his wife to show their love for each other. The name of his album is, 'Heart on the Homestead,' from the single we recorded together. You get the idea."

She clutched her chest, her heart pounding like a drum. *A photo shoot in Nashville? For another star?*

"Willow?"

"Yes, yes." She pressed a palm to her stomach, flip-flopping in a frenzy. *How would I get there?* "How would it work? I'm in Ohio."

"The record label would fly you out on Friday, and the shoot would be Saturday. You can stay with me. I have plenty of space, and you can have a private bedroom and bath. Better than a hotel. And fly back Monday."

She rested a hand near her sternum, steadying her breath. "I might need some lighting equipment."

"Text me a list, and they'll get it. You'll love Trent and his wife. They're good friends of mine."

Tears brimmed her eyelids, but she blinked them away. Was the universe giving her an opportunity to pursue her dream? "Thank you, Zach. You are my biggest supporter."

"You're way too talented not to be working at your craft. Call me tomorrow, and we can discuss more details." He cleared his throat. "What's for dinner?"

"You're missing pizza night."

"Darn. You guys enjoy it. We'll talk later, Dad. Love you."

"Love you, too, son."

After Willow ended the call, she remained motionless for a second, then faced George. "What just happened?"

"My son is your new agent." He chuckled and placed a napkin on his lap.

Willow jumped from her chair, spinning in a circle. "I'm going to Nashville!"

George shook his head, grinning, then reached for a slice of pizza.

And staying with Zach. But they were only friends. *Friends.* Her mantra needed to stick for as long as possible, even if she didn't want it to.

****

The next day, Willow dropped the letter to Charles into the mailbox on her way to meet Leah for lunch on the Riverwalk. She had tossed and turned the night before, not getting much sleep, as projected images and scenarios of spending the weekend with Zach clogged her brain. Doing a professional shoot for another country music star was beyond her wildest dreams. She swirled a palm across her chest, attempting to reduce the rapid pulse of her heartbeat before she had a panic attack. She waved at Leah and balanced their lunch in the other hand. Willow phoned her earlier about the weekend plans, so extra staff arrangements for George could be made.

"Hi." Leah took the drinks from Willow's hands.

"Glad you could meet me. I need some counsel before I leave." She settled on the bench next to Leah.

"Happy to be of service. Tell me the details again." Leah unwrapped a straw and jabbed it into the plastic cover of her iced tea.

Willow told her about the phone conversation with Zach and the upcoming one to review her schedule later. Her speech rate was fast, and she watched both hands shake as she talked.

Leah laughed. "What are you nervous about? I can see it in your body, and you haven't even left yet! You better pull it together before you arrive in Nashville, girlfriend."

"You're right. At first, I was excited. But now, as I've had some time to sit with my fears, or rather be bombarded by what-ifs and a million other scenarios rampaging my brain, I'm nervous about spending so much time with Zach." Willow removed her sandwich from her bag.

"Why?" Leah sipped her iced tea, then poured another sugar packet into the cup.

"Because I have feelings for him and don't want to get caught up in anything casual. I'm still healing from Charles." She told her about the letter and her decision to forgive him.

"Well, two things. I applaud you—letting go of what Charles did is a significant step. In forgiving him, you create space to find love again. And two, you need to trust yourself more, Willow. Acknowledge what you've been through and how hard you've worked." Leah paused to wipe a smear of mayonnaise from her chin. "Zach is your friend, first and foremost. You can be open and still stand clear in your convictions of what you deserve. I believe in you."

Willow unclenched her jaw, and the brisk pounding in her chest eased. Leah was right. By forgiving Charles, she felt her heart opening again, guarded now by a newfound strength. She now could maneuver around any situation involving love and attraction—at least, she hoped so. "You're right. Thank you for helping me see it all in a different perspective. What would I do without you?" Willow dipped a French fry into ketchup before eating it.

"Listen, you help me in other areas of my life, so we're even." Leah sucked on the straw in her drink.

"I'll focus on the work and let all this emotional stuff simmer on the back burner until I'm ready to deal with it. No need for additional stress."

"Now, you're ready for Nashville." Leah's watch pinged. "I have a client in fifteen minutes, so I'm out of here. Call me later, and thanks for lunch. I'll finish my sandwich later." She tossed it into one of the bags.

Willow stood, hugged her friend, and sat again on the bench to finish her meal. She needed a few moments to revel in the calmness of the water flowing in the river's current and decompress before life took her on a new adventure and, possibly, a new life.

****

As Willow stood by the sink washing the dinner dishes, she heard her phone buzz. *Zach.* She hurried and wiped the soapsuds off her fingers. "Hi."

"Did you get my email this morning with your flight information?"

"I did. Thank you. Could you rent my lighting equipment?" Her stomach still fluttered at the sound of his voice.

"Yep. We're all set. The weather forecast looks good for outdoor shooting on Saturday, which is what Trent wanted. Sunday might be miserable, though."

"No problem. Do you want to speak to your dad? We finished dinner."

"What did you cook?"

"I made a roasted chicken, so he would have leftovers. He's being very supportive about me leaving. He's amused I'm spending the weekend with you." Heat flushed her face with the realization of how she sounded. "You know what I mean."

"Yep. I'll pick you up at the airport, so no need for ordering a ride. We should be done with the week of promotions. Our song releases tomorrow, so listen for it on your radio. We already taped a session with one radio host but have a live session tomorrow morning. Fingers crossed."

"Can't wait to hear the song. Let me get your dad." Willow found him in the living room and handed him the phone.

"Hey, Pops. Everything all right? Are you mad I'm taking Willow away for a few days?"

"No. I'm delighted. She deserves this job. Thanks for arranging it. And Zach?"

"Yeah?"

"Take good care of this woman. She's special." George looked at Willow and winked.

"I will, Dad. No worries. I'll be the perfect host."

"Okay, talk to you later." He handed the phone back to Willow.

"What time is your interview in the morning? I want to set the station on your dad's radio and remind Jimmy to turn it on, so he can hear you live." Willow twisted a loose strand around her finger, biting her bottom lip.

"Very kind of you, Miss Mason. Nine o'clock on channel ninety-seven point six."

"Great. I'll see you Friday, then." She let go of her hair, pressing a hand to her churning stomach.

"Text me if you're delayed."

"Will do. Bye, Zach." Willow released a breath.

"Bye, Willow."

She returned to washing dishes but couldn't ignore the nervous sensation rippling throughout her torso. Talking was one thing, but staying composed in matters of the heart—when immersed in a real situation—was another story. Could she handle the chemistry of being near Zach for an entire weekend? Maybe. *Maybe not.*

Chapter Twenty-Four

On Friday morning, Parker Bates, the local radio host of Nashville's most popular country music station, signaled the start of the live show. Parker, in his early fifties with curly brown hair falling over his ears, had been an icon in the town for years. "And what inspired you to write, 'Heart on the Homestead,' Trent?"

"My wife and I are expecting our first child in a few months." Trent leaned in closer to the microphone. "I've been spending a lot of quality time with my family and soaking in all the love. I'm a blessed man, Parker."

"And how did you come into the picture for this song, Zach?" Parker's glance shifted.

Zach straightened his posture, even though no one could see him on a radio broadcast, his heartbeat racing. "Trent asked if I was interested in recording on it, and I jumped at the chance. Trent and I go way back to the early days when we first arrived in Nashville. I was honored to be included in the studio."

"Trent, when does the album drop?" Parker pivoted his gaze.

"Next month. I'm pretty sure you'll be the first to hear about the date." He laughed.

"And any new songs from you, Zach, coming our way?" Parker cocked his head.

"I'll be going into the studio soon to record my

next album. I finished a few new songs, including one I wrote with my dad." He grinned, feeling a warm sensation wrap around his chest.

"Oh, yeah? Sounds cool. What's the name of the tune?"

" 'Forever Kind of Love'."

"We look forward to hearing it. And now, here is the latest song from Trent Adler with Zachary Hayes, 'Heart on the Homestead.' The tune is sure to top the charts, so enjoy, folks."

The three men chatted while the song broadcast to the audience. Afterward, Trent and Zach stayed for another thirty minutes to answer live calls from the listeners. From the feedback they got in those conversations, they had succeeded in making a song listeners wanted to hear.

As he left the studio, Zach sensed a grumbling in his stomach and turned to Trent. "Want to grab some breakfast? This was an early call."

"Heck, yeah. I'm starved." Trent rubbed his belly.

They grabbed a booth in their favorite diner, but no sooner had they taken a seat than a woman appeared, asking for their autographs. They obliged with a smile.

"Never gets old. The fans are why we can make a living singing songs. We are two lucky men, Zach." Trent tipped his head to the server setting the water glasses and hot drinks on the table.

"We sure are." Zach picked up a menu, checking out any new specials.

"I'm pumped about our photo shoot tomorrow. When does Willow get here?" Trent laid his phone on the table.

"Four o'clock. I'm picking her up at the airport.

You'll like her. She's genuine, easy to relate to, and excited for this gig." Zach sipped his coffee, savoring the rich, earthy taste. The place was hopping with customers, but service was outstanding.

"After seeing the photo that she did for your album, Mary and I are psyched to see what she creates for my cover." Trent placed his order and motioned Zach to do the same.

"Thanks, Trent, for this opportunity." Zach brushed a stray strand from his face, then gripped his mug with both hands. "She's a longtime family friend who's endured a great deal of pain and heartache over the past year. I'm doing whatever I can to help her get back on her feet and believe in herself."

Trent tilted his head. "Sounds like you might feel something more you're not telling me. Are you sweet on this gal?"

Zach buttered his toast, shifting in his seat and avoiding eye contact with his friend. "She's awesome, but she's the kind of woman you commit to when you're in a relationship. And my preferences haven't changed—still happy sowing my oats, as they say."

Trent scooped scrambled eggs on his fork, then grinned. "One day, you'll grow tired of your wild lifestyle, buddy. When I met Mary, I wasn't ready to create a partnership for life. I woke up one day and knew I couldn't live without her. And the rest is history."

Am I helping Willow so she stays in my life? Keeping his testosterone in check over the weekend would be a challenge, but the bottom line was—he couldn't hurt her. Until he changed inside, he would never make a move. And change might not be in the cards.

After the meal, they paid their checks, signed another autograph on the way out of the restaurant, and left their separate ways.

Zach's housekeeper was at his place, tidying up in preparation for his guest, so he hurried to the grocery store to purchase supplies for the weekend. With a lilt in his step, he couldn't hide the smile plastered on his face, anticipating the arrival of a certain woman from Ohio.

****

Willow glided down the escalator to baggage claim on the main airport level and spotted Zach—hard to miss at six feet tall and wearing his signature black cowboy hat.

People milled around, waiting for luggage and hugging friends or family.

Willow waved, her heart rate accelerating when she saw him, but her mantra beat strong inside her—*friend, friend, friend.*

One young boy stopped him, bravely asking for an autograph.

She grinned, watching Zach take his blue pen and scrawl his name across a piece of paper.

As Zach approached, he offered both arms and hugged her. "Welcome to Nashville!"

"This is surreal, isn't it?" She grinned and lowered her backpack filled with camera gear.

"Yeah, surreal, but I like it. Let me get your bags." He bent, grabbing her carry-on suitcase and satchel.

"Seems you're always carrying my bags." She chuckled. Her butterflies danced in circles, and her heart pounded against her chest. She was aware of her feelings but was also feeling more confident in herself. If he wanted more than friendship, he would have to tell her. But for now, she planned on having a fantastic weekend and getting the best images ever for Trent. A glimpse of hope for pursuing her dream and succeeding as a fine arts photographer was within reach—one foot in front of the other. Hard work didn't scare her one bit. *Being alone with Zach does.*

"Let's get you settled at my place, and then we can grab a bite downtown. You can see the home of country music." He motioned her to follow, strolling toward the outside parking lot.

"Like a tourist?" She tilted her head, smiling.

"Yeah. We can talk more about the shoot over dinner, too." Zach opened the passenger door, helping her onto the high step of his truck.

"Sounds good." She would do anything he wanted but was comforted by his friendship and how hospitable he was being. When she arrived at his house, Willow eyed the sprawling estate and gasped. The mammoth ranch-style house spread out in all directions, surrounded by a few acres of dense, wooded forest. The trees were still green, their leaves on the verge of changing with autumn near, but the remote road to the house indicated privacy was a priority. She saw another side of this man—the man who liked to be alone and needed seclusion from intruding fans. *What is being in the spotlight all the time like? Does he get tired of all the fanfare?* She understood his respite in Ohio in a whole new way.

He grabbed her carry-on suitcase, backpack, and satchel, then ushered her into the house.

The living room spanned the main floor, hosting a

massive stone fireplace, leather sofa and chairs, and a large Persian rug with a rich, dark-blue coloring. Sliding glass doors along the side offered a view of the woods and rolling hills in the back. The open-style kitchen boasted a large island and six cushioned chairs facing a six-burner gas stove, walnut cabinetry above, and a formal dining room seen through a hallway on the other side. Willow gawked at it all. "You live here by yourself?"

"Yeah. Occasionally, I have the guys over for football or poker games, but the home suits me fine. I have a housekeeper once a week, so don't think I clean it." He curled his lips upward.

"I am impressed, Zachary Hayes. But I guess you *are* a big country music star and would have a place like this."

He shrugged and guided her toward another wing of the house. "Come on. I'll show you to your room."

She followed along a hall, passing several other bedrooms until she stopped at the end.

"This one has a striking view, private patio, and larger bathroom. Make yourself at home. When you're ready to go out, look for me in the kitchen." He placed her suitcase and other bags next to the bed.

Willow inspected the room, seeing a large queen-sized bed covered with a floral quilt, modern bathroom to the side, and a velvety upholstered chair in the corner. Then, she rested her gaze on a familiar photograph hanging over the dresser—*her* photo. He *did* have a perfect place for it.

As she opened the glass door to the backyard, she spread the corners of her mouth wide and breathed in the sweet country air, allowing a warm breeze to caress her skin. She couldn't believe she was staying with Zach and experiencing his very private life. *And the funny thing—I'm not wigging out.* She freshened up in the bathroom, put a few clothes on hangers, and changed her top. Dressed in jeans and a summer floral blouse, she opted for a pair of wedge sandals, giving her another two inches of height. She turned toward the mirror, applied a rose-pink lip gloss, then strode to the living room, taking deep breaths into her quivering belly.

Zach walked out of the kitchen, taking in a view of Willow, and widened his eyes. "You are…gorgeous."

"Thank you." She noticed he had changed into a clean dress shirt with his jeans. Willow stared, unrelenting, and a shiver crawled up her spine. The chemistry was palpable, but she was confident she could keep it under control.

"Let's go. I'll take you to my favorite restaurant, Benny's, on Broadway Street. They offer a variety of cuisine items—elegant but casual."

"Right behind you." Thrusting her chest out, she strutted with a swing in her step.

After arriving at the restaurant, Zach led her to a reserved spot in the back.

Willow scanned the area, passing a wrap-around bar crowded with people buzzing in conversation, and wooden tables scattered with cushioned seating. She grinned as people whispered or pointed, "oohing" and "aahing" over the well-known celebrity. *Is this what he goes through every time he goes out in public?* No wonder he found peace in Ohio—hometown folks left him alone. She breathed in the potent aroma of garlic and onions permeating the room—likely from grilled steaks and burgers. She felt a flutter in her stomach and swept her gaze across the table. "I'm beyond grateful for this opportunity." She reached out, covering Zach's hand. "You have given me faith in myself again and my abilities to make my dreams come true. Our new friendship is something I truly cherish, Zach." She squeezed the hand, then released it.

"You're very welcome. I've enjoyed every moment I've spent with you." He toyed with the silverware.

"You made a daunting task more manageable—and yes, even fun." She unfolded the cloth napkin, placing it on her lap. "Let's eat. I'm starved." Over the next hour, Willow ate, drank, and chatted about the next day's shoot. She ran some ideas past him and inquired about Trent and Mary's relationship since she'd never met them. She was grateful that he had even hired a skilled assistant.

After finishing his dinner, he excused himself and walked toward the men's restroom.

Willow sipped her glass of water, eyeing a woman approach Zach, then hugging him and kissing him on the cheek.

They chatted for a few seconds. When he exited the restroom, Zach paused as a different woman walked up to him, and the same thing happened. Were all these women past girlfriends or love interests? She shook her head, shocked she wasn't troubled by it all. No need for competing with Nashville women, but this reality also confirmed she needed to keep her boundaries clear. Yes, she opened her heart to Zach in Cedar Hill, but she still had time to protect herself. If she did, she wouldn't get hurt. That could never, ever happen again.

"Sorry. I kept seeing friends." Zach sat, leaning

back in his chair.

"No problem. You're a popular guy." She held her gaze on his face.

"Let's go for a stroll before we head home." He signaled the server for the check.

"Okay." Home. *What would making a home with Zach be like?* She let the fantasy drift in and out of her thoughts, its imagery tempting her deeper desire with this man. *I could get used to this—if the relationship was the real deal.* As Willow left the restaurant at Zach's side, she experienced the *click-click-click* of flashbulbs lighting up her face, indicating the paparazzi had been tipped off to a celebrity dining inside tonight.

"Who's the new woman, Zach? How long have you been together?" One guy shouted, insinuating taunts as he snapped another photo.

Zach slung an arm around Willow, shielding her from the invasion, and hurried her toward his truck. "Sorry about that. I wanted to show you the downtown. Another time?"

She noticed his disheveled hair and furrowed brow. "No problem. People sticking cameras in your face, I imagine, must get annoying."

"They're like vultures at times. But since I was with you, they all want a juicy story on my latest love interest—even if we're just friends. I'm sorry, but you might see your picture in the tabloids this weekend."

Willow flashed on the images of Marissa she had seen in the New York tabloids and shook her head. *That will never be me. I'm worth more than a fling.* Willow took a deep breath, then smiled.

"Are you okay?" Zach swiped at his sweaty brow.

She shrugged. "Doesn't bother me if they take my

photo. That's their job."

"You always surprise me in some way."

"Back at the house, you can give me a tour of your property and the grounds. We can enjoy some fresh air and stretch our legs at the same time."

"Anything for my guest." He avoided hitting the paparazzi while navigating his truck from the parking lot and drove home.

Willow stared out the window, lifting the corners of her mouth into her cheeks. She was enjoying this evening on so many levels—but perhaps, a little too much. *Uh-oh.*

****

The following day, Willow awoke to the smell of coffee brewing and bacon sizzling. She stretched under the covers and glanced out the window at a sunny day. *Thank God.* She bounced out of bed and slipped her robe on over her pajamas, then glanced down. *Can I go to the kitchen like this?* Of course she could. They're friends having a sleepover, and she grinned. She brushed her teeth, combed her hair, and began the hunt for caffeine.

Zach lifted his head. "Good morning. Coffee?"

"Please." She tightened her robe, readjusting the fit to cover any revealing skin.

"How did you sleep?" He slid a mug across the table in her direction.

"Like a rock." Willow bent her head over the cup and inhaled, savoring the bold aroma. "I love a classic roast blend." She smiled. "And I see the weather is cooperating, like you said, so I'm thrilled. How about you?"

Zach hesitated. "I slept fine."

Did he toss and turn as I did? She brushed the thought from her mind, climbing onto one of the breakfast chairs at the kitchen island, and took in his casual attire of sweatpants and worn T-shirt. Loose hair strands hung over his right eyebrow, and a dark trace of morning stubble shadowed his jaw. As she sipped her coffee, Willow watched while he fried eggs and bacon and buttered pieces of toast popping from the toaster. *This man's got skills.* She crushed her lips together, restraining a chuckle.

"Let's enjoy a hearty breakfast before leaving. No telling when you'll eat again." He poured two glasses of orange juice and placed them on the breakfast bar.

"What time are we going?" She breathed into her gut, drawing on her ability to calm herself. Every nerve in her body was on high alert.

"Around eleven, so you can tour the property and house for ideas of where to shoot." He dished out the eggs and placed some toast on a small serving platter.

"Great. Did I thank you again today for this gig?" She picked up a slice of bread, putting it on her plate.

"No, but I'm happy to help. Trent admired your work first and asked about the photographer. All I did was connect the two of you. Your talent got this gig, Willow, not me." He paused his movement, staring with a smile.

Heat warmed her cheeks. *Oh no. Am I blushing?* She bent her head slightly and continued eating her runny-centered eggs, even though her stomach was in knots, anticipating the day. She drew a deep breath each time her muscles tightened. When finished, she took her dirty dishes to the sink to wash.

Zach snuck behind her and took the plate. "No

need for cleanup duty. You're my guest."

As Willow changed direction, she grazed her left shoulder against him. His looming presence and smoky eyes behind the gaze peering at her made her blood race through her veins, sending shudders throughout her body. Willow scooted away. "I'm going to stroll your property before we go. Get my head straight about the shoot today. Helps me concentrate."

"Yep. A little walking meditation is good. I'll be in my office if you need me."

After dressing for the day, she slipped on a sweater, ignoring the tremor in her belly, and contemplated her host in the next room. She relished their deepening friendship and felt a satisfied warmth welling up inside her, settling in her chest. Whatever happened—if anything—she was proud of herself and her courage to move on with her life. *I can do this.*

****

Zach's phone pinged. *Marissa.* He ate lunch with her one day but had no contact since. For some reason, he didn't want anything more, including a romp of casual sex for the afternoon. Very unusual for him. He shook his head.

—*Dinner tonight? My place. I'll cook*—

—*Sorry. I have plans all weekend*—

—*Okay.* Sad emoji—

—*Have a good weekend. Talk soon*—

—Heart emoji—

Zach placed his phone on the counter and tidied the kitchen. He paused at the counter as another song idea surfaced in his mind. He wiped both hands on the towel, grabbed his guitar and notebook, and settled on the patio. He wrote one line, *You push and pull on my heart,* and found a promising melody, which was enough to start a chorus. As he contemplated lyrics, he glimpsed at Willow in the near distance, meandering throughout his property. *Is this song about her?* If he was being honest, he felt a tug on his heart each time she was near. *Is she my muse or something more?* He returned to his guitar and was wrapped up in a melody when he heard the *pitter-patter* of footsteps on the patio.

Willow tiptoed closer, until she landed at his side. "Enchanting melody. New song?"

"I'm getting it but not quite ready to share yet." He squared his shoulders. "Ready to go soon?"

"Yes. I'll be out in fifteen." She stood, hands tucked into her back pockets, shifting her weight.

He lowered his guitar back in the case and rose. "I'll grab a quick shower and be ready by then." He hummed, daydreaming about the day with Trent and observing the shoot. He had faith all would work out, not only for the gig but for his heart. Whatever was happening inside him was unfamiliar territory, but he trusted himself to do what was best when the time was right. *If I can.*

Chapter Twenty-Five

A little later, Willow looked out the window while cruising along the entrance road to Trent's farm. As the estate came into view, she gasped. "Oh my. This is beautiful." The house was a spacious, refurbished farmhouse, with a barn set in the distance and several horses grazing in the paddock. Lavish green fields bordered the back, their vibrant wildflowers dancing in the breeze without a care. Hay bales were strewn next to the barn and corral, and two dogs scampered out to greet her when the truck skidded to a stop.

Zach jumped out, giving the dogs a vigorous petting on their heads, then hurried to help Willow with her bags.

She lightly touched his forearm. "Thank you." She tightened the grasp on her purse's shoulder strap, still gazing at her impressive surroundings.

Trent, dressed in cowboy boots, jeans, and a T-shirt, bounded down the steps of the house's front porch with a petite woman with long blonde hair close behind. "Welcome to the Adler farm!" He slapped Zach on the back, then smiled at Willow. "And you must be the famous Willow Mason I've heard so much about." He offered a handshake.

"Thank you." As she greeted him, she grinned. *I can't believe I'm meeting Trent Adler—and working for him! Keep it together, girl.* "I'm not famous, but I'll do my best today to capture the heart of the two of you and your home."

"Hi, I'm Mary." Trent's wife stepped forward to take Willow's hand. Wearing a midi cotton sundress, she stroked an obvious belly bump. "Tote your stuff inside, then we'll explore the property. Okay?"

"Yes, thank you." Willow curled a loose strand around her ear, smiling.

"I have several outfits picked out, and my hair and makeup people will be here in about an hour. And when the shoot is done, I have a caterer preparing a barbecue for everyone." She clapped her hands together. "I love the photo you did for Zach."

"Thanks. I love it, too." Warmth spread across Willow's cheeks as she grinned.

"I hear you grew up with Zach in Ohio. You'll have to tell me about it." Mary threaded an arm through Willow's. "Come on. I'll show you the inside first."

Willow trotted up the steps alongside Mary, feeling like they had been friends for years, and entered the house. *Is this really happening?*

****

Zach glanced at Trent. "They'll get along, huh?"

"Mary's excited about the shoot. This is the first time she's been a part of creating my album cover. As we're doing it, I can't believe I haven't included her before. She's my rock and guiding light through life— every man needs one of those." He fastened his view on Zach.

Zach puckered his lips to the side, contemplating Trent's words—a gnawing feeling ballooned inside him with nowhere to go. He shrugged, and a half hour later, he was rocking on a porch chair with an iced tea, watching people bustle in every direction. He couldn't take his gaze off Willow as she walked the property with Mary, pointing out where different shots could be positioned. He smiled, watching her. *Why am I enjoying this so much?*

****

After deciding to shoot outside, Willow guided Trent and Mary from one spot to another around the farm. She directed them in natural poses, and soon, she had them chatting, hugging, and laughing as she led them around the property. At one point, she peered into the camera, clicking through several images, and motioned for them to look. She indicated a picture of Trent and Mary standing next to the corral by the barn, with one of their horses leaning over the fence. Mary was laughing and staring into Trent's eyes as he held one arm around her. Their faces beamed with love for each other, and undeniable joy leaped out of the photo. "This is it."

Mary peeked into the camera to see the image. "Perfect. I had no doubts you could do it. I love it." She threw both arms around Willow, squeezing tightly.

"I'll send you the proofs, so you can browse through all of them. But I have a good feeling about this one." Willow spread a grin wide across her face. *I did it.*

****

Zach watched from a distance, not wanting to interfere with Willow's creative flow. When he saw Mary hug her, he knew Willow had captured the perfect photo. He straightened, puffed out his chest, and stood tall before strolling out to meet them.

Willow waved.

264

Zach approached, tipping his chiseled chin upward. "Did you shoot the perfect photo?"

"Yes!" Mary and Willow spoke together, then laughed.

"Want to see?" Willow angled her camera.

"Heck, yeah." He peered into the frame and curled his lips upward. *Man, she's talented.* "You got it."

Mary caressed the small bump in her belly. "Let's return to the house. I want to change clothes and check on the caterer."

Trent hugged his wife once more and kissed her on the cheek.

Willow grabbed the shot.

Zach strutted alongside her in case she needed help, but the assistant had already put the lighting equipment away, ready for pickup from the rental company. "I can't wait to see the rest of the prints. Will you send them to my email?"

"You can see them on my computer tomorrow. I'll upload them tonight." She placed a light meter in her camera bag, then zipped it.

"I had faith you'd master the right shot." Zach shifted his stance, hands in his front pockets, and grinned. "I'm proud of you, Willow."

"You believe in me that much, Hayes?" She cast him a playful smirk.

"I do." He placed a hand on her shoulder. "And I think you're believing in yourself, too."

"You're right. This whole awesome experience was everything I've ever dreamed of doing with my photography career." She placed a hand on his arm. "Thank you, again."

He squeezed the hand. "You're welcome." Zach's

heart swelled, ready to burst.

"I'll meet you in the back. I want to talk to Mary a minute before the party begins."

"Sure. See you then." Zach was enjoying this day on so many levels. He was overwhelmed, watching Willow work, and stirred by a strange feeling—a shift deep within him, subtle but undeniable. *What's that about?* The change seemed related to his relationship with Willow or perhaps, the day's excitement. He struggled with an urge to grasp her, plant a fiery kiss on her luscious lips, and surrender any attempt to subdue his impulsive behavior. When she left on Monday, everything would go back to normal. *Or would it?*

He wandered to the backyard as some other people arrived—friends, band members, some studio players, and a few church pals.

The caterers arranged a buffet table with plenty of side dishes, and the meat was grilling, sending whiffs of mouthwatering barbecue out into the air. He grabbed a beer and joined his buddies—no sign of Willow yet. *Why am I always thinking about that woman?*

****

Willow freshened up in the bathroom and wished she had a dress to put on. She hadn't considered the party afterward—her brain always in work mode. As she left the bathroom, she collided with Mary.

"Let's go celebrate!" She side hugged Willow, sweeping her other hand up in the air.

Willow wiped a dirt smudge off her blouse. "I should have packed a change of clothes. I left my dress back at Zach's house. Never crossed my mind. I was too busy—and nervous." She grinned, now scraping a grass stain on her pants.

"Nonsense. You look great. But I have one you could borrow. Do you want to check out my closet?" Mary pointed in the direction of her bedroom.

Willow broadened her eyes. "Do you mind?"

"Absolutely not! Come on. I love girlfriend stuff. We're about the same size, so I must have something."

Within minutes of following Mary, Willow found the perfect midi-style dress. Yellow with tiny white polka dots, the garment cinched at the waist and flowed out into a loose skirt, swirling as she sauntered across the floor.

"Perfect." Mary clapped. "Now you're ready to celebrate."

"Thank you." Willow traced her fingers over the material, feeling like a princess. "I'll have it cleaned and returned before I leave."

"Don't worry about it. Check out my closet. I have plenty." Her walk-in closet was jammed with over a hundred dresses. "No problem."

Mary looped a hand through Willow's bent arm again and escorted her to the patio. She made it a point to introduce her to new people until she landed in front of Trent and Zach. "And here's our photographer extraordinaire." She released her hold on Willow. "I need to check on the barbecue. I'll be right back."

"Nice dress." Zach stared, scanning her body.

"Mary lent it for the party. I was a little grubby before." Willow could tell he liked what he saw—sending a slight shiver up her spine.

"You look good in anything, Mason." He grinned.

"You're beautiful is what he *wants* to say." Trent joked and punched Zach in the arm.

"Thank you." A sneaky warmth mounted in

Willow's cheeks, devouring any calm.

"And thank you for coming here to shoot my album cover. I'm stoked." Trent set his bottle on a nearby table, grabbing some peanuts from a bowl. "More artists might be interested in hiring you, so I'll get your number from Zach. Do you have an agent or manager?"

"Not yet." *Are my dreams coming true?* She expanded her lungs, calming herself, but couldn't deny an overwhelming feeling of joy bubbling up inside.

"Hmm. I'll ask around. Someone in Nashville might want to represent you. But your work speaks for itself, Willow." Trent grasped his drink. "Gonna mingle. Catch up with you two later."

Left alone with Zach, she lowered onto a nearby chair, grateful to be off her feet, and sighed. "Ahhh."

"Want a beer?" Zach turned, his brow lifting, then set his drink on the ground.

"Sure, thanks." She swept a hand over the skirt of the dress, releasing a tremor in her fingers.

He traipsed over to the coolers, grabbed a bottle, then returned to sit beside her in the Adirondack chair overlooking the property.

Willow grasped the drink and poured the brew into a cup he gave her. "Thank you. The expansive view is breathtaking here."

"Yeah, I do love the countryside of Tennessee— places like this spreading out into the hills, bordered by lush trees and dense woods." He reached for his beer again.

Willow sipped her ice-cold beer, sinking into the chair and observing the people at the party. Everyone mingled, greeting each other—a close-knit family of friends and relations coming together and celebrating in support of their friends' success. For an instant, she envied their closeness. She glanced sideways as another car pulled into the lot and nearly spat out her drink when she saw Marissa and another woman step out. Willow couldn't take her gaze off the woman in faded, ripped blue jeans and a close-fitting, tank top that hugged her curves, strutting confidently like a woman on a mission.

Zach whipped his head in the same direction, then dipped his chin.

"Your girlfriend's here." Willow straightened her posture. "I'm starved. I'm checking out the enormous food spread." Without another word, she sprang to her feet, leaving Zach alone.

****

Marissa hurried toward Zach, swooping in, and sat in the chair Willow abandoned. She pecked him on the cheek. "Hello, stranger."

"Hi." Zach tipped his beer bottle, taking a larger-than-normal gulp. "Sorry, we haven't gotten together. Trent and I have been swamped with media appointments, and this weekend, I have company."

"Yes, Willow was hired to photograph Trent and Mary, right? How'd it go?" She flipped her hair over a shoulder, tilting her head.

"Fantastic. She's quite a talent behind the lens." He shifted his body weight in the chair.

"So, are you back in Nashville for good now?" She slid her fingers onto his forearm.

"For the time being, I guess." *Why am I cringing at Marissa's touch?*

"Well, don't be a stranger. We still have catching

up to do." She stood and bent to kiss him again.

She's not giving up, is she? Zach couldn't ignore the way she batted her eyelashes before swaggering off to talk to friends. He guzzled his brew again and wiped a sweaty palm on his jeans. *She's still sexy, but I'm not interested. What's up with that?*

****

Willow stood at the food table, nibbling a cracker to tame her growling stomach, then heard a voice behind her.

"Hi."

Willow pivoted, coming face-to-face with Marissa. "Oh, hi. How are you? If you haven't seen Zach yet, he's sitting on the deck." She drew in a sharp breath, grounding herself against the swirl of nerves in her gut.

"We talked." She tucked a blonde strand behind her ear. "I'm happy he's back and have hopes we can rebuild our relationship. He's had so much stress with his dad and his career. Coming home will do him some good."

"A number-one hit on the charts can't hurt either." *Is she marking her domain?*

"Yes. The song climbed the charts yesterday." Marissa picked out a plate. "When do you leave?"

"I fly out Monday." *She's asking when the coast will be clear.* "Zach's been the perfect host." *Two can play at this game.*

"Yes. He's a considerate guy, most of the time." She tonged some carrot sticks, dumping them onto her plate.

"He's helped me quite a bit without asking for anything in return, so I'm grateful." Willow scooped coleslaw next to her salad.

"I guess since he's related to your best friend, he's like a big brother." Marissa grabbed some utensils and a napkin.

Willow was tired of the constant back-and-forth insinuations about her relationship with Zach. "He's more than a brother." *Now let your head spin.* "Enjoy the party." With a *swish* of her skirt, Willow sashayed away. *What did I say?* She was becoming a little cocky herself. She wasn't sure why she blurted those words out. Willow inhaled the mouthwatering aroma of grilled meat drifting through the yard, then strolled over to an empty seat next to Mary at a nearby table to eat.

Mary, the perfect hostess, invited Willow to sit, introducing her to all her girlfriends gathered for the event. Many were wives of players in Trent's band or people responsible for the recording.

Willow couldn't believe how comfortable she felt with these ladies. She relaxed her shoulders and got lost in the friendly chatter of women sharing details about their lives. The camaraderie of these country folk was so different from New York high society. Suddenly, her old life seemed to be drifting far away. *Is this my new beginning?*

****

Zach joined Trent and the guys at another table but often turned his head toward Willow, sitting with the other women. *I can't take my gaze off her.*

Trent nudged him. "Hey. When are you making it official with Willow?"

Zach jolted his head sideways. "What do you mean? We're just friends."

"Right. I see the way you gape at her. You're sunk." Trent's gaze remained fixed.

"We're good friends." Zach fidgeted in his seat. *Who the hell am I kidding?*

"Keep telling yourself that, my friend. I see more, but you don't want to see it. This might shock you, Zach, but you're head over heels in love. At least, from where I'm watching." Trent patted him on the back. "But I can see I shocked you, so I'll stop. *But...*she would be the perfect woman—you're not getting any younger these days."

"Okay, okay. I hear you." Zach squeezed the bridge of his nose with his fingers, closing his eyes, and shook his head. "Am I so out of touch with my feelings that I don't see what's happening in front of me? I'm not ready for a committed relationship, and I can't hurt her. She's been through too much."

"Well, your love life is your business. I'm just saying it as I see it." Trent stood. "You need another beer."

"Or a therapist." Zach shook his head.

Trent laughed as he headed for the cooler.

Willow strolled over, then stood in front of him. "What's so funny?"

"Oh, nothing." He squirmed in his chair, tightening the hold on his drink. "Are you enjoying yourself?"

"Your friends are awesome, and Mary has been so sweet. I like her."

"Yeah, Trent's a lucky man." He peeled part of the label off his bottle. "Holler when you're ready to leave. I can party with these guys anytime."

"I'm ready whenever you are. I want to give this dress back to Mary and change."

"Okay. I'll be here." Zach watched Willow turn, then stroll inside the house.

A minute later, Marissa appeared and lowered her body onto the adjacent chair. "Hi, again." She placed her left hand on his extended arm and let it linger for a second. "Congratulations on the hit."

"Thanks. You were a part of the success, too." Zach gulped the last of his brew, anxious to leave.

"Glad to be of service." She paused. "I talked to Willow earlier. She's a sweet girl, but you better be careful. She might want something more."

Zach wrinkled his forehead. "Why would you say that?" *Does Willow want more with me?*

"Something she said. And a gut feeling. So, when you're ready for some noncommittal fireworks, call me, cowboy." She brushed his cheek with her right hand, stood, then sauntered away.

Zach grabbed his neck, pinching the knots in his muscles. He cracked his knuckles, his body shifting side to side, and exhaled a heavy sigh. He didn't like these uncontrollable feelings consuming him—too disturbing and too uncomfortable. *What the heck?*

****

After changing clothes and saying her goodbyes, Willow left the house and waved at Zach.

He joined her, helped put her bags in the truck, and opened the passenger door.

As Willow rode back to his house, she discussed some of her shots in detail and noted that a few would make great personal photos.

Back at home, Zach glanced at the sky. "A storm's coming in. We made it just in time."

A rising wind rustled through the trees, and wisps of Willow's hair flew in her face as she climbed the steps to Zach's porch. "You're right." She brushed the loose strands away and hurried into the house. She put her gear away, changed into sweats and a cotton T-shirt, and strolled into the massive living room with a satchel containing her laptop.

Zach entered through the screen door from the backyard. "I secured some chairs and bolted the shed. The area could go under a tornado watch. Several years ago, a cyclone devastated downtown Nashville and some of the surrounding area. Scary stuff." He locked the door. "Do you need anything?"

"Do you have any herbal tea? If it's all right, I want to work on my photos in here." She lowered her computer bag next to one of the overstuffed leather chairs.

"Sure. I'll check." Zach strolled to the kitchen and motioned for Willow to follow. "I might have a box of chamomile in the cupboard. I don't drink much herbal stuff. Only when I'm sick." He grabbed the box out of the cabinet and edged closer, brushing against Willow's arm. "Here you go."

Willow turned toward him, lingering inches from his face, but then, she took the box and stepped away. *Friend, friend, friend.*

He put water on to boil and got her a mug. "Anything else?"

"No, thank you. I'm stuffed." She leaned against the counter, keeping a safe distance. "I'm anxious to look at the photos."

"Yeah, show me your favorites later. If you need anything, I'll be in my studio." He smiled, grabbed a water bottle from the fridge, then ambled toward his office down the hall.

While quietly waiting for the water to boil, Willow

scanned the large house—screaming bachelor pad, but homey at the same time. Zach was quite a catch—if he wanted to be caught. In the future, he would have plenty of concerts, tours, and women at his beck and call whenever he wanted. But seeing Trent and Mary's relationship gave her a small glimmer of hope that Zach could change. *What if he does change? Could I trust him?*

Once settled in the living room, Willow transferred her images from the camera's memory card to her computer, making sure to back up copies onto her portable hard drive, as well. A couple of hours passed while she organized her favorite images into a folder, concentrating on creating the best presentation she could for Trent. Later, when she looked out the window, she shivered, watching the rain slap against the window as the winds intensified and howled outside. She closed her computer, satisfied with her work, and tiptoed to Zach's studio. She could hear him singing and tapped on the door. An apprehensive tingle ran up her spine as she waited.

"Come in."

Willow stepped inside and saw him sitting in a chair, holding his guitar. "I'm going to bed. Thank you for the day and everything you've done." She twisted a loose curl through her fingers, swaying side to side, and grinned.

"You're welcome. Get some work done? Are you satisfied with your images?"

"Yes, to both questions. Do you want to see my favorites?" She felt a churning sensation reel in her belly as she prepared to reveal her work.

"Hell, yeah." He rested his guitar on its stand.

"Here." She passed her computer. "Just swipe to the left to see them. I put the best ones in that folder." She leaned back, watching him and attempting to mask the jitters in her gut.

"These are amazing, Willow." He looked up, then smiled.

"Thank you." She held his gaze but could feel warmth traveling up her neck. She still wasn't used to the praise. "Will you play me a song before I go to bed?" She didn't feel like leaving him quite yet.

"Sure. Have a seat." He pointed to the couch in front of him.

"What's the title of the new album?"

" 'Forever Kind of Love'."

"Play that one. You wrote it with your dad, right?"

He tilted his head, grinning. "You remembered."

"I did." She let her body sink deeper into the worn leather seat, her nerves finally settling.

Zach's melodic, baritone voice escaped into the room.

The song wrapped around her in a warm embrace, sending a sensation up her spine and landing in her heart. She closed her eyes and let the words reverberate throughout her entire being. When the music stopped, she stilled. She lingered in the quietness, breathing in the meaning and hope in the words: *And I knew in my heart, she was my forever kind of love.* She fluttered her eyelids open and met his gaze—unwavering, relishing the connection. Whatever the feeling, it struck her heart. "A…amazing." She did not break eye contact.

"Thank you. And thanks to Pops, too. This song healed a broken, distant, and shutdown part of me. And you were a part of the healing in how you cared for my dad and made it easy to slide into a relationship with him again."

Willow sensed heat seeping into her cheeks again. *Oh, God. I'm blushing.* "I'm happy you both found your way together. It meant everything to your dad." A warming sensation wrapped around her heart, absorbing in the tenderness of Zach's words.

He placed his instrument on the guitar stand and sat back, sighing. "I felt the same—more than you know." He stood. "Bedtime?"

"Yes, I'm beat."

He followed her into the living room. "Seems like the storm might be escalating. I'll turn on the news. If we're under a tornado watch, then I'll set my watch to receive an alarm if it becomes a warning. I want to be prepared."

"A tornado? Here?" Willow's pounding heart rate accelerated.

"Don't worry. I'll get a notification if we need to take cover." He stepped closer, resting a hand on her shoulder momentarily.

Willow fearfully trembled. She had occasionally experienced bad storms in Ohio—ones that ripped out trees with sixty-mile-an-hour winds—but she had never seen a tornado. "If you say so." She forced a grin.

"We'll be fine, Willow." Zach squeezed her shoulder, then released.

"Okay." She took a deep breath, calming herself. Before she retired to the bedroom, she angled her head. "Goodnight, Zach."

"Goodnight, Willow."

Her gaze remained fixed on him, unspoken chemistry raging inside her with no release in sight. *I doubt I'll sleep much tonight.*

Chapter Twenty-Six

Zach's alarm blasted in the middle of the night, pulsing a warning sound. He hurled himself out of bed, wearing only a T-shirt and boxers. He yanked on a pair of sweats, then rushed to warn Willow, pounding his frantic fist on her door. "Willow! Wake up! They issued a tornado warning. We need to go to the basement." He turned the knob and barged in to find her sitting—confused, but moving.

"Let me grab my computer." She slung on her robe, springing in his direction.

Zach hurried down the hallway, then jerked open the basement door, leading to wide carpeted steps. He flipped on a light switch, then offered a hand after the last stair, guiding her to a cushioned loveseat in a corner of the finished basement.

She glanced around the man cave with a pool table, giant television screen, bar, and leather chairs scattered throughout the room. She huddled against him, and minutes later, the electricity flickered off, darkness settling in over them. Willow shuddered, a jolt of fear running through her without control. Would the tornado hit them? Or was she more afraid of being alone this close to Zach?

"Are you okay? Don't worry." He turned on his phone's flashlight and patted her knee. "Good thing I was a boy scout. I've got some votive candles here, somewhere." He hopped up, opening drawers and cabinets until he declared a success. "Aha, here we go." He carried them over with a lighter and set them on the table in front of Willow. "This should do the trick." He lit them and plopped back on the sofa.

Willow trembled. Tornados were rare in her part of Ohio, and she quivered as the bellowing wind outside ravaged her nerves like a volcano on the verge of eruption.

"You're shivering." Zach put an arm around her.

"I'm not used to this kind of storm." She didn't resist and snuggled into him. Feeling the warmth of his body soothed her fright about the storm, but not so much her fear of being physically close. Somehow, her concern didn't matter anymore.

He intertwined his other hand with hers. "We'll be okay." He held her while the grueling sounds of thunder crackled with ferocious power, and the wind howled, shrieking chaos outside. "We should talk about something to keep your mind off being carried away to the next county." He grinned.

"Yes, I wouldn't be in Nashville anymore." She chuckled, then squeezed his hand.

"Tell me something I don't know about you." He scooped her in tighter.

Willow took a deep breath. "I never told you what happened in New York. I was too ashamed, but I'm sure you could have read about it online. No privacy on the Internet." She sighed, twisting a fallen hair strand in circles with a finger. "I received a letter from Charles, asking for my forgiveness last week."

"Oh?" He turned his face toward her.

She glanced and caught him lifting his eyebrows,

reflected from the candle's firelight.

"What did it say?" He traced slow, back-and-forth strokes across her shoulder as he held her.

"He asked for my forgiveness and apologized again. The whole experience forced me to close my heart and lose faith in having any relationship with a man." She stopped twirling her hair and looked straight into his gaze, steady and unblinking.

He rubbed his hand along her upper arm, then squeezed her. "I can understand."

"Trusting anyone again will be…very hard." She continued to hold his stare, quivering inside. "I forgave him, so I can move on with my life. I wrote him a letter and mailed it before I traveled here."

"And how do you feel about the situation now? Did writing the letter help?" He swept an unruly curl off her forehead.

"Yes. Somehow, the forgiveness has given me hope for a new life and one with love in it again. I'll have to wait and see what the universe brings." She angled her gaze away, dropping her head on his chest.

Zach released his shoulder hold and skimmed his fingers along her wrist and forearm, trailing his movement like a pendulum. "Mmm—velvety-soft skin you have."

Willow quivered, entranced by the mesmerizing movement of his fingers gliding across her skin. She didn't speak but lifted her head.

He stroked her hair, gliding his fingertips to linger on her cheek, and caressed her face as their gazes locked.

She tremored beneath his touch. She felt his warm breath caress her lips, then welcomed the slow toying and teasing of his tongue before he pressed harder. She fell into his embrace, allowing him to envelope her, sliding one hand behind her neck, and opened her mouth wider. She no longer could stop her desires. Easy at first, but the unbridled chemistry soon ripped open, and the kiss became a passionate fury as potent as the storm outside. Willow collapsed her body against his, feeling her heart on fire and wanting to meet his needs. She grasped at his shirt collar, easing toward his chest and arched up higher, wanting more, and not caring if she was in a dangerous zone.

As Zach released his kiss, he inched away in slow motion. "I'm...I'm sorry. I didn't mean to cross a boundary."

His look seemed to search hers for a response. She was sweating, moisture seeping through her nightgown, and her heart pounded. "I wanted you, too."

He grabbed a hand and drew her into a hug. "I can't..." Zach mumbled into her hair—his voice barely audible. Moments slipped by before he lifted his head.

At first, Willow felt a sharp stab to her heart hearing his words—not ones she wanted to hear but knew were coming. She studied the look in his eyes, and all she saw was fear. But somehow, she wasn't devastated that he wasn't ready for the kind of relationship she deserved. She slid her fingers over his jawbone, then dropped them to his chest. "This situation, a kind of life-and-death thing, causes people to do crazy things." She offered him an excuse, a way out, and she was strong enough to handle whatever happened. She drifted her palm down the front of his shirt, coming to rest on his right hand. She intertwined her fingers with his and rested her head on his chest.

Zach clutched her tighter, his breath jagged and uneven.

Ding-ding. His phone broke the silence, pinging with an alert.

He picked it up from the table. "The coast is clear. The tornado has passed our county." He dropped the phone on his lap. "Willow…"

She raised a hand, palm facing outward. "The kiss was long overdue. We both wanted it."

"I don't ever want to hurt you." He tilted his head, narrowing his brow.

"So, we remain friends. Stuff happens. We seem to get caught up in emotional moments." She shrugged, shaking off the disappointment that she refused to let him see. "But you did make me feel safer—and distracted me from what was happening outside." She chuckled. "Thank you."

"Happy to help." He held an unflinching stare.

She scooted away, gathered her computer, and grabbed a candle. "Mind if I take this to my room?"

"Of course not. I'll find some more and put them outside your door in case you need them. By morning, the electricity should be on."

"Thanks." She stood and made a concentrated effort to maneuver her wobbly legs, traipsing up the stairs. Yes, she was stronger, but that kiss knocked her off balance, making her head spin. She wanted more of Zach. Period.

****

As Willow walked into the living room the next day, she cinched her robe tighter at the waist. Last night's kiss lingered on her lips, her body still floating. "Good morning."

"Morning. I'm watching the local news—minimal damage happened last night throughout the county. The twister touched ground about five miles from here but only ripped out a barn on a rural farm—no casualties." Zach stood with the remote in his right hand.

"Glad to hear it." *Something is different about him. He's not looking at me.*

"Do you want breakfast?" He kept his view glued to the TV screen.

"Sure. Do you want me to cook? I am handy with a frying pan and stove." She tossed him a side-glance.

He finally focused his gaze in her direction. "Yes, true. But you're my guest, and I insist. Come on. Let's go in the kitchen." He turned off the TV, then motioned toward the kitchen. He opened the refrigerator, gathering eggs and ingredients for an omelet, and placed them on the counter. He shaved some cheese and chopped mushrooms.

Willow took charge of the toast and bacon, cooking by his side, like she had been doing it for years.

Zach cracked more eggs into the bowl and whisked away. "Might as well go big."

"Yes, all this natural catastrophe stuff has increased my appetite." She nudged him in his side with her elbow, unable to hold back her playful urge.

He jumped back, but not before he pinched her in the ribs.

She squealed. "Better concentrate, or we'll burn our breakfast."

"You started it."

"Yes, and now, I surrender." Her heart rapidly thumped against her chest, and she didn't care.

As they dished up their food, Zach's phone pinged

with a text from Trent.

—*Checking to make sure you both are safe from last night*—

—*All good over here. Thanks. And you?*—

—*All good. Are you two up for dinner tonight? Rosewood Grille. Our treat*—

He traded a glance with Willow. "Trent's inviting us to dinner later. Is that okay?"

"Yes! I'd love to see Mary again."

—*Yes, we'd love to. What time*—

—*Seven*—

—*See you then*—

They both resumed eating, saying little, each in their own world.

Zach poked at his scrambled eggs, then stopped. "I have an idea. You didn't see much of Nashville, but the countryside is breathtaking at this time of year before the leaves change. Do you want to hike one of my favorite trails? The path's not rigorous, I promise. And tonight, you'll see more of downtown when we go to the restaurant."

"Sounds good. I also want to send Mary and Trent some prints before dinner and get their input." She sipped her coffee, amazed at how calm she felt—even after the fiery, explosive kiss from the night before.

"Gotcha. After we return, I can work, too." He finished his plate and began clearing the counter.

In silence, she helped him. After the last dish was washed, she wiped her hands on a towel. "I'll get dressed and meet you in the living room. I won't take long." Twenty minutes later, she was in his truck, traveling toward the state park. Cruising through the country, she leaned her head back against the seat.

Broken tree limbs lay scattered in the fields and by the highway—evidence from the storm. One tree to the side had fallen over, missing the outer edge of the paved road. "We were lucky."

"Got that right." He pulled into the entrance.

Willow peeked over at Zach, still getting chills peering at his defined chin line, wavy hair sticking out over his collar, and sturdy hands gripping the steering wheel. No matter what happened in the future, she would always have a crush on him. *Who wouldn't?*

"Here we are. The trail is wide, but the ground will be wet." He grabbed a small towel from the back seat.

"No problem. I'm wearing my old sneakers." She stuck her foot out to show him.

"Always prepared, huh?" He hopped out of the truck and slid a hand along her lower back, guiding her. Strolling the path, Zach pointed out certain trees or commented on the land surrounding them.

A thickened silence, regarding their kiss's arousal, hung in the air, and Willow would not mention it. *Is he thinking about it?* She could tell when part of him was withdrawn and conflicted. Soon, she would be back in Ohio, and her life would return to normalcy without deliberating on matters of the heart—she hoped.

At the next bend, Zach pointed to a shimmering pond underneath the sun's rays with a bench in front, still damp from the storm. He wiped it with the rag and invited her to sit.

The water lapped against the shore, a lone dragonfly buzzed around the weeds, and fuzzy cattails lifted toward the sky, swaying in the breeze. A mourning dove *cooed in* the distance.

"When I need to reflect on my life, I come here."

He fixed his gaze outward.

"I can see why—very peaceful." Willow cupped her right palm over her eyes, blocking out the sun as she scanned the horizon. She took a deep breath, then lowered the same hand to her lap, letting tranquility wash over her as she was engulfed in a symphony of mesmerizing sounds—frogs croaking, crickets chirping, and the occasional bird's serenade.

Zach placed a hand over hers. "Listen, Willow. About last night."

"We don't have to talk about it, Zach. I'm fine." *Not really, but I'm not discussing it.*

"Willow, I like you. You're a remarkable woman. I'm the one with the major problem, not you. I'm not relationship material. I've never been." He squirmed, shifting his position.

"You don't have to explain. I get it. We're friends, Zach. Good ones at this point, and our friendship makes me happy. Whatever your inner angst is, you don't have to share it." She squeezed his right hand, then let go.

He kept talking. "What's wrong with me?" He dropped his head into his hands, moving it side to side. "Aargh."

She placed a hand on his back. "Don't worry. You'll figure it out. Someday." She smiled, then let a gurgling laughter escape her throat.

He straightened and twisted toward her. "I'm glad you have faith in me."

"I do, Hayes. I do." She gazed, a familiar warmth unfolding in her heart.

He sighed with a huff. "Want to head back?"

"Yes. I'm anxious to do some more work if you don't mind. That's why I'm here, remember?" She cast a flicker of a smile across her face.

He studied her expression. "Yes, I remember."

She stood, staying focused as she traipsed along the path, but inside, she was torn. Zach had a problem, and she couldn't fix it. At some point, she needed to let go.

****

After working all afternoon, Willow showered and got ready for dinner. She'd packed one dress for such an occasion—a pale-green one with matching heels and a sweater. Willow checked herself in the mirror and noticed the flattering color made her skin glow. She put on dangling gold earrings with tiny pearls etched around them, and her hair hugged her face, showing off its thickness and shine. Satisfied, she rejoined Zach in the living room.

He stood still, speechless for a moment. "You're stunning. I might be underdressed in my regular jean and flannel shirt attire."

"No worries. I'll still go with you." She snickered under her breath.

He swept an arm, facing the door in front. "After you, my lady."

"Why, thank you." She stepped in front, aware of his gaze following her. A shiver raced up her spine, sending a jolt through her butterflies as she made her way to the truck. The scent of his minty shampoo lingering in his damp hair and a musky aftershave on his body didn't help matters, either.

When Zach arrived at Rosewood Grille, he moaned, seeing a few paparazzi hanging around outside. As he hurried to the passenger door to shield Willow, he cuddled her body, nestling her against his chest, and rushed inside to avoid the annoying cameras.

"Sorry. It happens sometimes."

She smiled, tucking her chin closer to his chest. "No worries."

Trent and Mary welcomed them, and the flowing chatter commenced. Willow and Mary exchanged recipes and talked about farm life, while Trent and Zach schemed about the upcoming week, filled with more interviews and podcasts. Their song had climbed the charts, thrilling the artists and the record label.

As Trent finished his meal, he shifted his attention to Willow. "Let's talk about your photos. We chose the one by the barn with the horse and corral—our first instinctive selection—for the cover. The concept matches the title of my album perfectly." He grinned.

"We want to buy more, though." Mary placed a palm on Trent's forearm. "We want to frame some and place a couple on Trent's website. You do have a gift, Willow." She lifted the corners of her lips, her smile radiating.

"Thank you." Willow touched her cheek, her skin heating from the compliment.

"Your career is taking off, Mason." Zach held her gaze, unwavering.

"I hope so." She faced the happy couple. "I'm grateful for this opportunity to shoot you both on your property. Thank you, again."

"Thank Zach. When I saw his album cover, I was jealous. Now, I have my own Willow Mason print, so I'm satisfied." Trent socked Zach in the arm, busting a grin.

The server offered dessert menus, but everyone declined.

"I couldn't eat another thing." Trent patted his

belly.

"And my bed is calling." Mary yawned. "One thing about pregnancy is I could sleep anywhere, anytime." She grabbed Trent's hand, squeezing and gazing attentively at her husband.

"I have an early flight tomorrow, so I'm ready to go, too." Willow gathered her purse and sweater.

Trent opened his wallet. "This one's on us, man. Don't even try." He pushed Zach's arm away.

Zach tossed up both hands. "All right, all right. You win. Thanks, pal."

Willow took one last sip of water and placed her napkin on the table. "Thank you again for hiring me. I needed this gig to help launch my career, even with the danger of a tornado lurking in our midst."

"Never a dull moment in our sweet ol' Nashville." Trent enfolded his wife in a side hug as he stood.

The four approached the front door, then stopped. A swarm of persistent paparazzi were gathering outside.

The maître d' approached them. "Back door?"

"Yes!" They all chimed together in agreement.

"Let me call for you." He phoned the valet station from the host stand while the four guests strode to the rear entrance by the kitchen.

The valet drove their cars to the back, and both couples made an easy, clean getaway without a single photograph taken.

As Willow climbed into the truck, she turned to Zach. "Is it always like this?"

"No, if I'm by myself, they don't care. I receive more requests for autographs. Because two of us and a new woman stepped out, they figured they might have more of a gossip story. The headlines are what matters, whether true or not. They don't care. They make up stuff to sell the photos. Quite the opposite of your work."

For a moment, she lost herself, staring out of the window. She trickled her fingers across her face and across her chin, pondering about his life and hers and how different they were. *Could the two ever entwine into one?* Spending this much time together was leaving her with a longing. A longing to be with him—more time, more hugging, more kissing. And that couldn't happen. Ohio couldn't come soon enough.

****

The next day, Zach dropped Willow off at the airport and met Trent at a radio station for another interview. Arriving early, he sat in the waiting room, scrolling through his phone. He stopped on Willow's photo of him, taken after the shoot and right before the party. He let her goof around, snapping his picture, and when he wasn't paying attention—an unplanned moment was captured by her camera. But what knocked him for a loop was the expression on his face—the same one Trent displayed for Mary. One of sheer, complete, unmistakable love.

Had he been in denial these last few weeks of an inner change creeping up, taking root deep in his soul? He had many unresolved questions drifting through the uncharted waters of his mind, yet he yearned for answers. He couldn't ask her to be with him—too soon. Too soon after a painful devastation. Did she even want to be in a relationship? But her reaction to their kiss revealed she might be equally smitten. One thing was for sure—he couldn't make a move unless he was one hundred percent committed. He forced a breath out with

291

a heavy sigh. He was utterly, undeniably confused.

Trent strode in front of him. "What the heck's wrong, man? You look like hell, buddy. Good thing this interview is on the radio and not television."

"Oh, pondering stuff." Zach wasn't ready to share his innermost torments, even if Trent was a friend.

"About what? Willow?"

"Why do you say that?" Zach frowned.

"Man, anyone can see it. I've been watching you all weekend. The way you stare, with your head off in the clouds. Been there. You've got it bad for the woman, and I can't say I blame you." Trent lowered himself on a chair.

Zach tossed his hat onto the coffee table in front of him and shoved his hair away from his face. *I feel like crap.* "That obvious?" He shifted his body weight.

"Yes."

"I can't hurt her, Trent. She's been through so much. What if I'm not good enough? What if I screw up?" He wrung his hands in constant motion.

"You're plenty good enough. All your angst is pure rubbish. And if you don't want to hurt her, then don't. You're holding onto a lame excuse not to get involved."

Zach glanced at his friend. "You're right."

"I used to be that guy loving freedom. And look now." He thumped a thumb at his chest. "Have you ever seen me happier?"

Zach shifted his attention to staring at the floor, his voice lowering to a whisper. "No."

"Don't ruminate too hard about the logistics. Yes, she's in Ohio, and you're here, but things can change. A relationship can be fluid. Trust you'll figure it out. And if you can't trust yourself, trust in a bigger power at work here. Believe in that. Believe in your faith. And believe things will work out. They always do."

Zach bowed his head in a quiet acknowledgment, assimilating his friend's advice.

"Ask to be guided in your prayers tonight. The answer will come." Trent grinned. "Now, let's talk about the hit song we made together. Can't wait to play it live for an audience."

"Yeah. Me, too." Zach pondered Trent's words and knew he had received some solid advice. He picked up his hat and followed him into the station office but was conscious of slowing his ragged breath and relaxing his tightened muscles. He was becoming clearer about what he had to do.

Chapter Twenty-Seven

Several days after her return, Willow organized the table display of fiction paperbacks by the window. While she had been gone, Marcy and Deedee sold most of the store's inventory. The shelves were almost bare, and even the back storage bins were empty.

Marcy bent over a box nearby, sweat dampening the side of her face. She wiped it with her sleeve. "Willow, I found a few more copies of the cookbooks we were searching for. They sold fast on Saturday. One more weekend splurge, and we can close early."

Willow joined her, placing a hand on her hip, and observed the contents. "Selling out would be awesome. Here, I'll take them." She grasped the books, carried them to the side of the shop, and added them to the others.

Keeping busy was the best way to keep her mind off *him*. Over and over, she had analyzed the weekend—the easiness, the tornado, and *the kiss*. That kiss was way too powerful not to impact them both. *Is he thinking about me?* As much as she replayed all the events, somehow, her recent act of forgiveness numbed any doubt about the whole experience. By coming to terms with her situation with Charles, she found accepting whatever else happened in her life easier.

Marcy waltzed toward the register. "I'm finished. We're ready for any onslaught of customers and the weekend. All the inventory is out now."

Willow surveyed the store. She even sold the remainder of her photographs. "I put the ad in the paper for the weekend half-price sale this morning, which should wipe us out."

Marcy side hugged Willow. "I couldn't have done any of this without you. I feel bad I'm robbing you of your livelihood." She creased her forehead in a ragged frown.

"Don't worry. I viewed it as a promising sign from the universe to do what I love—photography. I received enough money from Zach's and Trent's gigs to last a while until I launch my website and do some marketing on my own. Zach and Trent are spreading the word in Nashville about my skills."

"Zach? *Hmm.* It seems you've spent a lot of time together, and you're beaming." Marcy cocked her head as she let go of Willow. "What's up?"

"Nothing. We're friends, and I'm happy we can be good friends. I didn't expect our relationship to turn out like it did. I'm very focused on my career now and don't need any distractions. I'll be fine." Willow straightened the pile of bestsellers by the register but couldn't ignore the rippling of nerves firing in her gut. *Am I fine?*

"If you say so." She picked up an envelope from the counter and grabbed her purse from the shelf below. "I'm going home and will call you in the morning. If I can stop by, I'll text you. Thanks for your help."

"Glad to be of service. When I first arrived, you helped me, and I'll always be grateful." Willow hugged her. "See you tomorrow."

"Yep. See you then." Marcy glided out the door.

Willow observed her for a minute, then returned to the front desk to finish paperwork before heading over to George's. He was doing okay, but she could tell he missed Zach even if he didn't say anything. They both did. *Does he miss us, too?*

****

Later that evening, Willow stood at the stove, stirring the spaghetti sauce, and breathed in the tantalizing aroma of garlic and bubbling tomatoes from the steaming pot. Whenever she was in the Hayeses' house, she couldn't help but mull over Zach and their time together. She missed him. She liked working for George, but if she was honest with herself, she couldn't deny how her heart pined for the country music man.

Yes, she was emotionally stronger now, but a new sadness wrapped around her heart—the sadness of an empty hole in her life without him. She shook her head. *I need to stay focused on my career. No distractions.* As she put the finishing touches on the salad, she heard her phone buzz. *Mom.* She put down her knife and answered it. "Everything okay?" Mom never called while she was working.

"Yes, dear. You received a priority mailing from the Sterling Center, and I couldn't wait to tell you. Could be good news."

Willow tilted her head. *I was runner-up and didn't win. What's this about?* "Strange. Everything was settled. Open it. Now, I'm curious."

Silence reverberated on the phone while Evelyn opened the envelope. "I'll read it."

Dear Miss Mason,

We are happy to inform you that your photograph selection will be showcased in the winner's exhibition

296

in November. Due to unfortunate circumstances, the first-place winner was disqualified. Since you were runner-up, you have now been given this coveted spot. Congratulations, and please get in touch with our office as soon as possible for more details.

Sincerely,

Martin Rexal, Selections Committee

Willow dropped the towel, hopping and spinning in circles. "I got it! I won!" Goose bumps rippled along her spine and tingled across her body.

"Yes, darling. Because you deserve it. You better finish that website and prepare for the launch of your new career. I'm so proud—and happy I called."

"Thanks, Mom. I'm glad you did, too. When I come home, we'll talk more." She swayed her body back and forth on her toes.

"Yes, we will. Now, back to George's dinner. Love you."

"Love you, too." Willow wiggled her hips in a little dance before she resumed stirring the sauce.

George shuffled through the doorway to the kitchen. "Hey, what's all the commotion in here? I heard you shouting from the lawn." He tossed his cap onto the hook by the door.

"Good news, George. Have a seat, and I'll tell you all about it."

Willow described the exhibition and the details leading up to the letter. She spoke at a rapid pace, like a speeding locomotive. Willow stopped, took a deep breath, and grinned. *Take it easy, girl.* While arranging plates and silverware on the table, she heard a car pull into the driveway. "Somebody's here, George." She leaned over the sink, peeking out the kitchen window.

A large, black SUV skidded to a stop, and Zach climbed out of the car.

Her breath caught in her throat, and she wrenched her neck farther to get a better look, her heart rate accelerating. "Zach's here." She pressed a palm across her quivering belly, willing her breath to slow before she exploded inside.

"Oh, good. Is he coming to dinner?" George turned toward her.

"Possibly. He's got a suitcase." *Is he coming back to stay? For how long?* Willow reduced the heat on the sauce and hurried into the living room to welcome him.

George followed.

Zach entered the foyer, dropped his gear on the floor, and threw up his hands. "Surprise!" He strolled toward his dad, bent forward, and hugged him. "Come here, Mason." He opened both arms, embracing her, and buried his face into her brunette curls.

Willow lingered in his hug. *Oh, God. This feels right. I missed you so much.* She tilted her head upward, meandering her fingers across his broad chest. "Couldn't get enough of us, huh?" She was just so happy to be near him again, she didn't care whether her future was mapped out or not. Yes, she had fallen in love with this man.

"You got that right." He released his hold. "I came back to finish writing the songs for my album. It seems my muse is in Cedar Hill." He tipped his chin, studying her. "You're more vibrant than ever. What's up?"

"Willow is having a photo exhibit in New York. Won some fancy contest." George directed his attention toward her, grinning.

Zach arched his eyebrows and spread his dimples

wide. "What happened?"

"I received a letter today. The first-place winner was disqualified, and I got the spot." She clapped her hands, raising on her toes, then lowering. "I'm stoked."

"I'm proud of you, Mason. You deserve this win." He lightly tapped her shoulder.

"Thanks." A giddiness filled her, sending shivers throughout her body.

George patted him on the back. "I'm glad you're back. Now, let's eat. I'm starved." He ambled back to the dining room.

"Right behind ya, Pops." Zach motioned his hand in front of him, looking at Willow, and sat at the table, engaging in conversation and retelling stories from his weekend escapades with her.

She let him do most of the talking, feeling more secure about her livelihood and future, with or without love. But she couldn't stop the pounding of her heartbeat, thumping hard against her ribcage. *He came back. Am I the reason?* Despite her excitement, she soaked in his commanding presence, relishing each smiling glance she caught. S*omething's different about him. What is it?*

After dinner, Zach helped clean up, then settled his dad to watch his television shows. He walked back into the kitchen and watched as Willow put the last pot away. "Can we talk outside about something private?"

"Sure." *What does he want? This seems personal.* Her butterflies had generated a permanent flight pattern in her stomach ever since he stepped out of the car. She followed him out to the patio.

Zach stepped closer, took a hand, then faced her.

Witnessing his intense stare, she shivered. A heart-stirring tremor gripped her body, exploding in every nerve cell. *What is he doing?*

"Listen. We've become friends over these last few weeks. Well, better friends, I should say, and we've gotten closer."

"Yes, true." Warmth radiated from his hand, coursing through her arm. *Is he struggling to talk? Oh, God. I'm shaking.*

"I have been thinking about you—a lot. My track record with relationships has been sketchy and unreliable. But these last few weeks, I've been looking at myself and wondering if I'm missing out on an important part of life—love. *Real l*ove with a woman. For the last ten years, I've had crazy fun with casual relationships, and finding a partner was the last thing on my mind. But since you came into my life, my emotions and thoughts have spun out of control with a fervor I don't recognize—and I've struggled to make sense of it. I know you experienced a devastating loss with your ex-husband, and a relationship is probably the last thing you want." He neared, cupping her cheek. "But…I've fallen for you, Willow. As soon as you left Nashville, I realized it. Yes, I'd felt chemistry before, but after spending the weekend together, I realized that my world could be so much richer and more fulfilling if I built a life with you. I want you, Willow. I want you bad."

Wetness pooled in her eyes, and she took his other hand. Her gaze never wavered. "Zach, I feel the same way but never imagined you would change. I can't be with you if you don't want a solid commitment. But if I hear what you're saying, then we might want the same thing." Her pulse raced—her heart threatening to leap from her chest—as she edged nearer.

He squeezed her hand, stepping closer. "I do want the same thing, Willow. I want the forever kind of love my parents had, and the only person who can satisfy my desire is you."

She stood silent as one tear escaped her eyelid. She could feel the heat of his body radiating against her and was in shock. *Is this really happening?*

He brushed the falling tear away, then enveloped her against his chest.

She could smell his musky cologne and sensed his breath tickling her neck, warming her body. His embrace felt so right. *This is where I belong.*

He eased back slightly, then entwined his fingers through her hair. "You're beautiful. I've been a fool all this time seeking to fill this void inside of myself with casual flings. What I need in this life is a woman who is pure at heart and worthy of a forever love." He bent over, sweeping his lips over her mouth, then pressing full-on to cover hers with intense passion, devouring her with wild abandon.

She met him with an ignited fire of her own, pent-up for weeks, but now, releasing into a joint explosion of their hearts—craving each other with a longing for the love they both deserved—no longer out of reach. *Is he really mine?*

As he leaned away from the kiss, he didn't let her go and kept his gaze locked.

He wants a verbal response. He needs to hear it. "I've fallen for you, too, Zach. For weeks, I tried hard to fight it, but somehow, you made your way into my heart. I could do nothing about it. After our kiss in the basement, I trusted a higher power to bring us together if a committed relationship was truly best." She laid her head on his chest, melting into the embrace of his muscular arms holding her. *I'm home—where I belong.*

Zach kissed the crown of her head. "*You* are the best thing in my life, Willow, and we can take it slow. Whatever makes you feel comfortable, I want to do it your way. I want you to feel safe. We can figure out logistics as we go. I want to spend more time here, and your career seems to have possibilities in Nashville. We can make this partnership work. I'm sure we can."

She didn't budge. *Is he serious?* "Okay. Slow." *Oh, God. He's saying everything I ever dreamed of.*

He squeezed her harder. "Yes, slow is good."

She lifted her chin to meet his intense gaze. "Can I trust you, Zach?" She held her breath, wanting to release the last bit of fear into his next words.

He cradled her cheek into his palm. "Yes, Willow, you can trust me. I promise."

Willow exhaled a relenting sigh and felt the tightening in her chest loosen. "Okay. Let's create our forever kind of love, then." She grinned and felt the accumulated pain and turmoil from the past year slipping away.

"Yes, *our* forever kind of love, Willow." His fingers traced the side of her face—his loving gaze unwavering—and pulled her against his chest once again.

She lowered her cheek onto his shoulder, trailing her fingers over the gold-lettered charm dangling against her neck—*Faith.* A serene calmness settled over her. She'd been through hell and back with Charles, but somehow, she regained faith in herself and trusted she and Zach would have a different story.

This she believed with all her heart and sank deeper into his embrace, not moving but basking in the strength of his grasp and his love ready and waiting. In forgiving, she had found love again. She thanked the heavens above for her happily ever after on the horizon with this man who helped mend her broken heart and who was now ready for *their* forever kind of love. Because…she was ready, too.

A word about the author…

Author Susan Bagby spent most of her life working with children and youth as a speech pathologist. After retirement, she moved back to her hometown of Akron, Ohio, and her lifelong dream to write romance books came true when she found a home for her debut novel in 2022. Two additional award-winning novels have been released.

Susan belongs to the Great Lakes Fiction Writers organization and to Romance Writers of America (RWA). She is presently working on a new small-town romance series and loves seeing new characters come to life. When she's not writing, she loves reading, walking in the woods, yoga, Pilates and playing the piano. She's a firm believer that dreams do come true.

www.susanbagby.com

www.ingramcontent.com/pod-product-compliance
Lightning Source LLC
Chambersburg PA
CBHW072116020726
47501CB00003B/851